"We only have to look at ourselves to see how intelligent life might develop into something we wouldn't want to meet."

\- Stephen Hawking

Contents

The Borsen Incursion

by

Julian M. Miles

Printed by Createspace, an Amazon.com Company

Available from Amazon.com and other retail outlets

The original edition is the Lizards of the Host Publishing paperback:

www.amazon.co.uk/Borsen-Incursion-Julian-M-Miles/dp/0957620071/

The ebook is available for Kindle from Amazon stores worldwide, and for all

other devices from Smashwords: www.smashwords.com/books/view/494651

Design and layout by Julian M. Miles

Original cover art by Genji Lim. All rights reserved.

Visit us online

Julian M. Miles (a.k.a. Jae): www.lizardsofthehost.co.uk

Artist: genjilim.deviantart.com

Lizards of the Host Publishing: www.lothp.co.uk

Prologue

Five hundred years have passed since the cataclysm that ended mankind's twenty-second century early. As the dust and ashes settled, the only cohesive force remaining was the United Nations; now controlling a military largely comprised of a homeless host. Nations had become mere footnotes in history. Indeed, history itself became an endangered thing during that first frantic decade. But stronger, more disciplined minds prevailed. The United Nations became the Unified Nations. Five years later it accepted the ruins of the United States of America into itself and became the USE: Unified States of Earth.

Earth Command was the power behind the throne. The military hardcore that had walked from the ashes of devastation, and rebuilt with ruthless determination, was not going to be derailed by the squealing masses this time.

For the following two hundred years, humanity rebuilt along old lines with renewed vigour. Science gave access to the stars before the end of the first century. From there, mankind went forth. By the end of the second century, mankind had encountered eight sentient races, but nothing to challenge its technological lead and fundamentally barbaric treatment of less advanced civilisations. 'We are a star-faring race with a colonial mindset' was how several swiftly silenced observers termed it. The survivors of the eight races would have agreed, had each of their single world 'reservations' been permitted the technology to access such data.

For the last three hundred years, mankind had been the unchallenged ruler of all it surveyed. Earth Command's early dynamism, forged in the crucible of conquest, decayed into bureaucracy, elitism and nepotism. It was hidden behind layers of needless complexity and over-regulation, which swiftly surpassed the same maladies that had riddled the governing bodies of the USE before the end of the second century.

Surviving observers quietly considered that the USE and Earth Command's time was done and, as is the way of all empires, a new order would rise to prominence in due course. They hoped that the genesis of this new order would be relatively painless for the inhabitants of the thousands of worlds and habitats, spread across incomprehensible distances, that depended upon the infrastructures and hierarchies of power for their safety and supply.

In the five hundred and first year, something happened at a far-flung outpost. The response was noted by the NewsNets as 'a rapid mobilisation of significant forces'. After that, there was silence. Eventually some disturbing rumours started to percolate in from the farthest edges of human-populated space. Rumours of strange occurrences: unexpected raids and devastated worlds.

Earth Command confidently predicted a quick campaign and easy victory. A few senior officers had concerns over the strategies chosen, but the heads of the monolithic military bureaucracy ignored them. After all, what could possibly challenge those who rule two thousand worlds?

Terms
(Y502 PA)

The sheer arrogance of an opponent that announced which planet they would attack next had initially been met with disbelief, treated as disinformation. Eleven planets later, Earth Command had decided enough was enough. Word was starting to spread and unrest was following hard on its heels.

They had asked their greatest commander-turned-politician to return, and orchestrate a salutary lesson for these brigands. Commodore James Harbon prepared a plan from his memories of mock battles and extensive reading, heedless of tactical objections from the few who had seen what these 'Borsen' could do. Then he waited for the next announcement.

He was mildly disappointed when his name-world, Harbon, was declared as the next target. While he regretted having to relinquish his Ambertree groves to make room for emplacements, he made a small fortune from some careful property acquisitions prior to the planetary fortification announcement.

Now he watched from the centre of a square mile of white marble, incised with the sigil of Earth Command in gold, as the enemy vessel

3

arrived and took synchronous orbit between the planet and closest moon. He waited, tapping his foot impatiently.

She just appeared. Naked and three-metres tall. Waist-length cobalt-blue hair seemed to move of its own accord. Her magenta gaze conveyed indifference. He thought that she would have been a true beauty but for the tentacles that served her as arms.

James swept a half-bow as he used the intelligence gathered about these alien beings to shape his opening line: "Greetings, Madame Athshper. I am Commodore James Harbon."

The woman-thing tilted her head to one side before replying.

"I am Sthtera, Mistress of the Borsen. My thanks for your flattery, but it will not save you."

James recovered his fabled diplomatic aplomb.

"Madame Sthtera, my apologies. I presume that you are empowered to negotiate surrender terms on behalf of your forces?"

"Your ignorance of honourifics is irritating, James. You may call me Sthtera. As for surrender, I am prepared to accept yours, disappointing as it is."

James straightened his robe and decided that, for posterity, he needed to emphasise the sheer genius of the strategy deployed.

"My dear Sthtera. You are now within range of more firepower than you can possibly conceive of. At my merest gesture, your vessel will be reduced to wreckage and you will be taken by our scientists, who are eager to get their instruments into you."

Sthtera seemed to contemplate for a moment.

"I recognise your proud defiance. Now cede this planet to rapine."

James sighed and brought his famous sneer to bear.

"Sthtera, I am a man of considerable military experience. Your single ship, although quite impressive, is vastly outgunned and outnumbered. Your situation is untenable. Let me be clear. The only way you will get this planet to 'cede' is to kill everything before my forces can react."

Sthtera smiled and her tentacles twined in discomfortingly suggestive ways.

"I am delighted! Foolish arrogance, but such a noble gesture. I accept."

Sthtera extended her tentacles to either side of her as she flung her head back and sang a single, pure note. While the echo faded, Commander Harbon watched uncomprehendingly as the warp-field swept overhead. As grey drowned his senses, the singing void rent his body to pulp and the pain continued far beyond his sanity's hold.

GX1342 stands as a monument to the two billion people who died on it. It is now known only by its planetary designation, as Earth Command has expunged the name of James Harbon from every record. The man who sacrificed twenty percent of Earth Command's forces with a single sentence has no memorial.

There is a single exception to this erasure: 'harbon' is now slang for anyone who brashly takes on, and spectacularly fails at, a task due to blithe disregard of the circumstances and their utter lack of competence.

Chant of the Betrayed
(Y512 PA / Y501 PA)

The hangar bay was gloomy, the lights having been stepped down to mark the arbitrary night aboard the troop carrier. At tables across the wide expanse, the warriors of the Ninety-First drank, shouted and carried on as if their lives could not end the next day.

In the shadows of the main power ducts, Commander Ethan Gould sat, sipping some of Sergeant Percy's finest distillate without a wince or a blink. His grey-green eyes regarded the gathered men, his enhanced optics running numbers and states on everything he saw. A stationary figure amidst the revelry caught his attention. At a table halfway down the hall, Major Garstang raised his mug toward him, while his other hand made a clenched fist against his chest. Commander Gould sighed as he braced himself, then nodded. The Major climbed up on his table and the hall grew quiet as ripples of awareness turned the men toward him. As the stillness amplified the sounds of the warship speeding through Hirsch to another bloody conflict, the Major took a swig of his mug and started in.

"It is time! Let the memory never fade!"

With a roar, eight thousand voices joined in the Chant of the Betrayed.

"Here's to the lads of the old Eighty-Two -

Blasted to dust when the Borsen blew through…"

As the familiar words tore at old scars, the sole survivor of that event, the one that marked the start of the Borsen Incursion, remembered the truth once more…

They had been waiting for something to appear, but a three-metre-tall, incredibly beautiful, naked woman with tentacles for arms was not on the expected list. The forward emplacements were nothing but steaming, screaming remains before she reduced the field of invisible mutilation about herself and apologised profusely, in perfect English, for her AI. She then introduced herself as Athshper, 'WarpMistress' of the Borsen.

Ensign Ethan Gould had run away that day, terrified beyond reason by the whispering in his ears. Just as some people could hear radio waves, he could hear the Borsen AIs private communications. His report on the encounter had been buried so deep he was still astonished that he was alive.

Anyone with the old skullcomms could receive transmissions from the Borsen AIs. Those transmissions were very persuasive, utterly sincere, and told the Eighty-Two that the Borsen were a race of females. The 'old Eighty-Two' stood there, stunned, as Athshper offered them consort status. Then the fighting started: the majority, who favoured acceptance, turning upon the few who balked at participating in treason.

Because of his sensitivity, Ensign Ethan Gould had never had a skullcomm. Because of that he missed the explanation. All he heard was Athshper's offer and her AI chatting with other AIs as skirmishes broke out around her. They were dispassionately making wagers on which of their wearers was likely to be the first to consummate her relationship with her new consort by giving her AI a new body.

The Eighty-Two were dead and gone. But there was a good chance that their bodies, or parts of them, would be involved in some of the killing tomorrow. Commander Ethan Gould checked the lowest set of status symbols on his optics. Each trooper had an immolator built into his armour these days. The Borsen would not be getting any more consorts.

The Power That Seeks
(Y521 PA)

The darkness sang with the power that bled from the walls. Great sheaves of cables and conduits drooped from the shadows above and curved away into the dim recesses beyond the Pillars of the Mothers.

Athshper made her way round the crumbling stone bier – and its long-dead, yet still-terrifying, resident - to stride through the short, arched entranceway that led to the heart of Avallea. Inside, a nest of tentacles ceaselessly traversed the acres of control surfaces. From within that writhing mass, a sibilant female voice emerged.

"Daughter mine, what news?"

Athshper genuflected and then prostrated herself on the floor: "The last of the consorts has expired, our Mistress. We have reaped five thousand Knights and ten thousand breedings."

"That is favourable hearing. Rise, my daughter."

Athshper sat up and wrapped her tentacles around her knees.

The voice came again: "They made rugged warriors, this Earth Command. What of them, since the challenge over the planet they called Harbon?"

"They ignore us. Despite our excellence in rapine, they refuse to limit us. It is as if they hope we will tire of them."

"We shall not. The decrees of the void delivered of Mother Eshnba are clear. They are the race we have sought since she uttered them. Like any stagnant pool, they are covered by scum, the dross who seek only to be above others and to secure their continuance. We must skim them: a culling in blood to rouse their ruling competences. When they rise, we shall see a change like none before."

"Could they become allies?"

"Not in their present forms. The decrees state that one will rise and lead Joyous Ghosts against us. The one who does that may develop some useful insights, but they are a short-lived race. I have not the cognition to see how they may overcome that. Goad them hard, my daughter. Their rulers are set like parasite upon host, with many deep-leeching grips that we must shake loose. When that succeeds and the ruling competences awaken, maybe I will be able to see."

"It shall be done, my mistress."

Arms Race
(Y529 PA)

The day was beautiful, a cloudless clear blue sky over rolling hills, the view interrupted only by copses of trees, and the occasional sheep.

Plus me, in One-Bushi. Standing a hundred metres tall, its gloss black finish detailed in matt grey, with the edges of its cooling vanes and detection arrays polished to bare metal - a detail stolen from pre-Apocalypse sports car design, I had been told.

My command channel clicked into life: "Okay, Manfred, your board is clear. Skies are open and the ground for a hundred clicks is ours. How does it feel?"

I stretched my arms and looked up, peripheral displays showing One-Bushi's arms mirroring my movement. I revelled at the detail on the heads-up display, telling me that my airspace had been violated at two hundred and twenty-seven point three metres by a hawk, that I was surrounded by thirty-nine probably non-hostile sheep within a half-click radius, that the nearest squirrel was one point oh-four two clicks due south and there were nine humans one point oh-one clicks to the west in full stealth suits, equipped with very advanced laser targeting equipment and commercial grade sidearms. That stopped me.

"Toymaster, I show armed intruders just past a click west of me. They are equipped to be hidden except for fancy laser painting kit. Are we expecting visitors?"

"Negative on that, Manfred."

There was a pause as the channel went mute at their end. Toymaster was talking to the owners of the 'toyshop'. Then the channel opened again.

"Mama Bear says you can lop Pinocchio's nose off any time you like."

I smiled. It was at this point my dermal sensors detected eight low power laser hits.

"Manfred to all players, being painted by hostiles, am about to go weapons-"

That was as far as I got. Next thing I knew, after a deafening metallic 'clang' followed by strange singing greyness, I was tumbling through the air while trying to puke myself hollow, as a resounding crash indicated where my now pilotless mecha had fallen. Then I landed - with a splash - in something that felt solid, and the lights went out.

I came round in hospital two weeks later. I was broken in most places and bruised everywhere else. The ninety-metre fall should have killed me, but by sheer luck I had landed in a shallow pond.

It seems that while my bosses had been all fired up to reproduce the Titan-class combat mecha from the last decade pre-Apocalypse, a rival consortium had been working on something obscure, reverse-engineered from captured warp technology. The idea had been to provide a warp-field beam weapon for use against Borsen powered-armour troops and their mecha-style command units.

I had the dubious distinction of being a side-effect to the discovery that the warp-beam could overload gravitic cores. The barely understood technology had caused One-Bushi's safety measures to eject me - straight into the warp-beam. Any effects of that - including my delayed landing - had been classified. I would need to be promoted three times before I could discover what, if anything, had happened to me.

Most of my recovery time was spent lying in bed, contemplating redeployment, as Project Samurai had been placed on hold 'pending review'. As that usually meant the project was over, Mama Bear strolling in to my room was a surprise. Reflex kicked in and my cast actually creaked as I tried to salute. She waited until I recovered.

"Manfred, I am told you will be up and about within a week."

"Should be, sir."

"Good. We need you back to pilot One-Bushi."

"I thought we were shut down, sir?"

She smiled.

"It seems that their trick device needs to be mounted separately to everything and requires a huge power supply for repeated use. Even when miniaturised as far as possible, it still looks like a twenty-metre-long assault rifle. So I made a few suggestions."

I grinned.

"Like adding an armoured power-feed and grips for One-Bushi?"

"Precisely, Manfred. Project Samurai and Project Wallaby have been merged. Welcome to Project White Knight."

Police Action
(Y535 PA)

It hangs there, blotting out the stars and everything else with its grey opacity. The great arc swings flawlessly across the sky and extends all the way to the ground. It marks the line between the living and the dead, as we wait to see which we will become.

We tried to reason with them, but they ignored everything after the first message we sent, to which this edict was issued in reply: "Your proliferation is contrary to the mandated density of a colony. Reduce yourselves or we will purge your planet. You have seven rotations to comply."

It took our leaders two days to work out that we had been given a week to cut our population sufficiently to meet the limit mentioned. The problem was that no-one had any idea what that limit was, except for the Borsen, who were not giving us any clues.

When the facts were leaked, the public went berserk. Our small Earth Command base had already thrown everything it had at, and been ignored by, the single Borsen ship that hung in geostationary orbit between Lacroix and our moon, Janette. They had also sent for help, but admitted that any effective assistance would be over a week in arriving.

My world devolved into anarchy and insanity. There were incidents of mass murder, but the experts agreed that any significant population reduction would have to be geographic in scale. As no-one was prepared to make that decision, most people resigned themselves to whatever came. It's horrific to see what supposedly civilised people will do when all hope has gone and the only certainty is death.

Alana and I are in my merchant company's flagship in low orbit over the northern polar cap, in formation with the rest of our fleet and the smaller fleet of what had been our main rival. Each ship carries specialists, families, friends and a lot of supplies.

We gathered on the observation deck as the warp-field appeared and proceeded to depopulate the southern hemisphere.

This sickening idea to save something, including us, occurred to me two days ago. I discussed it with Alana and some of my smarter people. They agreed with me. So, in utter secrecy, we set about the only option to save a bit of Lacroix.

We hinged our plan on population distribution. The most densely populated continent was Heremoste and it lay entirely in the southern hemisphere. It was a huge gamble, but everyone I spoke to agreed: a depopulation exercise, if applied as we would apply pest control, would start with the areas that had the highest concentration of 'pests'.

As soon as the warp-field started to spread from far to the south, after the sighs of relief, I opened a channel to the Borsen ship.

"This is Lacroix Colony. We can still be productive if you cease the purge when mandated density is achieved. We will endeavour to maintain correct density from today onwards. Please provide up-to-date colony mandates to ensure compliance." I shrugged at Alana. It was worth a try.

There was no reply. The field swept northwards for another hour, then stopped just after it passed the equator.

Since then, two hours have passed.

Suddenly, there is the hum of a channel opening.

"Lacroix Colony. Proposition accepted. Purge ceased as density is at mandate minus twelve percent. Data feed appended to this message contains colony mandates as requested and quotas to be met each anniversary of this day. Further failures to comply will result in full purge."

With that, the warp-field vanishes like a switch has been thrown. While we scream and shout, the Borsen ship departs. Shortly after that, the happiness fades as there is no real cause for celebration. Too many have died, and we have lost the Earth Command base because it was situated just off the coast of Heremoste. We look at each other, the joy of survival warring with the bleak truth of the horrifying cost.

I am still trying to get a grip on the Borsen's treatment of Lacroix. They did not make war on us, nor did they capture us. They treated us as if we were already one of their colonies who had merely broken a rule. We were no more than a minor adjustment for them.

Do they regard the whole of the USE as nothing but a rebellious faction to be brought back into compliance? Are they really that powerful?

Harsh Lessons
(Y540 PA)

"My fellow officers, you are aware that I have been analysing the confidential data of the first encounter for some time, in the light of further data garnered from subsequent raids. Today I come before you to present my findings and a plan that I feel certain to yield excellent, if not game-changing, results."

The circle of uniformed men and women turned to regard Admiral Maka Gentle, a master strategist who had dedicated his life to removing the taint associated with the name of his old friend, James Harbon.

"The clues were there in the Borsen's style of address and inflections of speech. In short, my extensive research indicates that they are bound by ritualised rules of combat. If we issue a challenge that precludes their use of warp technology, they will abide by it."

Looks were exchanged. Gentle's report was read repeatedly and analysed exhaustively by increasing numbers of people of decreasing competence. A week later, his proposal became Project Joust. Two weeks after that, the Borsen's warning regarding their choice of target made Romala the planet that would host the end of "these unwarranted and unwelcome intrusions into USE space", as Admiral Gentle put it.

The ship arrived swiftly and accurately into geostationary orbit with no corrective manoeuvring. She appeared just as she did in the video feeds salvaged from earlier encounters: naked - and without warning, detectable method or apparent effort. Her hair was ruby red and her arm-tentacles shaded to black at their tips.

"Greetings to you, envoy. I am Eshebth, Mistress of the Borsen. Your preparations merited a notable presence. I am here."

Commodore Baneff bowed: "We thank you. As our missive stated, we feel that James Harbon was overly hasty. We would contest for Romala with two limitations: firstly, no usage of warp technology. Secondly, let us fight for this world without the use of other weapons of planetary devastation."

Eshebth stood silent as her tentacles caressed her thighs and knees. After several minutes, she smiled: "My Mistress accepts your conditions. If it is agreeable, shall we say that hostilities will commence when our ships pass the outer moon?"

A voice hissed in Baneff's headset: "We have missile batteries on that moon. Tell her we accept."

Commodore Baneff bowed: "That is agreeable."

Eshebth smiled and disappeared.

"This should be something to watch." Commodore Drustin commented idly to Baneff, the next morning over breakfast.

"Oh yes. We've got the whole of the Fifty-Seventh through Ninety-First Brigades with full equipment, including the new anti-spacecraft batteries. We have the latest Charon class space interceptors and twenty battleships arrayed with their Battle Groups."

Drustin choked on his juice: "That's over a quarter of a million troops and two hundred capital ships! Just a moment, doesn't the Eightieth belong to Project White Knight?"

Baneff smiled: "Correct on all three. Admiral Gentle recommended an overwhelming force. The biggest Borsen fleet we have seen is four capital-class ships with an escort of thirty cruisers and auxiliaries. Never more than six troop carriers, which carry regiments of six or eight hundred effectives apiece. The Titan-class mecha and project team from White Knight are here to get some data-captured real combat in. We have also deployed several flights of surveillance drones to ensure we get the maximum intelligence and morale advantages from this battle."

A pale-faced orderly ran into the dining room and came to attention so suddenly he nearly fell over.

"Sirs. Colonel Dryer's compliments. Would you join him in the command centre immediately, please?"

Colonel Dryer looked like he'd eaten something that disagreed with him. As the Commodores entered the command centre, he saluted: "Sirs. The Borsen have started their approach. They will pass the outer moon within the hour."

"Excellent. Where are they likely to set down, given their approach vectors?"

"Everywhere."

Baneff looked at Drustin then turned back to Dryer: "Explain."

"They arrived in an englobement of the planet. It is closing to keep pace with the ship that the Eshebth was in, which is the vessel that will pass closest to the outer moon. We estimate eleven hundred warships from direct detection and mass-shadow analysis. There is nothing smaller than the *ECD Flanders*, Sirs."

Drustin stood thunderstruck while Baneff did some calculations in his head, using numbers from the capacity of his own ships to give estimates.

"Commodore Drustin, may I?"

Drustin nodded.

"Nearest reinforcements?"

Dryer checked the data: "Nothing useful can get here within ten days. Piecemeal reinforcement would just get shredded on the way in."

Baneff nodded as his suspicions were confirmed.

"If they were Earth Command ships, we'd be facing a fully supported force of over a million troops. We haven't seen the Borsen use significant armour, so we can only guess at what they have in the way of heavy weapons. My prediction would be for a small number of exceedingly dangerous items. Gentlemen, we are in serious trouble, with nowhere to run."

Drustin straightened up: "I'll fly over to take command of the second continent's forces. I'd recommend letting the Borsen have the open ground - after contesting their landings to try and bring their numbers down. After that, it's fortified enclaves and guerrilla warfare for as long as we can."

Baneff nodded: "Agreed. Our only option is to take as many as possible with us. Take half of Project White Knight's mecha and support teams across with you."

Colonel Dryer saluted: "I'll start deploying for rolling counterstrikes after interdiction of landing zones."

Drustin saluted: "Thank you. Gentlemen, let's make them pay a high price for their victory."

Baneff saluted: "Affirmative. Let's go to war."

As Drustin headed for his flight and Dryer started to frantically restructure thirty-three battalions from mass assault to roaming defence, without giving the hopelessness of the situation away, Baneff looked up at the ceiling and cursed in a whisper: "Damn you, Maka."

Within a day Earth Command battalions had renewed their acquaintance with the unpleasantness of fighting Borsen Knights: they had two-metre tall powered armour, wielded horrific energy blades, and used their armour's resilience to allow them to get into melee. Casualties from those battles were high, unlike the ones against the far more numerous Borsen warriors, whose only tactic seemed to be charge and fight with whatever was available until someone killed them or the battle ended. Battles against them went well for Earth Command troops. But for every Earth Command trooper that fell, there was no replacement. The Borsen horde seemed to be unending. Battles raged unceasingly, unless the Earth Command troops could somehow gain a small respite, which were only won at enormous cost.

The mecha of Project White Knight were devastatingly effective - for the short while they functioned. Failures under real combat conditions always happened at peak-demand moments and always resulted in the loss of the mecha and everything within a kilometre or so. They inflicted significant casualties upon both sides.

In the end, Fort Drustin was the last outpost. Commodore Baneff had named it that when he lost communication with Drustin mid-conversation, Drustin's last sentence having been drowned out by the scream of a Knight's energy blade.

Baneff had encouraged scavenging, and the place was well supplied with everything except troops. But they fought savagely and fended off two dawn-to-dusk assaults.

The next day, Baneff was woken by one of the hundred or so men he had left shaking him hard.

"We've got a problem, sir. But I think we've annoyed them."

Baneff grinned. Morale was ridiculously high and defiance was off the scale. He scrambled from his makeshift bunk, grabbed a ration pack from the communal stack and drank it cold as he made his way to the wall.

On the far side of the mist-shrouded nightmare landscape of mud and bodies, he could see the Borsen warriors in their usual pre-attack formations: arrayed in blocks that shared similar shades of brightly coloured armour. But this dawn had brought a new element: the Knights were in two groups, each gathered around a taller machine. About six metres tall with stubby arms and long legs; probably heavier armour than the Knights as well. These must be Mistresses. The tentacle-armed bitches had finally come out to play.

He switched to open broadcast: "Okay, people. Looks like we have royalty on the field. So anyone with anything that can range those two tall beauties should consider it their duty to do so as soon as they can. Apart from that, it looks like another day in the office to me."

There was muffled laughter.

The sun peeked over the horizon and the Borsen came in *en masse*. Baneff noted the lack of any reserve units in sight. So this was it. Nothing to do but fight until they stopped him or they went away.

The Borsen broke against the walls like a tide and the clamour of pitched battle rose, an all-consuming din punctuated by the louder moments: a dying roar, the crash of a Knight falling, the detonation of a grenade. Baneff kept his eye on the two new features. They spent the morning chivvying their troops. Come afternoon, their long legs revealed a breathtaking jumping ability. Both of them landed inside the walls, smoking but apparently unharmed by the very large amount of ranged unpleasantness that Baneff's troops had directed their way as they came in. The short arms proved to be deceptive as well. Great whips of energy sprouted from them, and the fall of Fort Drustin started.

Baneff noted that the two armoured machines flailed with an exquisite elegance. He guessed that the women used these weapons in the same way that they could use their tentacles, and with as much ease. The energy whips were just unreasonable. Five metres long and a quarter wide, they crisped, sliced or detonated whatever they touched. Baneff shook his head and ducked down to ready his *piece de resistance*. He had no idea where it came from, but the antiquated spindle-sabot anti-armour missile was going to be his sucker punch. He straightened up as one of the tall machines strode into view, whips tearing through everything. As if to order, she turned away from him. He smiled. Chivalry be damned, this was opportunity. He aimed the launcher and squeezed the trigger.

The half-metre missile shot from the tube and hammered itself into the back of the machine with an unearthly noise. Baneff saw the core penetrate the armour and the machine staggered, then everything above the point of impact exploded with colossal force, demolishing walls and throwing Baneff backwards. He stood up to see the other machine coming straight for him, energy whips lashing a pattern that he doubted pebbles could avoid, let alone aging officers. So he switched his pulse rifle to maximum output and let rip, screaming "One bitch down!" as he did so.

He heard his remaining troops cheer, then he was whipped into ashes and chunks as the cheers died along with their owners.

The Battle of Romala had lasted eight days. The Borsen ground forces lost nearly half their numbers - and a Mistress had fallen: an event so rare that Romala was the first place in USE space to be recorded in Borsen lore.

A single unarmed, automated reconnaissance scout was all that returned to Earth Command's main base. It was completely untouched. A single viewing of the solitary Borsen-created recording that had been appended to the datapacks caused consternation. Within minutes, it was declared classified information; at a level that would prevent access by anyone below the rank of Commander.

Commander Longard entered the main room of the embassy, contemptuously ignoring all the attendees at this tasteless and poorly disguised victory ball for the anticipated result from Romala. He smiled thinly, straightening the black armband that stood stark against the left sleeve of his dress whites. A few people turned to regard him with idle curiosity.

"Romala has fallen."

Those three words stilled every movement in the room and killed every conversation.

"How?" Admiral Gentle seemed more offended than shocked.

Longard turned to face him: "The Borsen accepted our challenge. They won. We lost."

"Good grief! What were our casualties?"

Longard looked pointedly at his black armband before replying quietly: "Everything."

"Pardon?" Gentle's face paled a little as he spoke.

Longard looked up, the anger in his eyes at odds with the expression of rigid calm on his face: "Three hundred and four thousand dead. Two hundred and forty-nine warships lost. All that returned was a single automated scoutship."

"Incredible! A robot scout escaped?"

Longard momentarily gawped at Gentle. Had the man not heard him?

"No. They let the vessel go after loading our surveillance drone data onto it. You missed two things, Admiral."

Gentle sputtered in outrage: "I analysed the data from Harbon for years!"

Longard winced at the man's lack of respect in using that name.

"Then I must presume you made assumptions. We only limited the weapons to be used, not the numbers of combatants. Our forces were slaughtered trying to overcome five-to-one odds."

Gentle paled further. In a voice gone hollow with shock, he asked: "You said I missed two things."

Longard paused while the tension grew: "You failed to predict what would happen afterwards. The ramifications of winning or losing."

Gentle regained a little colour: "What was there to consider? If we won, they would have withdrawn. As we lost, we get to keep fighting their damnable raids."

Longard shook his head: "The scout ship also carried a message from the Borsen. We lost Romala but something we did made them decide that we gave good account of ourselves. Because of that, we have been deemed worthy opponents."

Gentle waved his hands: "Always nice to receive accolades." He looked about, but very few laughed at his quip.

Longard raised his voice so nobody could miss his next words: "We are now regarded as equals. The Borsen have declared war." He paused before stepping forward, inclining his head to place his mouth by Maka Gentle's right ear. In a voice chilling in its whispered calm, he delivered the details that were not for public disclosure: "To mark the formal escalation of hostilities, the Borsen warpkilled Earth Command Base Seven and Earth Command Base Eight."

Maka Gentle staggered. Those were their two main garrison planets in the outer territories. They had been home to over ten million troops, their families and sundry personnel. It was a catastrophic loss.

Longard finished with a mutter of trenchant contempt: "A monumental harbon, Maka. James would be so proud."

Admiral Gentle's face turned waxen: "Excuse me, ladies and gentlemen." He walked toward the balcony with a stiff-legged stride, and nobody turned to watch him go. A few moments later, the muffled impact of a body hitting the ground several storeys below was heard.

Commander Longard came to parade attention and executed a formal salute toward the balcony door, as conversations restarted and glasses clinked. Apart from that, the last casualty of Romala went unmourned.

Dreadnought
(Y542 PA)

"Twenty-nine, twenty-eight…"

Captain Janet Rossiter felt the first bead of sweat follow the nap of her close-cropped hair, before running cool and smooth down her jaw and into her uniform collar. It was so quiet on the bridge; she swore that her exec had heard it.

"Twenty-five, twenty-four…"

Sixty people made less noise than a creeping cat as they watched the dizzying host of screens. Beyond the shutters, warp space sang to their dreams. No-one had slept much in the last eight months.

"Twenty-one, twenty…"

It had taken Project Lancelot twenty years to reverse-engineer Borsen warp technology, and five more to work out navigation, in parallel with the building of the first warp dreadnought. Even now, the Borsen still did things with warp that made grown scientists cry.

"Seventeen, sixteen…"

This was the crux. The first warp dreadnought, Excalibur, hurled like a vengeful spear at the Borsen homeworld, loaded with atmosphere igniters and stealth fighters for a genocide raid to finish a conflict that Earth Command was no longer confident of winning.

"Thirteen, twelve…"

Providing the bastardised warp technology brought them out at all, of course. Earth Command had decided that, since the Romala debacle, speed was of the essence. This test flight would also be the greatest raid at the furthest distance by the biggest warship ever built.

"Nine, eight..."

She thought of spring in Providence, her daughter playing on the swing while her husband made Irish coffee on the range. This was why they all fought. For all the families: ensuring their children had worlds to grow up on and a future worth living.

"Five, four..."

A vibration ran through the two kilometres of the Excalibur, causing wide eyes and white knuckles for every one of the thousand-plus crew. She prayed to a god, hopefully nearby, that they would see real space again.

"One. Phase transit."

With a disconcerting lurch, the Excalibur arrived in the Borsen system. Sensors awakening galvanized people into frantic motion. They had to be on target in moments. She smiled a thin smile as the shutters withdrew. Time to see what colour your air is, you bastards.

"Oh God. Sir?"

At first, she just could not absorb it. The system had no planets. The reason was right there, waiting. It reflected the distant sunlight from its myriad surfaces, and she was sure that she could see the Excalibur reflected in one of the facets facing them. She gathered herself, years of training and bitter, bloody combat experience culminating in a defining command moment of grace under pressure.

"Exec. Shipwide, please."

The general broadcast fanfare rang hollow.

"Ladies and gentlemen, we have arrived and I am sure you see what I do. No-one could have envisioned this. Please, stand down and make your peace with whatever gods you hold dear."

She regarded it. So big. Could you call something the size of Jupiter a spaceship? The movement and weapons detectors homed in on the behemoth's one acknowledgement of the Excalibur's presence. The figures coming from the mass detector alone lit the board red with scale queries.

Her Second expressed the thoughts of all present with the poignantly appropriate line of defiance, prayer and dark humour: "Sweet Lord, for what we are about to receive..."

She felt her face become calm as she watched a railgun five hundred kilometres long send a projectile twenty-five kilometres wide at them. Her words ended the data stream that reached Earth eighteen years too late: "Dear John, remember me. Raise Millie well. Love from Captain Mum."

Sacrifices
(Y551 PA)

As from last week, all orphans and other children in care are to be automatically enrolled in Earth Command's 'Youth Division' if they're eight years or older. Criminals under the age of sixteen will go to career training camps, while non-violent offenders are to join the labour divisions. Thankfully, they're keeping the violent ones locked up. But the new rules mean I cannot roll on down to the USE refuge office and punch the advisor who suggested that I put Graham into care because we'd both be better off. My son's not for recruiting until he decides that he is.

Rationing started today. Nothing major: everyone has to live frugally within set maximums and recycle as much as possible to stop their personal limits being reduced. We are all making sacrifices, we are told.

"Mama, why is Dada late?"

Because, my beautiful boy, he's always been a thieving git, but this time he couldn't dodge the penalty. Earth Command took him and he's on his way to a planet called Gethsemane with the rest of Labour Division Sixteen.

"You know your dada, Graham. He comes and goes as he pleases."

"Then who's bringing the shopping home?"

Good question. I lost my legs when a freight exoskeleton failed due to lack of maintenance. The owner got jailed and his assets were taken by the USE 'for the good of all'. I got an unpowered wheelchair from the charity shop. I want to know which people are getting the good, because around here it only seems to be going to the toughs and the crazies.

A lot of folk are of the opinion that these Borsen, 'this threat to all humanity', are giving a lot of nice people the chance to clean their pretty neighbourhoods of all the things that they feel make their cities look untidy. But I may be a little biased.

There's a knock at the door: "Who is it?"

"Charlie Sivers."

I like Charlie. He ran the charity shop, until they closed that a couple of months ago, again taking everything 'for the good of the people'. I roll myself behind Graham, because he can undo the chains, but only my retina print can release the lock. Charlie comes in with a big bag of groceries, far bigger than I can afford. He smiles at Graham, who is concentrating hard as he puts the chains back on the door, trying not to tangle them.

"That's too much, Charlie. With Davy gone, and refuge payments halved because of the war, I just can't afford it."

Charlie grinned and started to make tea: "I know you can't pay. That's an advance."

"Advance?"

"On your salary."

"For what? Ballet?"

"Did I mention that I moved back to my parents place in Henley?"

Henley? Charlie's folks were rich?

"It's not all mowing the lawn and cream teas. Dad's in USE headquarters and mum's in a vodka bottle most of the time. So I live over the garage and do repairs for the local servitor community."

"Community? How do robots have a community?"

"They don't. Earth Command requisitioned all robotics and similar tech six months back. Got a load of people that work in the fancy districts now, and they all need stuff fixing, or finding."

He turned and looked at me: "Or lifting, or stacking, or delivering. So I thought, who do I know that is licensed for freight handling, exo-cleared, and doesn't need lower body modification to fit the short harnesses designed for servo droids?"

Well I'll be the legless wife of a failed thief: "Charlie, I could kiss you. When do I start and how do I get to work?"

"Well, as to the kissing thing, that's a bit hasty. But the garage has two apartments. You'd have the smaller one, which is about twice the size of –"

He glanced about, waving his hands, searching for an inoffensive condemnation.

I filled the blank: "This mouldy shoebox that I'm forced to raise a son in because a certain absentee – who we won't mention in front of small people – is a deadbeat?"

Charlie grinned: "That works. Can you be ready to leave by eleven tomorrow?"

"We can be ready to leave in eleven minutes. Put the groceries back in your car. Graham! We're going on an adventure."

"Before or after dinner?"

Ghosts
(Y555 PA > Y562 PA)

They always told me that if I found a wounded Ferine, I should drop a grenade on it, if any organics were visible, otherwise back off and call for an air strike. They never told me what to do if I was running from a massacre and fell into the same pit trap as one. I landed in the hole where its turret used to be. It was shot to hell and gone, but as I shook my head to clear my vision a growling voice scared me clearheaded.

"Hullo, Alpha Commander. Sir."

I looked about to see a single internal repair optic gazing at me.

"Hello hunter. Identify."

"Ferine six oh four, Alpha Commander. Regret non-mobile and non-combative due to being in a hole. Sir."

That made me smile. I ransacked my memory for the details I had received on these savagely effective assault cyborgs: Second generation CRITTURS, their biocomponent rumoured to be spliced from wolverine and wolf. Independent hunter-killers also capable of devastating pack tactics. Famous for entering a homicidal frenzy when damaged or trapped. Yet Ferine six-oh-four seemed calm.

"Ferine six oh four, state time at present location."

"Residency at current location thirty-eight days. Sir."

Thirty-eight days! This Ferine had been in the first wave. Amazing. But a commander should never converse with his troops by number, no matter how brutish: "Ferine six oh four, what is your callsign?"

"My pack name is Smokewalker. Sir."

That struck a chord with me: "My great-grandfather was Walker-in-Smoke."

"Am privileged. Sir."

I checked myself over. Thankfully, nothing permanent. Then I looked up at the edge of the pit, ten metres above me. The walls sloped inwards, too. Looked like Smokewalker and I were going to have time to get acquainted.

"Smokewalker, why are you not in final rage?"

"Was in final rage for three days, nine hours and eighteen minutes. Then it passed. Sir."

Passed? Ferines could recover? That was essential intel. We were executing cyborgs for going into a temporary traumatic frenzy!

"Define current mentation."

"Ignoring body damage markers, all metrics exceed CRITTURS norms. Intellectual balance plus twenty, total Turing plus twelve, Feigenbaum plus nineteen. I have also realised empathy and faith. Sir."

"Faith?"

"Our trainers told us many tales before downtime. We liked the stories about Wakan Tanka, the Great Plains, hunting and living free to roam the land. Now understand his words about invisible world of Great Spirit. Have walked the spirit path and returned from my rage a ghost warrior. Have brought Wiwanyag Wachipi for all CRITTURS."

Now that would give the psych-techs something to chew on: a Ferine claiming he had achieved enlightened warrior status by undergoing the CRITTURS equivalent of the Sundance Ritual.

It also led to a nightmare stack of ethical and moral considerations regarding Earth Command treatment and usage of CRITTURS. They were regarded as cannon-fodder, a way to save good soldiers from pointless deaths. That was something you didn't do to K9 units, let alone comrades; even if they did have treads for paws and a turret for a head.

Of course, Smokewalker could have been an anomaly. A one-off miracle induced by surviving its episode of 'final' rage. But why shouldn't his experiences be valid as stated? I realised that I was no longer prepared to leave the hole without Smokewalker.

Could CRITTURS actually have embraced a bastardisation of Lakota ways as a collective identity: a new *oyáte*? If so, how could Project Pavlov's researchers have missed their burgeoning high-function faculties? All I had read indicated that CRITTURS were mindless or possessed the most rudimentary intelligence, at best.

Ingrained customs from my youth reminded me of something: the telling of a warrior's name should always be reciprocal.

"I am honoured, Smokewalker. My pack name is Knife-in-the-Night."

"You understand The Way, Knife-in-the-Night. We were meant to meet. I shall watch over your ghostwalk, sir."

He had a point. Stuck down here, it could be a while before we were found, because the war raging across this planet would need to complete. I may have been an Alpha Commander, but the fate of this world had to be decided first.

It took the rescue teams three weeks to find us, not that they were looking for anyone except me. By then I had recovered from a week in delirium, and had been sustained by rainwater and Smokewalker luring local wildlife into the pit so I could drink their blood, and sometimes eat them raw after stabbing them to death. Either or both of which was probably the reason for my deliria, but I had survived.

We knew each other's life stories and had shared every 'fire tale' we could remember. The stories Smokewalker told of suppressant drug regimens and shock devices made me decide that my next command was going to be overseeing Project Pavlov. I had seen the request on a daily basis for months, but, like all the other commanders, I had ignored the transfer to what we had all thought would be effectively the end of our careers.

I was convinced I was making the correct choice when I had to order the troops escorting the 'handlers' from Project Pavlov to restrain them at gunpoint, thus preventing the ground blasting they proposed as the only method of dealing with Smokewalker. As we set up a hoist platform to get him out, I heard his growling tones and noticed that the initially reluctant volunteers standing on his body were now crouched down and chatting amiably with him.

He was mobile when out of the pit, after asking for two sets of damaged tracks to be burnt away so he could roll on his wheels. To my surprise, the two troopers who had ridden up with him asked to ride along. So the three of us trundled along behind the very annoyed Project team, comparing notes and chatting with this revelatory CRITTURS.

My next obstacle was debriefing, which I entered only after accepting the request for a ranking officer with combat experience to oversee

Project Pavlov, and receiving confirmation of my new command. I completed debrief at record speed, thanks to only junior ranks being available to ask the questions, then called my two companions from the ride back. I offered them promotions and a chance to make a difference, but only if they met me at Project Pavlov's field base in full combat gear, and ready to ruck, in under five minutes. I had hobbled half a kilometre before they slowed down next to me, and I jumped onto the command half-track they had requisitioned on my behalf.

Arriving at Project Pavlov, I was grateful for being accompanied by two heavily armoured and very suspicious veterans. The staff there just did not want to admit me, would not admit they had Smokewalker, and quite definitely did not agree with my judgement of his capabilities. I was just entering the early stages of what promised to be an epic sense-of-humour failure when Corporal Anderson took off at assault speed, straight through a controlled door on the far side of the room.

Corporal Theakston levelled his assault rifle at the staff in front of me, before commenting: "Anderson caught Smokewalker on tightbeam, sir. One word: 'vivisection'. Permission to massacre something, sir?"

I raised my hand as all the people in front of me went white.

"Let me be clear. I am Alpha Commander Jackson Spence. My new command is Project Pavlov and if Ferine six-oh-four is harmed there will be summary executions today. Am I understood?"

Their faces blanched even more. One tech was reaching for an internal comm when the harsh sound of a Jarvis assault rifle on full automatic, and an ear-shattering yowl of fury, induced utter stillness.

"Panthac."

The word, whispered in fear by one of the techs to my right, meant nothing to me. A few minutes later, a crash from the corridor Anderson had dashed down announced his return.

"Sir! Smokewalker has been secured. The techs and handlers in the operating bay were stubborn, and I would have been face down without the assistance of Panthac niner-niner-two."

He stepped to one side as he said that, to admit a sleek, dangerous-looking quadrupedal armoured form that resembled nothing less than some mecha cat from the animes of the twentieth century. The creature gracefully touched its chin to its right forepaw before straightening up again. Rubescent sensor eyes regarded me from two metres off the floor.

"Commander Knife-in-the-Night. I am Death-From-The-Shadows."

I heard Theakston's awed whisper as the feminine voice purred into silence: "Yes, you probably are."

I took a very firm hold from that point onwards. I spent a month sorting out the field base on Corrigan IV before boarding my new command ship, the incredible half-kilometre CRITTURS warship Hyfin two-oh-two. He introduced himself as Sings-The-Night, and used his extensive communications arrays to identify and prioritise the Project Pavlov sites that needed my attention. I have never been as disgusted with mankind as I was over the following eight months. The culture of fundamental cruelty and casual abuse I found should have been unthinkable, even if the victims had only been unmodified animals. After presenting my first formal assessment, Project Pavlov was halted, and I was placed in charge of the new CRITTURS initiative, Project Spirit. The CRITTURS themselves identified the good and the bad personnel. After my hundredth summary execution, Earth Command asked me to show leniency. I informed them, somewhat brusquely, that I already was.

I was present the day that Smokewalker mentored our first Ferine through final rage on Amadeus II. The critical thing was that the Ferine, Spark-Dancer, knew that it was not 'final rage'. She knew it was the Ghost Dance. Just changing the words did it. With that event recorded and quantified by the psych-techs, I had due cause to institute a full-spectrum analysis of sentient structures in all CRITTURS. What they found made history.

A completely unreported verbal culture with chants, poems, songs, mythology, faith, apocrypha and heroes was revealed. I was staggered to find that I already featured heavily in the mythology, along with Smokewalker and Death-From-The-Shadows.

It was about this time I realised that I loved this assignment. I also found that certain people actively manoeuvred to serve on my command. So when I moved from Sings-The-Night to the immense CRITTURS dreadnought Thunder-Star, I brought my family along, and encouraged other members of my command group to do likewise. Seeing children with these incredible war machines was at first jarring and worrying, but the response of CRITTURS to human 'cubs' was astonishing. I can only say that they loved them. The only image I have on my desk is of my daughter Katie, laughing uncontrollably as she slides down a snow covered hill on Bachman III, riding on the Halhatta scout Never-Caught, who had flipped his raven-shaped form onto his back to make a better sled for her. Such moments of wonder were so frequent in the early days. When Sings-The-Night died to a Borsen warpcore, the eulogy at his rites reduced me, and the other human members of my command, to tears. The Afya surgeon Weaving-Hannah - author of the definitive treatise on the treatment of battlefield trauma by multi-limbed surgeons - has kept me up late on many nights, discussing the intricacies of Sun Tzu. But even she can shed no light on why exactly his 'The Art of War' should hold such a fascination for CRITTURS.

The ridiculous rescue of the survivors of the Twenty-Fifth, staged by the Gora Punch-Drunk riding on Smokewalker, earned them both Command Crosses, despite the fact that they were in no danger. We noticed early on that the Borsen would not engage CRITTURS in combat. Smokewalker and Punch-Drunk simply used that fact to roll up the siege which threatened to eliminate the battalion. I received a terse missive from ECOC a few weeks later, to the effect that the entirety of the surviving Twenty-Fifth had requested a transfer to my command. They expected me to turn down nine hundred siege-traumatised veterans, but like hell was I going to refuse that many CRITTURS friendly troops. By way of petty revenge, ECOC also transferred every ancillary person and item that could plausibly be linked to the Twenty-Fifth into Project Spirit. A three-week logistical nightmare ensued, which revealed some novel skills in men and CRITTURS and cemented the core of my First Ghost Commando: squads of troops trained to operate within and around CRITTURS deployments.

I ignored Earth Command unit designations, applying them on the rosters but allowing the clan, cadre and pack structures of the CRITTURS to mature. The results were ferociously good. Our encounters proved that the Borsen could not cope with CRITTURS, and would not engage in combat if confronted by CRITTURS forces.

Something about them scared our previously unshakable opponents rigid.

Three years after I took command, CRITTURS legions were regarded as an essential part of any battle formation. Troops seemed to take the 'company mascot' emotional tag and apply it to these strange fellow grunts. They went from a necessary evil to the one thing you wanted to have your back when the Borsen came down. ECOC actually had to issue a blanket edict that Ghost Commando regiments were not an option as first-in reinforcements.

Four years after I took command, I had the pleasure of taking representatives from all of my clans to Lakota tribal lands. I watched them assemble, with every sensor array spread to capture the slightest nuance, as they broad-beamed the event to every CRITTURS pack.

Smokewalker made strange growling noises as the elders painted an invocation to Wakan Tanka along his eight-metre armoured flank. True to custom, they erased it at the end of the ceremony. Death-From-The-Shadows received an eagle feather from the chief. It was an unparalleled gift and, after enquiring as to its proper use, Project Spirit gear and all CRITTURS displayed a representation of that very feather. But only Death-From-The-Shadows had the emblem blazoned on her forehead. Since then, human members of Project Spirit who have been give names by the CRITTURS are referred to as 'feathered'. Only after that can they add the eagle feather patch on their uniform.

I also noticed that the invocation daubed on Smokewalker's flank became the standard pre-battle ritual for all teams that included CRITTURS. It is written upon the ground using materials native to wherever we are, and its erasure means the end of the ritual and the start of bad things for the enemy.

Earth Command currently seems to believe that CRITTURS are either high-function sociopaths, or emotionless morons. I know there is a massive variance in intellect realised by 'awakened' CRITTURS. Despite the rumours, most CRITTURS can be considered, at best, as rather serious teenagers. But many of them would be considered geniuses within certain narrow specialisations. Emotionally, they are rated as possessing a greater stability than humans, possibly linked to their collective espousal of the bastardised Lakota spirituality partially outlined by Smokewalker.

Some problems arise from my people's tendency to over-anthropomorphise their cyborg companions, attributing them with greater understanding than they actually have. This causes confusion when things thought to be mutually understood turn out to have been interpreted very differently by those involved. Time will ease that, I hope. We are both still learning about each other, after all.

My one concern, which has no real foundation yet persists regardless, is the small number of CRITTURS that do not manifest sentience. Remaining as enhanced cyborgs, they are referred to as 'Silent Ones', and are deployed as defence units for high-security facilities. Why they do not 'awaken' is as much a mystery as to why their siblings do.

I feel that their particular mystery will not yield to time, but to revelation. The cause and nature of that event is, I suspect, what really worries me.

I am writing this memoir to clarify my thinking, as the fifth year of Project Spirit comes to a close. The units under my command are the only ones that report clear victories these days. The Borsen will actively retreat from our presence in a theatre of war. If we could only understand why, we could win. But I am seeing jealousy arising amongst my fellow commanders. Ghost Commando units are being deployed to win non-strategic battles, while Earth Command continue to throw away essential victories.

It saddens and angers me, this profligate waste of good men and women, sent to their deaths because their leaders fear the unknown. I hear rumours that we can only be so successful by being in league with the Borsen. I do not understand why Earth Command has not quashed these rumours, but thanks to the insights of my curiously gifted command, I see the probable outcome a little too clearly.

I have taken advantage of the pervasive, unspoken animosity to bring all CRITTURS units under my command, along with those troops now derisively referred to as 'animal-lovers'. When they finally decide to examine the rosters, they will realise that I control a substantial percentage of the entirety of Earth Command's forces. It is not enough to overthrow them; it is definitely insufficient to defeat the Borsen. But it is enough to ensure that we will survive. I have my own survey vessels and colony ships, plus the finest CRITTURS labs ever built. Those labs are housed in vessels bigger than Thunder-Star, but Earth Command will never see them, as they are rostered as mundane bulk freighters, and they are far outside the contested zones, establishing bases where my command can settle.

They were ghosts before I discovered them. Me and mine found them and, in the end, joined them in spirit as brothers and sisters. Before our own side turns on us in almost-superstitious dread, while the Borsen continue to win, we will do what ghosts do best: disappear.

To Kill and Kill Again
(Y556 PA)

I awake, the warmth of satiation fading, as hunger drives me forward again. What is this ceaseless need I am driven by? I sense the seals ahead of me, and the hunt is on. I move fast to prevent them scattering, or clustering to defend their weak. One is lagging slightly. I drive myself in to sink my teeth into the soft hide. The bliss of the kill overwhelms me and I give myself over to the frenzy boiling within me.

"Whoa! What was the window of opportunity?"

"Nine picoseconds."

"That's incredible. Nothing could have detected that."

"It did. Scratch one juicy supply ship."

"So what happens next?"

"We load the hunt data across to Graw oh-oh-nineteen and activate it."

"Why not activate all of 'em?"

"I need to monitor each one."

"But the convoy is off at flank speed."

"Yup. Flank speed into a squadron of Charon Threes. Simple chase-into-the-net stuff."

"But you said you were activating another Graw?"

"I did. This one's over in Aurigae theatre, in the drive-shadow of a resupply cruiser. They ignore it because it shows as space debris caught in their drive effect."

"Do we do the Charon Threes first?"

"No. They're real fighters, the most reliable of our piloted interceptors. Now sit tight. If you thought the last one was good, watch this."

I awake, the warmth of satiation fading, as hunger drives me forward again. What happened to basking, as the sun warmed my back and filled the water with ripples of light? I sense the squid ahead of me, and the hunt is on. I move fast to prevent him turning on me, or diving too deep. He senses me. I drive myself in to sink my teeth into the soft hide. The bliss of the kill overwhelms me and I give myself over to the frenzy boiling within me.

"Sensational! It never stood a chance. What payload do they carry?"

"Ten-kiloton nukes. No worries over safe distance, contamination or EMP in free space, so they have simple mechanical impact detonators. Nothing to detect as a threat."

"Sweet. So twenty is next?"

"You got it. Now give me a moment while I send the kill intel to ECOC."

"I heard some odd stuff coming from Corrigan IV about discovering the CRITTURS were aware?"

"Animal rights propaganda. These systems use only the most basic mentation of the source creatures to provide hunt senses and reflexes that we cannot duplicate with our current technology. These missiles are no more awake than your average ant."

"Thought it was NewsNet filler. So, where's twenty?"

"Over by Bachman Three. Some big stuff just came through the debris belt there and twenty got picked up in the drive field of something huge if the passive sensors read correctly. Shall we take a look?"

"Hell yes."

I awake, the warmth of satiation fading, as hunger drives me forward. When will I reach the gathering place to mate and rest? I sense the whale ahead of me, and the hunt is on…

Childcare
(Y563 PA)

Dear Tara,

If you're reading this, then I have just died again. I am sorry that I will miss Luke's sixth birthday and even more upset over missing our eighth anniversary. That brings me to evens now, I promise to try and make the ninth.

Never forget that I love you, and I only do what I do for you and the children's safety. Yes, I know about Eva. The update reached me just as we dropped out of Hirsch. So I guess that I am going to be in serious trouble for missing her birth as well.

By the time you read this, I'll be wombed on board the Fulminator or Inceptor, so you can leave updates there and they'll drop them into the personal feeds, but remember to keep the words simple. You used the word 'disgusting' last time and it hung my induction up for three weeks while the meds unravelled my fixation with multi-syllable constructs.

Time to finish as we are about to launch the hammers; I've finally qualified for a Charon Five, the only upside I can see from dying heroically so often. My death-point learning and psychological resilience is too useful to waste, apparently.

So, until I race up the path into your arms again, be strong and kiss the kids for me.

All my love,
Jack.

Tara put the worn note back into its stasis frame as the sounds of childish argument started in the kitchen. Sure enough, Luke and Jack were fighting again. She sent Luke to clean his room while she firmly put Jack down for a nap. Another few months and she'd need a matron droid to help control him; Two metres tall, two hundred pounds of muscle making for three, the mind of an eight-year-old with the sleep cycle of a two-year-old.

Jack had been on the Fulminator when the Borsen had punched a hundred-metre warpcore through it. She should feel lucky, that her man had died so many times in the line of duty, that Earth Command had actually bothered to retrieve him from the wreckage: the sole patient saved. He had been ex-vitro for too long when they got him back to advanced regen, so he had to finish growing back the long way.

All the memories were there, but their release was keyed to physical brain age. He only remembered what he knew at that age, with occasional prescience. Thankfully, the insights drawn from Jack's prescience were enough for Earth Command to pay his family's way for the next twenty years.

It was going to be difficult, raising her man to be the husband she had loved.

My Name is Vengeance
(Y564 PA)

The trail of blood led back down the ramp and continued far out of sight behind him. He had no idea of how far he'd crawled, but he'd rather bleed out than quit because some steel-clawed automaton thought it had a soul.

The day had started uneventfully, the CRITTURS and their animal-lovers filling the compound, with his team feeling uncomfortable and remaining near their ship. They had dropped in on a surprise inspection and found a lot of things amiss: there were huge quantities of supplies, way too many people and several transports that he didn't recognise. He estimated that this 'research outpost' had over double its complement of effectives and way past triple the rostered number of non-combatant personnel. They were polite and well-disciplined, but he and his team had felt watched since the moment, the previous evening, when they stepped off their transport.

He clawed his way over the lip of the ramp and looked across the empty landing field. They had even taken his ship!

49

Things went wrong just after midday, when he noticed that the transports were loading heavy: evacuation style. He sent his men in pairs to investigate what was going on while he prepared a report for express routing to ECOC. Something was very wrong.

An hour later his men hadn't returned. So he let himself out of the belly hatch of his ship and slid down a vent into the underground areas of the facility. He came out in one of the storerooms and found it empty. He progressed cautiously from there.

The rumours from chatting with his fellow ECOC officers said that Jackson Spence and his strange command were coming under increased suspicion of working with the Borsen. That was why his team – and several others – had been assigned to an 'inspection' tour of as many Project Spirit bases as they could reach in one Hirsch jump.

He entered the twentieth room of the surprisingly large underground complex, expecting to find it stripped like the others. Instead he found his men, tied up and unconscious. From there it had been a simple step to realise that Project Spirit were about to go AWOL. Their mission became simple: break out. Reach their ship. Get a warning off.

They nearly made it. The running battle had gone their way, as many seemed reluctant to fire upon them, something he and his team had no problem in taking advantage of. But when he gunned down a group of techs and orderlies to reach the upper level that lead to the main ramp, one of the damn CRITTURS felines went for them. Actually, it went through them, with an ease that still froze his blood when he thought about it. The combat abilities of these cyborgs had not been exaggerated, even if their intelligence had.

He came round a lot later, under the remains of his team. They had been savaged to bits. Given that he was badly ripped up, extricating himself had taken a while. Thankfully, one of the bodies had an accessible medipack. He had used everything in it to keep himself alive, to get back to a ship that he now found had been stolen. With a sigh, he let his head drop. Rest for a while, then decide what to do next.

"Captain Leng! Captain Gadison Leng!"

The voice called him back from the warm darkness. He opened his eyes to see an Alpha Commander standing over him. He tried to salute, but his arms were immobilised with bandages.

"Yessir." His voice sounded weak; beaten. He hated that.

"What happened here? I have reports of CRITTURS attacks and unscheduled Project Spirit vessel departures."

Gadison Leng's voice strengthened as his anger rose: "We were attacked by Project Spirit forces, sir. They've either fled or defected. My men and I tried to reason with them, but they wouldn't stand down. In the end, we had to defend ourselves. Did any of my -?" He let the question hang.

The Alpha Commander shook his head sadly: "Sorry, Captain. None of your boys made it."

Leng cursed: "Let me at them, sir. Give me a command that can do that."

The Alpha Commander looked down at him, his glance travelling the length of Leng's torn body: "You're going to need surgery, some replacement parts and a lot of healing time, Captain. Then ECOC want you back. But be diligent and if an opportunity arises, I'll bear you in mind. So far, you're the only survivor from the few who shared ground with CRITTURS yesterday. Which means you have qualities that we may need. Be strong."

Leng smiled. He'd be the dedicated ECOC officer who survived Jackson Spence's betrayal. From ECOC, he could go anywhere. Up until now, he had intended that to be a senior posting back on Earth, at the heart of Earth Command. Now, he had a new ambition. He needed to be an Alpha Commander. Alpha Commanders got battle groups. His battle group would eventually be manned only by people who felt the same way he did about the animal-lovers and their cyborg pets.

Revenge is a dish best served cold. The cold emptiness of free space would do nicely: a cold so intense that it burned like his hatred.

A Farewell to Fools
(Y564 PA)

"What do you mean, 'they've gone'?"

"Precisely that, Commodore. Project Spirit is no longer locatable within Earth Command theatres of war or within USE territories. They are, for want of a better word, gone."

"Dammit, man. That's not acceptable. Tightbeam Alpha Commander Spence and inform him that I want an explanation."

"We've tried that sir. They are not on the tightbeam grid either."

Commodore Servan muted the comm and swore. He'd told the damn fools in the general assembly that Spence and his circus were up to something. No one could win that many battles against the Borsen without collusion.

He had never believed Spence's animal-rights sop about the cyborgs being sentient. Damn the man, Earth Command needed that technology. Under proper control, something useful could be salvaged from the mess made by those bleeding-heart animal-lovers. He turned back to the comm.

"Convene the general assembly and get me schedules of whatever assets were assigned to Project Spirit. We're going to need to patch some holes and I want to be the man with the details, not the guesswork."

"Yessir."

Four hours later Commodore Servan sat in the general assembly, heartily wishing that he had not called it before he gauged what Spence had made off with. The numbers were frankly shocking, and he had already spent an hour disciplining people for letting it get so out of hand. He looked up as Admiral Longard stood to open the session.

"We are gathered to discuss the loss of Project Spirit. If you check your pads, the assessments of capability, capacity and remediation are laid out. It is not pretty reading and I thank Commodore Servan for his alacrity and honesty in providing it without delay."

Servan glared daggers at Longard as he sat down, then glanced at the other assembly members. His gaze pointedly avoided the eyes of Admiral Tsander, Spence's long-time advocate.

Over the next few minutes the assembly got louder, as those present came to understand that Alpha Commander Jackson Spence had just under fifteen percent of Earth Command's entire combat capability under his command, with far more than the maximum logistical support that such a concentration of effectives would usually require. It was an army within an army, and it was arguably the most effective anti-Borsen aspect of the whole of Earth Command. Admiral Michaels stood and waved a chubby hand at Servan.

"Good god, man. He's gone AWOL with damn near a quarter of our personnel. How did that happen, and why?"

Now it was time. Servan stood ramrod-straight and let them have it, vindicated in his formerly isolated opinion at last.

"The man is in league with the Borsen. I have suspected it for a while but have been ignored by all of you. Well, now I am unhappy to say that I was right. Spence and his circus have done the dirty on us. High treason is an ugly term, but I believe in this case that it is the only suitable epithet."

"Bollocks."

The clipped rejoinder focussed all attention on Admiral Tsander, sitting in a relaxed pose as if all this was merely business as usual. He raised a diplomatic datapack.

"This was delivered to me as I made my way here. It had been in deferred storage within our secure courier unit. The conditions for delivery were: after a date that passed a week ago, and on the occasion of Commodore Servan calling an Emergency General Assembly. I have only checked the routing information, and firmly believe that we should let Jackson Spence speak for himself."

Servan nearly passed out as his rage rose to new heights. He had been Spence's commander! How dare Spence bypass him and go directly to the assembly! He mastered his wrath and slammed his hand down on the desk in front of him.

"Objection! I need to review my Alpha Commander's communiqué for time-critical information before it is presented to the assembly."

Admiral Longard stood, a look of anger finally disturbing his usually imperturbable countenance.

"Denied. You have accused your own, highly respected, Alpha Commander of treason. Let us hear what he sent us, as the manner indicates this is the first audience he desired."

Servan sat with ill-grace. Tsander walked to the display unit and inserted the datapack. Then he stepped back.

"It is known that I am a supporter and friend of Alpha Commander Spence. Admirals Longard and Purbetch, would you please verify the authenticity and untampered nature of this datapack?"

They looked startled, but did so. Servan simmered as another gambit was blocked. Longard looked about at those present, then actioned the playback.

Alpha Commander Jackson Spence sat in full view of the recorder, his desk behind him and his office on the CRITTURS dreadnought ECD-308 clearly visible. He was alone and the sigils in the corner of the hologram indicated that his office was sealed against all surveillance and comms at the time of the recording, three months previously. He sat forward and placed his cap on the floor before he looked up and started to speak.

"By now you will be aware that Project Spirit is out of communication and detection range. I would guess that some fairly vigorous attempts have discovered that we are not on the tightbeam grid or any of the tactical nets either, and our locator beacons are dark."

He smiled as he sat back.

"You will not believe the amount of agonising I have gone through prior to making the decisions that have resulted in this datapack being recorded and sent. Suffice to say that I have not taken this situation lightly, and with all of the talent, training and experience I have accrued in my rise to Alpha Commander status, I evaluate my actions to be the only ones acceptable for the continued existence and safety of those under my command. I will break this declaration down into simple sections that are unambiguous. Please do not attempt to read hidden meanings into my words. To do so would cheapen the intent. Please also accept that my statements are the absolute truth from my standpoint. In several cases, they are supported by testimony that is included in the appendices of this datapack. Brace yourselves. You will not like this one bit."

Servan glanced about the room. The faces showed curiosity and vague unease. He was aghast. The man was plainly manipulating them. He would insist that the recording be checked for subliminals.

"I, Alpha Commander Jackson Spence, Commander of Project Spirit and thus of the First through Eighteenth Ghost Commando Divisions and all CRITTURS-related aspects of the Earth Command military, do hereby formally declare my and our secession from the Unified States of Earth with immediate effect."

Longard paused the playback as the room erupted. When the furore died down to a level where he only had to shout, he interrupted: "Let's get the whole recording out of the way before we react. Sit down everyone."

"I, Alpha Commander Jackson Spence, hereby level charges of gross incompetence against Commodore Elgin Servan. Please refer to appendix one for evidential testimony."

Servan felt the colour drain from his face.

"I, Alpha Commander Jackson Spence, hereby level charges of gross negligence against Earth Command Operations Control, usually referred to as ECOC. Please refer to appendix two for evidential testimony."

Admiral Michaels looked like someone had punched him in the gut.

"I, Alpha Commander Jackson Spence, hereby level charges of discord causing actual loss of strategic and tactical assets against Alpha Commanders Juval, Mattern, Reddison and Danders. Please refer to appendices three through six respectively for evidential testimony."

Jackson leaned back in his chair to add truth monitors to his brow, chest, neck and wrists. Their readouts joined the privacy sigils in the corner of the hologram.

"Testing. I was Alpha Commander Jackson Spence. I am Commander of the forces gathered under the aegis of Project Spirit."

The readouts showed veracity. Servan immediately decided that this formerly accepted method of proof was suspect.

"At no time have I or any member of my command engaged in any activities with the Borsen except those of direct and unmitigated hostility. I am not a traitor and nor are any of my people. What we are is marginalised, shunned, demonised and about to be subject to formal sanctions under charges of sedition being brought by Commodore Servan, a man singularly incapable of accepting facts that contradict his biases or shortcomings. That is not something I will be party to. To prevent this, I have taken the decision to quit your army and indeed your empire. As of now, I am the first leader of Ghost Command. I pledge that we will not engage in hostilities against Earth Command forces, unless under attack by said. We will also continue to engage the Borsen whenever we can. Should the arrangement be beneficial to Earth Command forces in the same theatre, I trust they will accept a single-skirmish alliance against a common foe."

The readouts showed truth without variance except for deep emotional turmoil. In the holo, Jackson removed the monitors, then leant forward to stare hard into the recording, his gaze radiating suppressed fury.

"You fools. Bloody idiots the lot of you. The Borsen actually retreat from CRITTURS. If we understood the reasons, that could have won the war for us. But your bureaucracy, jealousy and bigotry made that impossible. I will not let my people be victimised as a scapegoat for your inadequacies. Unless you evolve to meet this threat, you are doomed. Learn from this, please. Save millions of lives by changing your wholly ineffective tactics. You have the people with the abilities to do so. I shall not name any I consider capable, for fear of them being regarded as traitors."

He paused as a huge grin spread across his face.

"Plus, I've already recruited several of them into Ghost Command, because I really don't think that you can change. Not yet. After a lot more defeats and deaths, maybe. But after a datapack from an AWOL Alpha Commander? Not a chance."

Servan was disgusted to see Tsander smiling at that. Some changes were definitely required, the first of which would be to classify everything associated with this fiasco so high that it would never see the light of day.

Privateers
(Y567 PA)

We spear down from behind their moon as the night side swings across the planet below. Our monitors pick up their alarms as we perform low-atmosphere braking and drop under their radar. That's when we split up and arrow to our chosen targets, widely separated and a long way from our arrival point.

"Shame-The-Storm, what's our window?"

"Thirty minutes, give or take twenty-three."

"Funny fish. So seven minutes for us?"

"Correct, Fly-to-Live. We are the hare."

Like privateers of old, one ship attracts a lot of attention and draws the authorities, while the rest of the fleet steals what we came for, quickly and quietly. Alpha Commander Spence's rules are for minimum casualties, especially amongst civilian populations. Ghost Command may be forced to raid while it establishes its infrastructure, but he sees no need to do further damage to our reputation.

So, tonight we're the ones to draw the Earth Command pickets after us, by breaking unpopulated things and being obvious, all the while pretending to be a big, nasty threat.

"Shame-The-Storm, make some noise. What's on the playlist?"

I launch a couple of freight skiffs, rigged to be detected as loaded for looting, toward their main fuel depot. Going for their fuel always seems to provoke them.

"I have half a dozen bridges, a dam and the spaceport apron lined up for our whistle-stop tour of Cadmius Two."

"Then let's rock 'n' roll. All hands: prepare for stupid manoeuvres without warning."

I reconfigure myself for better atmospheric traction and slam a left, shooting the other pair of skiffs toward their central armoury. Not a chance either will make it, but the amount of stuff they'll redirect to make that happen is less stuff to come our way.

"Bridge one, a fine single-span of the classic freestanding arch school. Your preference?"

"Drop a screamer in the centre."

A screamer is a big, ominous, armoured box that makes all the right noises to sound like a fission bomb or collapsile field generator. It'll take them a while to figure it out.

I pull my nose up into a near stall, pop the screamer, check it's going to actually hit the bridge – I only made that mistake once, but I'll never live it down – and then arrow off toward the next bridge.

"Bridge two, in the viaduct style with spectacular central arches."

"Take it off at the knees."

Which means I slam through the centre arch, with the obvious results. The impact is hard: they must have run some modern reinforcing through the old metalwork.

"That was rough. Damage?"

"Nothing that a couple of days work won't fix, but my manoeuvring is down by fifteen percent."

"That brings you within range of their interceptors, doesn't it?"

"It does. But I can still outrun them."

"Then do it. We hit what we can on the run, with no fussing. Let's carve a line they can follow."

Five minutes later and the dam has a screamer sinking down toward its base on the wet side, an elegant suspension bridge has severed cables and the spaceport apron looks like something ploughed it.

"Three, two, one. Upship!"

I point my tail at the ground and give it everything I have. I reach escape velocity before I hit the clouds, and the interceptors that have been dogging my trail give up. I bring my shields to forward and flank, just in time to lose the entire front shield as I go through a heavily stealthed large satellite in low orbit. Not sure who owned that, but as even I didn't see it, the people below are probably better off without it lurking up here.

Heading out into the system at full speed, I pick up tightbeam confirmations from the rest of the fleet. All targets have been hit. A good operation. I activate the sensor-deception systems that give me a mass-shadow equivalent to our arrival and head for the next planet out, which would be a logical place to rendezvous with a carrier. Sure enough, I soon have company – and it's big.

"Shame-The-Storm, is that a battleship I see?"

"It's an old H-class, so it's either the *Basilisk* or the *Rhino*. Either way, we don't want to meet it."

"You said it's old."

"It is. But those two remain in service because of their armour and armament. The stats are coming up on your sidescreen."

"Good grief. They could hammer their way through a couple of moons and not break a sweat."

"Precisely. Now can we go?"

"Are the raid packs clear?"

I check via the tightbeam.

"They're heading out now."

"Okay, let's react to the battleship and do a runaway round the nearest object that will give us a long-enough detector shadow to enter Hirsch off their screens."

"It's going to be a rough ride. Did you see the range of their main guns?"

"I'm sure you can cope. Take us home, Shame-The-Storm. All hands: brace for impact, drastic evasive manoeuvres, and Hirsch transit without warning."

"Pictures-by-Moonlight is going to love you."

"I told her last time that liquid paints weren't suitable personal kit on raid runs. If she ignored me again, then she deserves to wear 'em."

Out of Time
(Y570 PA)

"They've got reinforcements!"

I checked my chrono. Down to one thousand, eight hundred and forty-three instances. I was warning Flank Axel Leader when Scout Axel Second cut into our channel.

"Looks like two full regiments."

Damn. That meant twelve hundred grunts. I instructed Scout Axel Second.

"I need to know when they're ten seconds out."

"TEN seconds? Ye gods. That's cutting it fine."

"I know, but this is where we hold them, or this sector is history."

"Tick tock, sir. We're on it."

I smiled. One thing about working with two thousand temporally shifted instances of yourself was that you never failed to get the in-jokes. The battle was going as well as could be expected. We had the kill ratio up to one of me to two of them. A new record. Scout Axel Fourth came on.

"Lost Two and Three, sir. You are fifteen from enemy engagement on my mark... Mark!"

I counted down on open channel so all of me could synchronise.

"Five, four, three, two, one, Hawkin!"

With a purple flash, eighteen hundred instances of me appeared in six-hundred-me deployments, at the flanks and rear of the enemy reinforcements. There were cheers on the open channel.

"Pick it up, Axels. We have five minutes to finish this."

From then on, things got brutal: pitched battles always do until one side gets the upper hand. That moment came and I was just about to singularise chrono-me when Scout Axel Seven ruined my day.

"Two hundred Knights incoming, sir!"

Left with no choice, I phased in the last forty-three instances of me. The world around me slowed down, as causality and a few of its friends finally noticed that I was cheating. The rules were simple: I could use idle time from my past to get an instance of me to fight now. Of course, everyone has only so much free time. Behind my eight months, three weeks and four days in combat lay twenty years in training, which included at least two hours a day standing at full combat readiness but doing absolutely nothing. While the latest me was alive, causality took the path of least resistance and any instances of me that died just vanished, temporal ghosts that never existed. Of course, as they never existed, idle mes were available for the next battle.

Assault Axel Nineteen came on the tactical line.

"We're getting pasted, sir. The Knights have the advanced reflective fields."

Scout Axel Thirty-Two confirmed that we were done for.

"They've got Mistresses! I see at least five!"

They were coming for me. It was the only explanation for such a costly manoeuvre. My chrono worked overtime, as I ran temporal and flat strategy predictions. But they all agreed. I was dead. The only variable was how many of them died too. So be it. I overrode the chrono and set it to get a me from tomorrow. With a smile, I phased an impossible instance of me into existence. Causality put its foot down hard and deleted every me, all the opposing forces, and the planet we stood on in a wave of singing grey chaos.

I appeared, naked, in a maintenance locker on the regen ship *ECSV Alexandrya* at the exact time I'd entered the battle on a planet that never existed in this timeline.

My body is much younger. I suspect twenty years, eight months, three weeks and four days, if it could be gauged accurately.

A month has passed and they're still taking notes. In this causality-adjusted timeframe, the chrono-trooper project was abandoned ten years ago. Because the entire first intake of volunteers developed chronic multiple personality disorder – with all the other personalities being me.

Truth in Blood
(Y572 PA)

We rolled into the Dachboro' war zone that night, feeling like hammers of the gods, and no one noticed. The lack of attention displayed by pure civilians never ceases to amaze me.

The rumours about why our military personnel are being gathered elsewhere are wild, but until someone clears the air and issues orders, I'll just shut up and soldier.

Corporal Tankle taps my arm and points through the one-way armoured glass of our bus: "Looks like our contact, sir. Yellow hat and a cigar."

True enough. In the slum areas of any city, standing out was something you just didn't do. That applied double when your bit of the city had been declared a war zone. So, this big bloke in the custard-yellow sombrero, sitting on the bonnet of a long-dead urban racer, was probably our man. The hat kept his cigar dry as he casually ignored the rain, looking our way as we rolled up.

As agreed, Corporal Tankle went out to chat. She couldn't wait to get back in the truck and change into combat rigs, but we all appreciated the view of her fine legs in the tiny skirt and tall heels dictated by her role as a lady from a rolling brothel.

She and Mister Cigar chatted for a bit, then he made a cutting motion with his hand, and she threw her hands up in apparent disgust before storming back into the bus. Beautiful imitation of a whore turned down, I thought, until I saw her face.

"Problem?"

She shook her head and visibly calmed herself before reporting, ignoring the fact she was dripping wet.

"He says his name is Darkmane, which matches with our intel. A dealer in education and stories by trade, apparently. While he's got no issues with the CRITTURS presence on-planet, he objects to our side using it as a cover to line our pockets. His words."

I raised an eyebrow. Corporal Tankle withstood me for a minute, before her shoulders slumped.

"He's very good at what he does, sir. Knew about my holiday on Sairsgard. I got a little hot over that. Sorry sir."

"Then he's far better than you think. What he provoked from you was the perfect reaction to fit his and your cover. Flag Mister Darkmane as an intel asset and query his background. To see through the scaremongering about CRITTURS on the NewsNets, and to know how to bait you, indicates a man who either needs to be co-opted or watched very closely. Now go turn yourself into a soldier."

She nodded and scrambled. I noted she had a fine arse to complement her legs, as she dumped the soaked ensemble and shimmied into assault gear. With a sigh, I moved myself back to the topic of tonight's entertainment.

"Heads up! We are here to deal with a CRITTURS incursion that has turned nasty, just as our psych-techs predicted when their Alpha Commander was convicted of treason."

I held up my hand as my company's faces registered disbelief, then pointed to the uplink mounted in the corner. Its active light was glowing softly.

"To that end, until dawn, Dachboro' has been declared a war zone. You know the rules. If it isn't a civilian, it's hostile. If you suspect that a civilian is actually hostile, you make the call. Be prepared to answer afterwards, but come the moment, I expect nothing except soldiering. Remember that CRITTURS have been known to infiltrate Earth Command planets with allied-human fire teams. Plus, we don't know what goodies the Borsen have given them. So be ready and always shoot first."

I lowered my hand as the uplink's light went off. With a quick move I grabbed and hung Tankle's discarded wet knickers over the pickups. There was muted applause at her choice in lingerie. She glowered at all and sundry, until quiet returned.

"Right. Now for the unofficial briefing. The CRITTURS presence on this planet is small, and ECOC considers it nothing unusual. However, we do have a problem. Analysis of the raid data after an anonymous tip-off showed – in amongst the usual targets – a crop of very attractive hits for a group who wanted to improve their pension funds. This group has no qualms about aggravated looting from friendlies, or even murder. This cannot get out because, without a doubt, it is a small group of Earth Command personnel who are perpetrating these hits under the cover of CRITTURS raids."

Corporal Candy raised his hand: "So we clean house and let the whole thing be blamed on Ghost Command?"

I shook my head: "I'll pretend that you did not use that banned term, Corporal. Otherwise, you are correct."

Candy glanced about and shook his head without further comment. I wasn't surprised. His brother had left when Project Spirit had vanished. No warning, no details given. I knew that former Alpha Commander Jackson Spence had communicated with Earth Command after deserting with a significant chunk of their forces. The contents of those communications were classified so high that I guessed you would need oxygen tanks to be able to read them. I had lost half my company in what was unofficially termed 'the Exodus'. Those that remained were considered to be of questionable loyalty, and I knew most of them wished that they had been given the option to go with Spence and his forces to form Ghost Command.

Even I admitted that I would like to ask Gemma why she went. Her last message to me, sent on the day they went dark, had been interdicted. But enough reminiscing. I had bad guys to kill. Politics aside, we were here as a kill team. Because we were expendable. It was possible that ECOC would order Dachboro' slagged if it made the embarrassment go away. With that, I had a sudden thought.

"Saunders. Have you sent that flag about Darkmane up the line yet?"

"No sir."

"Then hold it until we're on the way out."

Everybody realised the implications of my decision.

"Right, enough of the wasted air. Ladies and gentlemen, we have criminal activities to curtail. Stand to."

The company got itself sorted in record time. Something really annoyed them about members of our own military ripping off our civilians for profit, while blaming those who could not respond, but had been comrades until eight years ago.

We rolled silently through the rain-pummelled streets until we reached our patrol zone. In it lay the four remaining premises that had the right target profile for our thieves. The timing was good: CRITTURS raids had begun in two other cities within the last few minutes. We battened down the doubts and got ready to do bad things in a good cause, parked two hundred metres from tonight's target of choice, if Darkmane had been correct.

Because we were dealing with troops from our side, we could not rely on any of our usual tech. Tonight was going to be done the old-fashioned way: manual observation and local headsets.

It was a wet two hours until my headset clicked twice. Private Yall had a contact on the far side of the building. I had just motioned for us to move out, when a Ballista III anti-vehicle missile ruined my hopes of facing an embarrassed and reluctant enemy. I saw it come round the corner, seek twice, lock on to us, and accelerate. By the time it had completed the turn I was screaming: "Bail bail bail! We are blown. Get stuck in if you want to make it to breakfast!"

As I had been focussing on throwing everybody off the bus except myself, the explosion shot me out of the open door like a human missile. It was a shame that my flight path was obstructed by a wall a few metres away. I hit it very hard, and the lights went out.

When I returned, I had flashbacks of the scenes described by survivors of pitched battles against the Borsen. I was lying against a stack of abandoned crates looking at less than half of my company fighting for their lives. You could see it in their expressions. They were going down, but determined to make someone pay dearly for the privilege.

I sat up very carefully and decided that I was good to ruck except for being deaf in my right ear. Then I noted that my left thigh was visible and covered in field trauma patches. I revised my opinion of my state tomorrow – from stiff to bedridden – and slid myself over to Corporal Tankle. The amount of firepower coming our way was ridiculous. Who had been running the looting? I tapped her boot and she ducked away from the window and crouched by me.

"Sitrep."

"We're stuffed, sir. The raiders are mixed special forces and tactical ops. We were giving as good as we got, then they pulled the rug from under us. Reported they had intercepted the raiders and needed support as they were taking heavy fire. Our main comms were in the bus. Every bastard on this planet thinks that we're the bad guys. We tried to surrender twice and got mown down. They can't let us live, and the support units are letting specials and tactical run the show as per standing orders."

I actually had to rest my forehead on the cool floor as the situation sank in. We were going to die, and posthumously be dishonourably discharged. The company would be blacklisted, and our families on Buenos Inicio would be downgraded.

I was reaching for my assault rifle – to go down fighting with my people – when a movement caught my eye. In the darkness beyond the stack of crates behind us, a pair of ruby-red sensor eyes sparked to life, freezing the cry of warning in my throat. The first pair were followed by half a dozen others, and I sensed movement around them in the dark. We were so fucked it was almost comical.

Then Gemma stepped into view, seemingly unbothered by the crap flying about, probably due to the suppressor field that surrounded her with a faint green glow. I raised my hands, after slapping the floor to get everyone's attention. Our firing tapered off, while the opposition took it up a notch in response. I realised that the movements behind her were of a group far bigger than what ECOC had considered to be a standard raid.

She walked forward accompanied by a huge grey steel feline. At her back was a tall gent in full special operations rig. I heard Tankle curse and I put two and two together. He smiled as he spotted my realisation. Gemma patted the armoured flank next to her.

"Pull all raid teams back to the ships. Everyone out except us." Then her attention turned to me: "Hello David."

I just sat there, as war raged outside, and stared at my ex-fiancée, who now led the Ghost Command group that had just captured what was left of my company.

"David. This is Stalks-The-Dark, and you are aware of Dark-Mane. By now you have worked out that you are getting framed. In memory of what we had, and what I think you could be, I offer you Ghost Command support."

I just fell backwards and lay on the floor, looking at the ceiling. The remains of my squad crawled nearer as the firing intensified. I heard Gemma's voice rise.

"Rides-The-Sundown, do we have the comms?"

"That we do, Eyes-of-Midnight. Permission to interdict?"

"Granted. Please pass details of Forty-Four company dependants on Buenos Inicio to our relocation teams. Standard offers with disclosure and bereavement support. I'd like to route Skies-Of-Dawn to back them up. The blacklisting went out before we were prepped."

I sat up and looked at my command. Nine men, five women. All wounded, dirty, bleak-eyed and destined to be executed as criminals, while their families became labour force for Earth Command. I looked at Gemma. My God, she was beautiful. She stared back and gestured towards the windows, where the crap didn't seem to be getting in any more.

"We've run a suppressor across the front of the building. Just don't ask for finer details now. We have about three hours to wrap and run. The only question is; are you and yours coming? As you heard, we are approaching your families now with the same offer. No-one gets dragged, and they will be given assistance if they choose to stay, although it will be very limited. Earth Command doesn't like us very much." She smiled as she said it.

I looked at my team: "I cannot answer for my people and will only answer after they have decided."

Gemma nodded, the dip of her head not quite hiding her smile. Tankle looked hard at Dark Mane: "Can you do what you said you could?"

He roared with laughter and choked out an affirmative while wiping his eyes.

Candy raised a hand: "Do you know my brother, Sergeant Bathlem Candy?"

Another huge feline stalked gracefully into view: "You are a sibling of Kills-Without-Sound? He will be dancing until dawn. I will personally take you to him. I am Slaughter-Child."

One by one, the remains of my company asked some very unusual questions before accepting. Then they all looked at me.

"I accept on one condition."

Gemma stiffened.

"There are a lot of bastards outside who think they can get away with killing my people. I am going nowhere until those who betrayed me and mine are ruined. We may not be able to redeem our name but we shall write the truth in their blood."

Gemma staggered as her feline companion head-butted her gently.

"He is with us. He is Truth-in-Blood. A warrior calling for righteous revenge for his cadre's betrayal is not one of them."

Gemma smiled and shook her head.

"In one thing I am outranked. If a CRITTURS feathers you, you're in, and your wish is their wish. Looks like we get to make a mess after all. Let's get your cadre ready to fight."

Those deployed outside included the criminals from special forces and tactical ops, indistinguishable from the other special forces and tactical ops with them. Both 'factions' had Earth Command regulars in support. It was likely that some of them were guilty too. The combined force had us pinned down and were expecting nothing but a wait before we came out for a final confrontation.

We talked for nearly an hour before realising that distinguishing between the guilty and the innocent by sight was going to be impossible. It was Candy who had the idea. An idea that Gemma's command approved in seconds, and I liked so much I laughed until I split my dressings.

ECOC were mildly concerned when they lost contact with Dachboro'. It occasionally happened when a war zone got a little rougher than predicted. When they lost contact with the planet Staten they scrambled forces to investigate. By then, every resident of Dachboro' not in hiding was staring up at the CRITTURS warship Rides-The-Sundown, and expecting the worst.

The conflict we had been involved in had stopped when what seemed like every rooftop sprouted fire teams of human troops backed by Panthacs. Ferines lazily cruised the main roads with their entire ordnance deployed. Continuing to attack us, into the teeth of this level of reinforcement, would have been suicide and – by inference – any retaliation by the CRITTURS would inflict huge civilian casualties.

Two monstrous Gora, called Able-Doom and Slam-Dunk, acted as supervisors when the time came to separate the criminals from the Earth Command forces they were hidden in. It was surprising how many people actually suspected, and it only took a polite request from either of the eight-metre tall gorillas in shining armour to get people talking.

We sorted the bad from the duty-bound and sympathised with our former comrades. They knew we could not stay, but now they knew that we had been driven into it. The fact that Earth Command would execute us anyway was never explicitly mentioned. My command were the ones to burn the criminals down without mercy. We had lost twenty-five friends to their betrayal. All the local NewsNets were given full access, and the footage of children climbing over the Panthac known as Screaming-Vengeance caused a sensation.

Gemma actually had to turn down requests to join Ghost Command. We cautioned all involved that they had to portray us as traitorous bastards if they wanted to survive the inquisition that Earth Command would bring.

Then we loaded up, and, as we lifted, Rides-The-Sundown broad-beamed the details of our framing and the execution of the criminals through every Earth Command frequency we could access. Then we got the hell out and disappeared like the ghosts we had to be.

Just as we pulled our disappearing act, Buenos Inicio misplaced ninety-three inmates of its detention facilities, all related by blood or love to the late Forty-Fourth. A small but devastatingly fast ship lifted off, punched through atmosphere, and made transit into Hirsch before the planetary defences could react.

Meanwhile, a small freighter made scheduled departure and transited without attracting attention. On the dark side of the furthest planet in the system, it dropped back into real space and made rendezvous with the CRITTURS dreadnought Skies-Of-Dawn.

I was in bed, with Gemma sat beside me, on board the transport Touches-The-Stars, when Earth Command ignited Staten's atmosphere. She held me as I screamed in fury, when I was named as the traitor to Earth Command who had taken the decision to torch Staten, to show Jackson Spence and the Borsen that I was ruthless enough to join them.

My feathered name is Truth-in-Blood. I will write the truth of Staten, in Earth Command's blood, on the pages of history, if it is the last thing I do.

And Far Away
(Y573 PA)

My new home still looks like a very fine place to live, even after walking through that rainstorm.

"Sir! We have fourteen incoming, twelve freighters and two escorts."

I guess I'm not going to get any more time to sightsee today.

"Sergeant, the crop carriers are to be rerouted to Nirvana; you'll need to provide co-ordinates. Then split the remaining freighters evenly between our spaceports. Are the escorts for permanent roster?"

"No sir."

"Then they orbit Asgard and swing out to refresh at Loki before heading back. No communication, as per regulations."

"Yessir!"

I turn to walk back down the path between the grey rock formations. This place reminds me of somewhere on Earth – the Blue Mountains – that I once saw on a nature show. High above me, two raptors circle in the late afternoon breeze, their bat-like wings tilting to maintain position. I smile: they would certainly ruin an eagle's day.

"Sir, Colonel Williams of the battleship Roanoke requests downtime for his crew."

"Request denied."

"Sir, he's insisting."

I stop and look about for rat-cats. No movement: "Put him through."

"Alpha Commander Peters, this is –"

"Colonel Andrew Williams. You are about to quote regulations regarding crew furlough on inhabitable worlds. Those do not apply here. You will refresh at the station in orbit around Loki and depart within ten hours. That is not a request. Peters out."

Harsh, but necessary. Speaking of which, the light has changed. Afternoon is about over.

"Sergeant."

"Sir?"

"Have Leftenant DeGorsi come and pick me up. I have overextended my walk and will not have time to return to base by nightfall."

"Will do, sir. Spectacular out there, isn't it?"

"It most definitely is, Sergeant. And if we do this right, our grandchildren will get to enjoy it."

"DeGorsi lifting off now, sir."

"Very good, Sergeant. Carry on."

A small part of me says that I should be pining for the front, desperate to be fighting the Borsen alongside my fellow Alpha Commanders. Instead I find that I am looking forward to Melanie arriving to share these sights.

I am Alpha Commander, and lead officer, for the establishment of civilisation on eighteen new worlds without any of the detritus of history: a literal green-field restart. We can make this work. We must make this work. For the sake of mankind, Project Thule must succeed.

Observers
(Y575 PA)

The noise is what gets you first. You can hear the damn thing slam into the opposite side of the ship, a hundred metres away. The groaning of framework and scream of venting atmosphere. The rhythmic thuds as it plows through bulkheads, each one getting louder. The breach sirens play catch-up with its savage progress through the *ECS Eindhoven*, spurring people on as they struggle to reach the nearest protection from the airless cold which accompanies this doom.

I had suspicions from the moment the announcement came. I tried to get everybody else in the squad on my side, but the Captain wasn't having it from the outsize suit-trooper who needed double everything. Budgetary grudges won out over tactical precautions, it seemed. So I just volunteered for every duty in the locker room, where our armoured battle suits were racked. Looks like I'm going to be smug and alone.

My suit seals with a hiss and the heads-up displays come online. Just as I heave a sigh of relief, it arrives. The cerasteel bulkhead to my left bulges impossibly, then tears like paper. The sound of that is something which will haunt me for a very long time. The intruder plows through the hole it has punched, a vast tentacle of some impossibly tough alloy shaped into huge interlocking plates. It twitches from side to side, scattering kit and fitments like they weigh nothing.

I crouch and bring my arms up to defend my head. A battle suit is the best protection you can get, but a two-ton girder will go through most things smaller than another two-ton girder. I'd rather lose an arm than my head, so arms up and duck is the way to go.

The tentacle crashes onward, going for the now-infamous through-and-through, before it curls to rip the guts out of the ship. We'd watched in horror as *ECS Dunkirk* was gutted in the same way, ripped asunder by four half-kilometre tentacles radiating from a sleek warship nearly a kilometre long. It had taken the entire fleet's firepower to stop it. The blue-green flash of its alien power source detonating had melted the *ECS Carnegie* down to its centreline. They had been mobilising rescue craft when the Carnegie's gravitic core lashed out, through it's compromised containment, and reduced the half-kilometre battleship to a super-dense toroid barely a metre across. Not one bit escaped the implosion.

ECOC stated that the Borsen had only one of these terrifying ships deployed, because our use of warp suppression was such a surprise to them.

We had never seen the Borsen fight conventionally in free space. Their dominance of warp manipulation made things like traditional warfare above a planet's surface irrelevant. So we hauled into orbit above Afiven, equipped with the first example of an answer to their mastery, fully reassured that the Borsen were all bark and no bite if we took their warp capabilities away.

The warp suppression field worked like a charm. We let the Borsen deploy, then turned on the field. The armour-suited Mistress down on Afiven hesitated for a moment, then she tore our command group to pieces with her energy whips. Everyone died, except for a trooper named Almiraz.

He dumped his guns and pulled out a wicked machete. I was told afterwards that it was a family heirloom, carried into battle by each first son of his family for generations. To our surprise, the Mistress stopped her armour, climbed out and produced a pair of long knives from somewhere. What followed was breathtaking. I have never seen such artistry with blades. In the end, Almiraz went down, his entrails spilling, before she finished him with a coup de grâce that nearly decapitated him. But she was bleeding by the time she did it. We all watched in amazement as she stopped and caressed his corpse, carefully wiping and scabbarding his machete before laying it on his body.

After that she went back to slaughtering and ECOC ordered the space offensive. We sat back and waited for when we were needed to secure the planet. The Borsen ships were driven back for about half a day, then detectors warned of warp traces at the edge of the system. What came was the tentacled horror, and several other vessels of unique design. The initial counterattack cost us the Carnegie, but after that they concentrated on holding their orbital status. ECOC were crowing that we had overawed them when a single missile hammered in from behind our deployment. It was huge due to the massive engines that sent it into the *ECSV Pompey* at a significant fraction of the speed of light. Detection-to-impact was less than three seconds. The detonation of the Pompey sent an expanding sphere of blue chaos through the fleet. Sensors crashed, systems overloaded, and ships lost station. ECOC started screaming about being prepared for warp attack. We closed formation as best we could, but the expected warp incursions did not occur. Instead, two huge tentacled vessels, both bigger than the one we slew at such cost, emerged from warp outside our formation and attacked at flank speed. They started ripping the fleet to pieces while the other Borsen ships swiftly moved into an englobing formation.

We fought, launching every form of ordnance that could assist our fight, along with every Charon interceptor. Their smaller vessels fared badly against ours, but their bigger ships were just overpowering. All through this, we grunts sat and prayed that whatever happened either allowed us to make atmosphere, or at least provided a quick death.

I had made my way to the locker room as the globe closed around us. After seeing Almiraz, I had been inspired to finish working on the huge axe I had been making for use with my battle suit. Having nothing else to do except listen to the communications of a fleet fighting a desperate last stand, I thought I may as well finish it.

I had just done that when I heard the tentacle hit us. As the tentacle passed through the locker room, I suited up, grabbed the axe from where I had dropped it and moved toward the silver ship-killer with a mad intent filling my mind.

The tentacle ceased moving and I saw the side against the floor start to contract, interlaced alloy plates flexing like armour over an elbow, as the tentacle started to curl.

I leapt onto the tentacle. My thinking was simple. No last gesture of defiance, just a crazed survival drive. When I reached the top of the tentacle, I drove the spike of my axe into it, between the plates, twisted it in a shower of sparks and freezing fluids, then hung on for dear life as the tentacle tore downwards, eviscerating my ship and killing my comrades, yet shielding me from damage with its massive girth.

Sure enough, a few minutes of hell later, I was in free space, as the tentacle curled away from the crumbling remains of the Eindhoven. I had no wish to take too many chances, so, gauging the clearest piece of space above me, I tore my axe free and pushed off with everything my battle suit could provide.

I shot forwards, finding the axe useful for batting debris out of my path, or for changing course by hooking a larger piece of wreckage. I rose rapidly above the plane where the combat was occurring and looked down at the end of Earth Command Battle Group Ten.

About half an hour later, it was all over. The Borsen did not even attempt to salvage or investigate: they just swooped down upon Afiven. Three hours after that they departed, their grim work done. I saw the warp-field sweep around the world, killing every living thing. I also saw the single, tiny ship that travelled above the leading edge of that field. I amped my gear to capture every detail that it could. I had never heard that ship mentioned before. Maybe someone could salvage the record from my suit, when they finally recovered it. I would probably be long dead, but the thought of leaving something possibly of importance appealed to me.

When the vessel passed out of range, I spent some time checking my axe over. I found that it had survived it's field-test with nothing worse than scratches. After a moment's thought, I adjusted my suit's long-barrelled weapons rack and the life-saving melee weapon came to rest, head-up, behind my left shoulder.

I had been drifting for a further six hours when I finished the Combat and Strategy manual I had always meant to read. The suit hummed quietly, obeying my directives to keep me alive as for long as possible. The peace out here was incredible. Shame I could not wander back to the squad, refreshed after this break. Quietly I sounded off the names of my squadmates, then expanded to include everyone on the Eindhoven that I had known. I've never been a religious man, but speaking their names into this calm seemed fitting.

"Holy shit, sport. How many of the poor buggers did you know?"

The woman's voice over my comm came close to finishing the job the Borsen had failed at. I brought up my tactical and found I had company. Firing my manoeuvring jets I slowly rotated to face –

An angel.

My sensors saved me from discovering religion. It was a battle suit, something so far beyond mine it was ridiculous, with huge wings that arched up and back adding to the visual impact.

"Bloody hell, miss. You nearly scared me to death. Which would be a shame, given the day I've managed to get through."

Her laughter was deep and sent a tingle up my spine: "Fair comment. Now, how about a shower and some hot food?"

I looked about. Just her. Then again, those wings may have been impressive but I guessed there was a mothership somewhere.

"Sounds good. Your mob need another suit-trooper? All of a sudden I'm looking for a unit."

A rainbow ripple in space behind her faded as the ship it concealed rejoined the accepted visual spectrum. It looked like a big bird too, with a lot of interesting-looking bits sticking out.

"You had the smarts to avoid being part of the ruin of the Tenth, so you're good by me. We'll have to see what the boss says."

She flew in easily and offered a hand. I took it, and soon we were heading for her ship, which turned out to be farther-off and a lot bigger than it first appeared. I saw its name as we passed the prow. *ECSV Thunderchild.*

A while later, my pint-sized and very shapely rescuer stared me squarely in the solar plexus before tracking her gaze upwards.

"Sweet mother studly. Did they make you out of two normal-sized people?"

I laughed. I come from a family where genes from both sides bequeathed me a double-dose of massive. At seven feet tall, I had decided to be muscular rather than lanky. Five years of hard training had been augmented by three years in the military, who liked the occasional monster that looked good in a dress uniform. The end result was me, who had been forced to become an expert modifier of every piece of gear they gave me because it was all sized for normal people.

Fortunately, I had recognised the rank blazons on her suit. I came sharply to attention before replying: "No, Colonel. Maori and Norse blood, plus a bit of hard work."

She stood back, nodding her head in approval: "You're actually about the size of a Borsen Knight. Which makes me happy, because we have a shitload of Knight gear that no-one can use. So I think you're in. Commander?"

She turned her head up and back as she finished the sentence. On the crossway above, a figure lit a cigar before leaning forward to regard me. He hadn't been there just now and I hadn't heard him arrive. That was worth remembering.

"We're an information-gathering outfit, Colonel. Apart from your curiosity about his personal performance, does he do anything other than be unfeasibly large?"

"Sir, I observed a small vessel tracking the leading edge of the warp-field across Afiven. I gathered all the data that I could with what I had available. Thought it might provide something useful when someone found my body."

He nodded: "That was one of our drones trying to detect anything that we missed the last half-dozen times we've witnessed a warpkill event. It didn't, but good spotting on your account."

The Colonel looked up at the Commander and placed her hands on her hips. There was a whole conversation in the posture that backed her stare.

"All right, Colonel. If you promise not to shag him down a dress size, he's in. Welcome to the madhouse, Trooper. We're the invisible people who watch others die, while gathering as much information as possible about the Borsen. That intel we pass to Earth Command, and to Ghost Command. Do you have a problem with that?"

Ghost Command? These people acted as first-in recon and intel gathering for both human contingents? I was in.

"Not a bit, sir. I think that it's a good idea. We need everything if humanity is to survive."

The commander waved a hand: "Glad to hear it. He's all yours, Colonel."

I looked down at the Colonel, who was still trying to adjust her blush.

"Okay, I'm busted. So we can either do the rank thing, or you can call me Isla, except when other crew are about," she said with a very improper grin.

I grinned right back at her: "I'm Svalten. If I may be forward, why don't you give me a guided tour of the shower facilities?"

Leng's Crusade
(Y577 PA)

Gadison Leng looked up from his command couch at the wasp-waisted form standing at parade attention, feet perfectly aligned on the "Wait" chevron.

"Yes?" His voice displayed no emotion other than a hint of boredom. It was one of the many attributes that made him terrifying.

"Lancer Coundre, sir. You requested my presence."

He sat up and grabbed his jacket. The massive scarring of, and tech repairs to, his torso were briefly visible in the bright light from his displays. He donned the jacket in a single smooth motion and stood to glare down at her, his nose barely a decimetre from her forehead.

"Lancer Gillian Coundre. Transferred to Project Safari with the highest confirmed-kill rating of any Earth Command pilot in her flight categories. You requested this posting. Yet today you let a CRITTURS limp off home. This is the third skirmish where you have permitted that to occur, I am informed."

Gillian swallowed, visibly, while her mind teetered on the verge of terror. Alpha Commander Leng had a reputation for being merciless, just as those who served with him did. It was why he and Battle Group Five had been given Project Safari, the ongoing mission to seek out and destroy any and all threats within Earth Command territories. She hadn't realised how personal some of his motivations were until she saw his body. Those had to be scars from a CRITTURS attack! She also realised that people did not serve *with* him. They served *under* him, or not at all.

"We had broken their attack, and I decided that the surviving flights were better deployed in defending the convoy against potential secondary incursions."

He grinned: "Tactically sound, given their damnable habit of ambushing pursuers from multiple directions with layered precision."

She relaxed a fraction. It was a mistake.

"Tactically sound for normal battle groups. I do not care what normal tactics are. You will never surrender an opportunity to kill CRITTURS. No matter what. All my personnel know the risks and accept them. No mercy, no question, no quarter, no hesitation. Go for the throat because they will do the same to you."

He placed a hand on her shoulder. Despite her reinforced skeletal structure and armour-skin suit, she felt the power in his grasp. But the real punch was in his gaze. This man was a fanatic, and finally she was going to find out what his cause was.

"We were officially sent out here to have a look about and make a nuisance of ourselves with any enemies we encounter. But, in reality, Commodore Servan himself instructed me to seek out and utterly destroy anything of Project Spirit that I could. The Borsen are only a distraction, to be avoided if at all possible. The scum of Project Spirit are traitors, cowards and lunatics who call cybernetic animals equals. They must be excised like the cancer they are. So here's your chance to shine or shoot, Lancer. Rise to the cause we are tasked with or GET THE HELL OUT OF MY BATTLE GROUP!"

His roar actually blew her hair back and a mist of saliva sprayed her face. Her expression did not move.

"Very well, Alpha Commander. I see now that I made a foolish decision, as I am unsuited for the rigours of the counter-incursion duties undertaken by Battle Group Five."

His look of fury softened into a cold, thin smile: "Good choice. Your inbound transfer is revoked. Get your gear and get gone before we haul arse out of this system."

Down in the vast hangar, Gillian strode quickly to her craft. She saw that it was fully prepared for long haul work, yet had a full weapons load as well. Her tech, Brion, was already strapped in and had full combat harness on, with survival packs. As she settled into her seat, her question about the unusual preparations died unspoken. She spotted a note taped under the control panels, where only someone properly seated could read it. It was in Brion's handwriting:

> We need to scramble FAST.
> Have removed the demolition
> charges from our drives.

A chill ran up her spine. The rumours about the total commitment of Project Safari personnel were true. Which meant that combat losses were part enemy action and part removal of any who disagreed with Alpha Commander Leng's merciless intentions. Definitely time to go. She stroked the controls and the Hellion III came alive as its motivating artificial intelligence, Sabre, returned from wherever AIs went when they hibernated.

"Gillian. I detect targeting arrays beyond the bay doors. Have we fallen into enemy hands?"

Good question, Gillian thought: "Define as hostile arena, Sabre. Maximum defence, no retaliation."

"That reduces our chances. Brion, may I have full combat control until we are clear?"

"Gill?" Brion's voice was steady, but she caught the edges of panic.

"Yes, Bri."

"Sabre, you have combat helm."

"Sabre, you have flight helm."

Brion gasped. Gillian had never relinquished pilot duty before.

She explained as the drives powered up: "They have our records, Bri. They will have factored my psych-profile into their evasion plotting. So we have to do something unexpected."

"This should be interesting, boss. First time I've done a full duck-and-run from one of our own flagships."

"It's a first for me too, Bri. Brace yourself. Sabre: FLEE!"

That one-word directive was standard in all of Earth Command's new generation of vessels. It gave the onboard artificial intelligence a single objective: to escape from the current tactical arena with all personnel unharmed, using all systems under its command to do so.

Gillian and Brion felt the cockpit G-dampers activate as the Hellion lifted, assuming full flight configuration within the hangar – something directly contrary to regulations. Just as the comms lit up, the Hellion departed with a roar. The drive plume warped deck plates and melted sensor arrays.

Immediately upon exiting the hangar, it corkscrewed itself diagonally upwards, oriented itself to the hull groove that ran the length of the vessel, where the core defensive weapons were housed, and went to maximum acceleration. They passed turrets with millimetres to spare and shot over silo doors even as they started to open. By the time they cleared the battleship's drive apertures, they were moving faster than any ship that Project Safari had available. Sabre completed the escape by shooting every piece of sensor-deceiving munitions they had in every direction, and left several anti-pursuit mines scattered in their wake. This proved to be a sound decision, given the number of detonations that blossomed behind them.

Three minutes later, Battle Group Five headed out at flank speed. The Hellion and its crew found themselves flying through an unnamed and deserted system.

"Relinquishing flight and combat controls. Flee directive enacted successfully."

Gillian gently rolled her neck. G-dampers were life-savers, but when they were maxed out, you emerged feeling bruised and stiff.

"Sabre, log that manoeuvre. Flagships should not be evaded that easily."

"Noted, Gillian. Awaiting further instructions."

"Bri? What next? Our lift home just abandoned us after trying to murder us. I presume that the pickup request that would usually accompany our transfer was not sent. By the time we get to any USE habitat, we'll be flagged as KIA at best. As Leng has Servan's backing for his genocidal crusade, I have no doubt that he has ways to ensure that those who disagree and escape do not blemish anyone's perceptions."

"Well, as I see it, we have five choices: scoot about in-system and die of starvation. Try and piggyback on a Borsen warp jump, hoping it takes us somewhere with better options. Pick a star, aim at it and max the drives. Find a liveable planet, set up shelter and start a new colony. Join Ghost Command, after we telepathically locate one of their ships."

Gillian snorted. Brion had the worst covered with humour as usual.

"Gillian? I have detected four incoming traces at the edge of our range. They are Hellion Twos. Scans indicate that they are not ECEI - they're only ECI: single pilot with neural interface, no artificial intelligence."

She punched the console frame. Damn Leng and his bloody crusade, of course he'd have volunteers for a one-way glory run to dispose of problems!

"Sabre, we're out of countermeasures?"

"Correct. If I had not used them all, we would be dead by now. Alpha Commander Leng's fire control was optimised to kill us."

"Sabre. Tactical options?"

"Likely outcome: one hundred percent probability of demise, with seventy-five percent enemy casualties. Factoring in combat data from Project Safari reduces casualties to fifty percent, on their side. They are very effective."

"Bri, I think we're stuffed. Anything to add?"

Brion worked his boards mercilessly. AIs like Sabre were superb at straightforward battling. For the barmy stuff that saved your skin, and possibly snatched victory from catastrophe, humans were required.

"Gill, I've got a bloody huge anomaly lurking at the three o'clock position of the gas giant at five o'clock to us. A detector-void that absolutely cannot be natural. Sabre, stealth-scan starboard rear quadrant."

Stealth-scanning was a new science. It looked for traces of the various technologies used to hide something from detection, not for the object being hidden. It was called a 'noisy' technology because whoever was being detected would know it, due to some sort of feedback effect between the stealth-scan and the cloaking fields.

"Confirmed, Brion. There is vessel of larger than capital-class size under advanced stealth protection in that quadrant."

Gillian cursed under her breath. Alpha Commander Leng was cunning as well as fanatical. To leave one of his dreadnoughts behind was a move she hadn't predicted. Then a cold dread stole over her: "Sabre, did Battle Group Five depart with full complement?"

"Confirmed, Gillian. All rostered vessels left at flank speed in Standard Formation Eight."

Gillian felt Brion jump as realisation hit him. If Leng's fleet departed with full complement, then this capital ship was from a different fleet, or it belonged to either Ghost Command or the Borsen.

"I have twenty contacts moving to englobe the Hellion Twos. Scans indicate that they are CRITTURS strike craft with a variant profile. Full sweep for logging?"

Gillian quickly weighed the chances of antagonising the CRITTURS against the minimal benefit of accurate information: "No."

"I have incoming comms. Accept, deny or countermeasure?"

Brion snorted mirth and Gillian smiled. As if countermeasures would be any good against something which could dispense twenty ships that moved like *that*. She watched in awe as the formation roiled around the four Hellions, their movements reminding her of birds. No, something else.

"Sharks. They're shark-template interceptors."

"You're right, Bri. God, but that's an elegant massacre. Sabre, accept incoming comms."

"This is Ghost Command Dreadnought Storm-Surfer. Who do I have the privilege of conversing with?"

Gillian twisted herself to catch Brion's eye. He shrugged. The voice was conversational, warm, even slightly amused.

"This is ECEI Hellion Three, designation Sabre. Lancer Gillian Coundre."

"Who is your gunner?"

"Specialist Brion Matherson."

"Then I presume that Sabre is the resident entity."

"That is correct."

Gillian started. Sabre had replied without requesting permission. Which meant that -

"We're not speaking to crew, are we, Storm-Surfer?"

She could almost hear the laughter underlying the reply, in a woman's voice: "You weren't, but you are now. Captain Elvira Turner. You seem have had a serious falling out with your command line, if I may say so."

Brion cut in with vehemence: "We discovered that we're allergic to genocidal maniacs, ma'am. The leader of the fanatics has a rather final way with those who don't make permanent roster."

"Oh, Gadison Leng has always been a bit intense, apparently. Can I offer you a lift anywhere?"

Gillian twisted to look at Brion again. His hand came down on the mute button.

"Hitching a ride with Ghost Command, or Sabre getting our bodies home in time for unmarked disposal. I vote we go to the zoo, boss."

Gillian smiled in spite of her fears.

"Sabre. Do you have an opinion?"

There was a noticeable pause: "You have never enquired that of me, nor queried my hibernation time. I am surprised and grateful that you request my input. I have obtained from Storm-Surfer the parameters of technological intelligence environments within Ghost Command. He has given me sufficient data that I would like to witness them directly."

Gillian nodded and Brion lifted the mute from the comms.

"We need a place to park for a bit and freshen up. After that, destinations can be discussed."

"Fair enough. Can you three wait while I get my Hanfins back on board? They get twitchy if they have to queue."

"They do not. The evil queen tells you lies. My pack are civilised hunter-killers with conversational skills and manners to match." The voice that cut in was deep, almost growling, but strangely clipped.

"Gillian, Brion and Sabre, may I introduce Bites-Down-Hard, leader of the Brightwater pack and one of the few Makos."

Sabre commented: "Port side and parallel."

They looked. The ship alongside screamed 'predator': from its red and blue stripes to its twenty-metre length, it was a needle of focussed hostility. No cockpit marred the perfection. Thrusters, vents and nozzles revealed hypermanouevre capability, streamlined blisters hinted at countermeasures, while stubby fins had the concave tips that indicated heavy weapons hardpoints. The business end had a single pulse weapon that Gillian guessed ran damn near the length of the ship, directly fed from the oversized gravitic core near the tail.

"It is a pleasure to meet a Hellion Three. We watched your escape, would like the parameters used." Bites-Down-Hard was clearly intrigued.

"That will be subject to negotiation, apologies." Sabre was mindful of their unusual diplomatic status, and Gillian released a breath she wasn't aware of holding.

"No problem. Chat later." With that, they watched the twenty sleek strike ships angle toward the massive ship that finally emerged fully from concealment.

"Oh my." Brion's voice was reduced to a whisper of awe.

"Yup. That fits the infoburst on a Generation Four CRITTURS dreadnought. Makes the numbers seem silly, doesn't it?"

"Hell, yes. It looks like a whale. A really big one in chunky armour, with a fortified bunker city on top, turrets all over, and way too many fins."

Gillian chuckled again: "Let's go and see if the rumours are true."

"Which ones?"

"Bri?"

"Yes?"

"Shut up."

Leader of the Pack
(Y579 PA)

The troop carrier bay is rockin' to the latest release from 'Mad Dogs and Englishmen' and my squads are leaping to the beat. It's absolute mayhem and louder than a firefight in an echo chamber, but that's the way we do relaxing. I never really appreciated why my troops – and pretty well all Dog-T's – love this stuff so much, until I decided to make my command posting permanent and had the aural modifications necessary to integrate fully with dog soldiers.

Psychobilly played by Dog-T bands uses the whole auditory range that Dog-Ts can hear. A human just misses too much: including the savage humour that is included outside human hearing range.

I've commanded human troops who I am proud to call friends and have experienced the familial bonds of combat squads. But here, I am with my pack. I step out onto the deck and the music stops.

"Alpha on deck!" The call is made by Chase-The-Stone, my Lead Captain. With a staccato series of crashes, the whole regiment falls in, leaping vehicles and rigs to assemble in record time. I grin as Fox-By-Night skids to a halt in front of me, snapping her forearm across her chest, the belts from her arm-mounted machine gun clattering against her stomach plating.

"Seventh Ghosts ready, sir."

I look at them, gleaming in the ready lights – where they have not broken their outlines with intricate tribal style patterns in matte camouflage colours. Their organics are mainly Alsatian and Rottweiler, with splashes of Chimpanzee and Leopard for bipedal co-ordination and climbing. Their mechanics are a two-metre bipedal combat chassis with modular hardpoints and the special tech that allows them to become quadrupeds for fast movement. They are damn-near literal dog soldiers. I move in front of them, gesturing Chase-The-Stone and Fox-By-Night to fall in.

"Heads up, puppies. Chalfont has a Borsen problem and the big CRITTURS can't fit down the little holes. Now Earth Command got their arses handed to them before us, so this one's a bit warm. The snake-armed bitches and their pussy-whipped boys are refusing to bug out and thinking they have us outfoxed."

I grin as a low growl starts, coming from eight hundred places at once.

"But I told Knife-in-the-Night himself that I knew some dogs of war who could ferret as well as they foxed. Was I lying to our Chief?"

The roar of negation nearly blows my eardrums. I come to parade attention and the whole regiment snaps to.

"We call Wakan Tanka on the ground this time, puppies. Knife-in-the-Night has given us coup on Chalfont, if we can take it. Are you ready to put the first world on the Seventh Ghost Regiment banner?"

I'm glad I muted my pickups as the whole deck goes crazy. Counting coup is an old tradition. Ghost Command awards it as battle, campaign or world emblems added to the regimental banner and sub-banners of the group or groups who contributed most. Alpha Commander Knife-in-the-Night makes the decision after reviewing recommendations from all the commanders involved in each action. The world emblem is the second highest accolade possible. For my Dog-Ts, it would at last be a visible recognition of their worth.

I gesture for quiet: "Another thing. We may have packmates down there. Chalfont was the home of Project Pavlov's Tosak facility. Knife-in-the-Night says intel confirms that the big dogs did not go quietly; a few small packs and loners may have survived. Getting the Borsen off Chalfont will be a feat to be sung. But returning a breed to the *oyáte*? How many banners are feathered?"

The response is savage and I grin into it. Woe betide anything that gets in our way down there.

The Tosak CRITTURS breed is legendary amongst the fighting units of Ghost Command. Organically hybridised from Karabas, Tsang-khyi and Tosa, their four-legged chassis had an experimental linked-alloy charged armour, a weave between chainmail and scales. I had seen remains, but, to date, not one of this breed had been found functional. In many ways, finding live Tosak would be counted a greater victory than chucking the Borsen off Chalfont. But just in case, me and mine were going to do both in style. I grinned as the noise died down. The last piece of news was where I would beat my retreat, because I wouldn't be able to get any more orders followed for a while.

"Puppies! Pay attention! We downship in thirty hours, so I want everything ready to rock in ten and ready to roll fifteen after that. Finally, a bone for you: we get Chalfont, finding Tosak or not, and Knife-in-the-Night has already approved the orders for Mad Dogs and Englishmen to play at Seventh Headquarters after the coup ceremony. So get it done. Dismiss!"

It got way too loud very quickly. I beckoned Fox-By-Night and stepped out of the bay, with her following close behind. While the pack howled, I needed someone to help me sort the battle orders.

We came in fast, or, more correctly, Wanders-By-Night came in fast, Kilos deployed and her Battle Group behind her. As usual, the Borsen ships in-system lit out as soon as they detected that the attack force was entirely CRITTURS ships. It was discomfiting that we still had no idea why they did that.

We were just down and looking for trouble when Wanders-By-Night gave us the bad news. An Earth Command Battle Group had just arrived and our standing offer of an alliance against the Borsen had been viciously rebuffed. The Battle Group was Leng's! We all knew Project Safari was a front for Commodore Servan's CRITTURS genocide programme after the massacre at Ulan. Looked like things were about to get desperately interesting.

Wanders-By-Night agreed and said she had called for reinforcements, but until they arrived she was going to be tied up with the space and air side of things, so we had to deal with the ground show.

I called my rankers in.

"Something new, boys and girls. Project Safari is going to be dropping in. Until we get reinforced, the ground battle will be ours. So crank it up, because we may actually have a fight on our hands."

My pups didn't miss a beat.

"We get to pound on Leng's executioners?" that from Drinks-No-Water, Fox-By-Night's leftenant.

"We get to pull their arms and legs off if we can. I'm not minded to be polite. Worst case we have Borsen under us and Safari around us. So we are going for the throat until someone says otherwise or we run out of bad guys. Am I clear?"

"Yessir!"

With that, we formed up and headed out, sneak mode on and everything watching for anything. I had revised the battle orders to keep us together, but eight hundred Dog-Ts is not something you can hide. We were spread in ten- and twenty-dog packs across about four kilometres of ground, chasing the sundown and heading for the biggest Borsen burrow that had been found. I expected hostilities before nightfall, and wasn't disappointed.

"Contact left! Long-range patrol!"

"Shut them down."

Forty Dog-Ts just rolled over the ten-man Safari scout team as the rest of the Seventh Ghosts picked up the pace and kept moving.

"Contact right! Knights!"

"Contact left! Skirmish group!"

"Free fire."

Firefights blossomed to either side as we upped the pace again. With Borsen on the right and Safari on the left, the burrow looked increasingly like a good place to take and hold.

"Units Two and Three, four-step and get me that bunker!"

Ahead of me, two hundred Dog-Ts dropped into four-legged sprints and disappeared into the dusk.

"Contact rear! Safari incoming!"

Here we go: "All units, this is Wolfman. Kill at will. Keep your packmates alive. We roll until we take the bunker, then we dig in and hold our turf. Alpha Pack on me."

With howls that echoed through the twilight, six hundred Dog-Ts became a moving mass of trouble for anything that wanted a piece of us. I kept my pack about me and headed for the bunker at a run.

"Bunker over ground and first level clear. Activity below but no-one wants to play."

"I can live with that. Ready to cover pups incoming under fire."

We raced up the ramparts of the bunker and joined Units Two and Three in setting firepoints and then assembling heavy weapons to go in them. Whatever came at us was going to regret it.

"Unit Four, Wolfman."

"Go Four."

"Safari is armed for bear in a full-force deployment. I swear they're actually frothing at their mouths."

"If they're that rabid, see if you can sucker them into spinning off heroes and small attack groups. Let's start wearing them down and mixing them up. The angrier they are, the less thinking they're doing."

My pups played lethal games of tag until darkness fell completely. A moonless night gave us the advantage and Leng knew it. He withdrew his fireteams and bivouacked. As for the Borsen, they were gone, again.

"Unit Seven: give the Safari kids enough time to get smug then punt some noisemakers over their lines. I want them to have a sleepless night, but take no chances for kills, unless the opportunity is clean. Unit Five: cover Seven and put down some tanglewire and anything else to make their morning difficult while you're there."

High above, something blew up. Wanders-By-Night was doing her job, and I just hoped we weren't wearing the thick end of the beat-stick up there.

The night was uneventful for us, I rotated the resting at unit level and, by dawn, everybody had managed at least two hours. The last shift, from Units Seven and Five, wandered in looking smug. I pinned their NCO, Leap-No-Cliffs, with a glance.

"Give."

"Drummer-Dog and Thistle-Maw got inside their lines, Wolfman. Safari will be walking today if they don't check their vehicles."

As if on cue, a series of explosions thundered from the east. The Seventh howled in approval.

"Good work. Commendations for initiative and bravery, two weeks latrine maintenance for disobeying orders."

He grinned: "They bet one week. They're going to be short of cash too."

I laughed. This was what made the pack. The commendations went on record; the scutwork for bad behaviour was worked off. It kept the rosters clean and the discipline tight. I knew damn well that some of Drummer-Dog's and Thistle-Maw's packmates wouldn't scat for a couple of days before they started their term scrubbing the toilets. CRITTURS may be mainly tech, but those with significant organic components need to eat and thus to void themselves, and I swear that Dog-T 'output' is the nastiest goo ever conceived.

"All units, this is Wolfman. Today, Project Safari is going to be knocking on our door, after they have tramped all the way here. They are going to be angry bigots and I expect nothing less than stone-cold fury from the lot of you. We haven't lost a tail yet, and I'd like to keep it that way."

We watched for about two hours before Unit One's scouts slid over the wall. They reported Leng's Battle Group were on the way and loving every moment of the traps left for them by Unit Five, and also reported that a large group of Borsen Knights were shadowing the Safari teams. Damn it, why did it have to be Project Safari?

"Spark-Ear, open me a line on Earth Command's general tactical channel."

Chase-The-Stone's head came round so fast his neck nearly snapped: "You're warning them?"

I shrugged: "I'll not bring dishonour to the Seventh."

He nodded reluctant agreement.

"Earth Command leader, this is Ghost Command leader, be aware that you have Borsen Knights on your right flank."

"And your scum on my left, no doubt."

"We're wherever we need to be. But helping the Borsen is no part of that."

"Of course. Why would traitors and animal-lovers lie?"

I could almost hear the sneer. I decided a cheap shot was worth it.

"Whatever keeps you going, Gadison."

"So you know me. Then you know what's coming, animal-lover."

"Watching you getting a singe-cut from Knights, I expect. Have a nice day, arsehole." I waved my hand across my throat and Spark-Ear cut the link.

"Well, he seemed like a-"

"Whip flare! Right flank of the Safaris."

So those Knights had been screening a Mistress? That should make Leng's day. The Borsen didn't have the numbers for a win, but dealing with them would cost Leng dearly.

"Scratch-Back, got anything good for a Mistress at this range?"

"Sorry, Wolfman. Nothing."

"Oh well. I tried."

There were chuckles at that. The battle lasted a good fifteen minutes before the Borsen backed off. As I expected, Leng defied Earth Command's standing orders and immediately continued his advance toward us, ignoring the Borsen.

"All units. Free fire. Kill at will."

The Safari formation picked up speed as it approached, just closing round the gaps created by our remaining traps.

"The mad bastards are going to charge us!"

Well, that was unexpected. I guess our little aggravations had given them a battalion-sized humour amputation.

"Flank and rear fire teams, keep your eyes open. The last thing we need is visitors up our chuff in the middle of what's coming."

With that, Leng's regiments actually stormed the ramparts. Troopers screaming with hate came at us like nothing I had ever seen. So we killed them and kept killing them. Then the fallen bodies started exploding, and I got a clear look at fanaticism. They just kept coming because – dead or alive – they were a danger to us. Troopers are covered in kit that converts handily to shrapnel. The battle went from unpleasant to nightmarish, and we started taking serious casualties.

"Fire teams, chop their legs out from under them, keep them off the top of the ramparts!"

That worked. No legs, no climb. Or no climb quickly, anyway. Plus, death and detonation occurred at the base of the ramparts.

In the middle of this, I heard the rattle of armoured tracks. Looking up, I saw three battle tanks approaching. You clever bastard, Gadison. Get my fire teams hooked into anti-personnel, and then change the game by stealthily rolling in armour until it was too late to deal with them. With a roar, their main guns fired, and several metres of my rampart became an inviting entranceway. Damn, this could get unpleasant.

"All units, breach backed by armour! Go underground!"

We made an effective if messy withdrawal. The problem with shooting them in the legs was that they could still fire back when prone. Runs-The-Rivers solved that, setting up his teams as pairs: one for legs, the other for heads. For a short while we had near-precision charges by using their own rigged corpses against them, but the tanks were beyond anything we had available.

We dived down two levels after collapsing the entrance. Scouts reported that there was still movement below, but nothing had come our way, so we'd live with it.

"All units, status to rankers and then get resupplied, patched and sorted."

The Seventh Ghosts weren't done yet.

A couple of hours later, Leng's mining teams discovered that collapsing the entrance to the upper level was our opening gambit. The mines we left in the debris were a special bonus for the enthusiastic. That should slow the genocidal bastards down.

"Five hundred and thirty-eight effectives. Sixty-one walking wounded. Nine critical. One hundred and ninety-two down." Chase-The-Stone was grim-faced as he reported.

Gods above! That was an evil number of tails gone to Wakan Tanka.

"Estimates of their casualties."

Fox-By-Night smiled: "Best projection is over seven hundred out of action. Low bound is around four hundred. That exploding trick must make their medical teams skittish; I wonder what the attrition rate for their orderlies is?"

I smiled: "That's why there's a delay between death and detonation. So friendlies can duck and cover."

Chase-The-Stone snorted: "Less of them is a good thing. Wolfman, we may have taken a fierce blooding, but all units are viable."

That helped. Losing a whole unit would dent morale far worse than getting a pasting. Enough of the sitting on our butts, time to soldier some more. This battle wasn't over.

"Right. We're down here and Leng will be coming for us. My guess is that he'll try to get a cracker dropped on the bunker, to give his teams access without having to worry about traps. So we need to be two levels down and half a kilometre over before that happens."

Fox-By-Night looked off toward the badly wounded: "What about our non-combatants?"

"Two effectives to assist, six walking wounded to cover. Packmates by preference."

She nodded: "I'll make it happen."

I turned to Chase-The-Stone: "Everyone ready to roll in ten, point teams from the unit with the least casualties. We got anything that can help us navigate?"

Chase-The-Stone looked at the ceiling: "Wakan Tanka."

Not as immediate as I'd have liked, but serviceable: "Then get two scout teams off to investigate the movements we've been picking up from below. You never know what the Spirit in the Sky has left for us."

I saw my words being repeated by the inevitable eavesdroppers. Judging by the grins being exchanged, I'd said the right thing.

The tunnels were big: eight metres round with a levelled floor taking a metre off the vertical diameter. Even so, we were stretched into a long operation by the time everyone had moved out. Fox-By-Night had got the invalids moving with their units, something that made everyone happy. Our low-light vision was supplemented by glow-sticks and we were getting a move on. The scout teams had scent marked their trail, and I had the tail-waggers leaving souvenirs for anything coming up behind, scent-marking them to make sure none of ours got caught if we had to came back in a hurry.

We had just passed three-quarters of a kilometre away, and two-hundred metres down, when the ground shook and dust spurted from all over the place. That would be the gatecrashers.

"Pick it up, puppies. I'd like to be somewhere wider than my dick when Leng comes calling." There were howls of laughter, and some less than complimentary replies, but everyone upped the pace.

I was just wondering where my scout teams were, as the technology to talk through metres and tons of dirt without wires was still a dream, when one of them came our way at the four-step.

"Wolfman, we've found the source of the movement. You were right. Wakan Tanka left us the motherlode."

I kept the surprise off my face: "Where?"

"Down two levels and about two hundred north."

"Room for all?"

"No. But we need you and Alpha Pack. Scout Two is carrying on trailblazing."

"Heads up! Alpha Pack and Unit One, Pack One on me. Everyone else, Chase-The-Stone has command. Keep following Scout Two's markers and let's get a move on!"

Something was making me nervous. Time to shift. The Seventh split and both groups raised their pace to a lope. We had just descended two levels when a runner caught up from the main group.

"Gas! It's not close enough to be dangerous yet, but its coming."

The bastard. We couldn't close tunnels without giving away our positions.

"Tell Chase-The-Stone to treble the scouts and four-step as he sees fit. We can't block it, so we have to outrun it. Given the size of the tunnel system, the lower levels will be endangered first, so we won't be hanging about."

"Yessir!"

He was gone quicker than he arrived. Good pup.

"Okay, let's get our business done and get gone. Pack One, you have the tail-end and spread back to us."

Twenty grunted assents were all I got. Alpha Pack were the command group, but Unit One's first pack were my personal guard; real pleasant, savage, metal carnivores to a dog, the lot of 'em.

We headed down more of these curiously uniform tunnels until we came to a junction. The scout team were gathered there, casting nervous glances round the left-hand corner and looking very relieved that we'd arrived.

"What have we got?"

"Take a look, sir."

I crouched down and did just that. The tunnel ran for about twenty metres before turning right. Gathered at the end, in front of the opening to the right, were a group of CRITTURS like I had never seen. Heavy quadrupedal combat chassis at the very least. I ducked back.

"Tosak?"

"That's what we thought, but they're the size of horses. Plus, they will not move from that opening and do not communicate like we do. We don't understand them, sir. That's why we came for you."

Okay. What did I know about Project Pavlov? They were infamous for abusing the first and second generation CRITTURS. They refused to believe that their creations were sentient. So, any survivors of the final days of the project, when self-serving sadists sought to cover their abuses, would have been through wholesale slaughter, the loss of packmates and friends. They would have no information about Project Spirit or Ghost Command. Or would they? Every Pavlov installation had trainers drawn from a common cadre, that much Jackson Spence had determined. The regular reassignment of those people had disseminated a lot of the mythology that formed the basis of the CRITTURS belief system and grounded their collective identity. I stood up and brushed myself down.

"I'm going in. Fox-By-Night, on me. Be prepared to run, pups. Those do not look like dogs we can take head-on."

I turned the corner with Fox-By-Night by my left shoulder. To all appearances, a human officer with a CRITTURS bodyguard. Now to see how well my trance-learned Pavlov speak had settled into memory.

"Animates! System status!"

The vague mass resolved itself into ten distinct CRITTURS: three massive, the rest just big. The massive ones stepped away from the opening and lined up facing my approach. The growls were unmistakable. There had to be wolf in their splicing, somewhere. I stopped five metres away and looked up at these monsters: four metres to the top of the head, compound eyes, segmented alloy armour.

The central one spoke, the accent clipped and almost muffled by a tendency to growl its words: "Tosak Beta Two, full function, intellectual balance plus eight, total Turing plus four, Feigenbaum plus eleven."

The one on the left started to speak the moment the central one had finished: "Tosak Beta Fourteen, full function, intellectual balance plus nine, total Turing plus twelve, Feigenbaum plus ten."

The one on the right segued in perfectly: "Tosak Beta Nineteen, full function, intellectual balance plus forty-two, total Turing plus twenty-five, Feigenbaum plus thirty."

Okay, the one on the right was a genius in CRITTURS form.

"Query request." This from the central one.

"Granted."

"Status of Project Pavlov? Contradictory data gained by Beta Nineteen requires further input."

Here I go: "Project Pavlov was abandoned in five-five-seven. All assets transferred to Project Spirit. Project Spirit upgraded to independent entity 'Ghost Command' in five-six-four."

Beta Nineteen stepped forward: "Are we transferred or do we retain rogue status?"

I thought hard and decided to try it on: "Rogue status vetoed due to invalid authority of assigning officer. I am Wolf-Man-Wendigo, Alpha Commander of the Seventh Ghost Command Regiment. Your transfer to my command is approved."

Fox-By-Night snapped her fingers in delight.

"You walk with Wakinyan?"

Oh, thank you, anonymous CRITTURS trainer.

"We all do. This is Fox-By-Night."

The central one touched his chin to his right forepaw before straightening: "I am Tundra-Ghost. To my right is Fury-Bushido. On my left is the brains of our pack, Apple-Tea."

"Your packmates?" I gestured to the seven behind.

"From your left to right, Digs-Like-Mole, Thunder-Howler, Bleed-No-More, Faster-Than-Dawn, Twilight-Killer, Truck-Stopper and Bold-By-Nature."

"They are smaller than you, because...?"

"We are Beta units, sized to prove the concept. Control decided that we were not cost effective, so they downsized the chassis and reduced the armour and sleight-interlacing for Gamma series. This compromised the design, and they scaled all later units to fall between Gamma and Beta in size. For the Delta series, they removed intrusion and countermeasure options. No Gamma series survived the reset."

"So your packmates are Delta series. You are Betas, but are you specialised?"

The great head dipped: "We are, Alpha. Fury-Bushido and I are assault class. Apple-Tea is a full-spectrum warfare server. But like the Deltas, we retain the combat effectiveness of our core design."

Ye gods. If all the fancy designation titles meant what they could mean, I had just acquired a pack of battalion-eating monsters. Time to go.

"We need to move out, Tundra-Ghost. Opposing forces have dispersed corrosive gas."

"After you have decided about our captive. We had no ECOC guidance, so resorted to containment and awaited command presence."

A prisoner?

"How long have you been on containment?"

"Since five-five-eight."

That was when the Borsen first hit Chalfont, and started the interminable battles for this dirtball!

"Safe to observe?"

"Affirmative, Alpha."

"I'm callsign Wolfman."

"Affirmative, Wolfman."

I walked down to the opening, between the massive Tosaks. Their armour looked a lot more formidable on live specimens. I also realised that all Ghost Command had ever found were the remains of Gamma series. I crouched and peered under the foremost Tosak, into what was a quite well-set-up bivouac. A woman, with a crude prosthetic right arm and a tentacle in place of the left, sat naked on a lounger, reading a datapack. Then the revelation hit me. The Tosak had captured a Mistress!

She looked up: "The Joyous Ghosts' master appears at last. I was beginning to think I would be here until my victuals ran out."

I straightened up. My improved view showed me the stacks of Earth Command ration packs at the back of the room. Twenty-one years on combat rations? I was sure that constituted some form of torture.

"Greetings. I am Colonel William Fairen."

She stood up slowly. The captivity had not been entirely easy, I saw. She was very thin and, as she turned to put the datapack on the makeshift table, I saw that her back was a mass of healed scars. Her tentacle seemed withered as well. She walked forward until the Tosak growled.

"I am Fshnepri, Mistress of the Borsen."

"You present a problem for me, madam. Your presence explains why the Borsen never fully relinquished this planet like all the other uninhabited ones they have raided. Simultaneously, I cannot let you go. Yet taking you to any of my homeworlds or installations would be a significant risk, given the persistence of your folk."

She smiled: "I accept that you will have to kill me, after torturing me for information. It is a shame: I would have liked to die in combat, so my brood would know of my fate."

Another crazy idea surfaced: "What if I were to offer you the chance to die in battle, in exchange for answering a few questions to meet my personal curiosity?"

She considered, her tentacle caressing the back of her knee: "I see no barrier to that noble offer being acceptable. But I would ask for clarification of the death-in-combat aspects."

"We are Ghost Command forces. At our backs is a large Earth Command Battle Group that is intent upon our demise. They even ignored the opportunity to retaliate against another Mistress, just to continue pursuing us. They will be coming down these tunnels soon, following the gas they have dispersed. That gas is deadly to my CRITTURS, inconvenient for me, but should prove harmless to you. In this scenario, I get to buy time for my regiment to find a place to stand and fight, while you get to meet your end in a suitable manner."

She nodded: "It is a fitting thing. I accept. Ask your questions."

"You called these Tosak 'Joyous Ghosts', in a way that makes me think that it's a title?"

"Correct. For us, who see the shape of what lies within each physical form, your charges are abhorrent and terrifying. They appear like revenants of the dead, yet are patently in the real and quite at home in their mechanical bodies. What you have done in creating these beings is beyond us. They are aware, spiritually alive, and not wracked by agonies untold. We cannot countenance their existence. We do not know how to kill the dead and suspect it may be a ruinous thing for us to do. I do not have the time or material to take you through our society and its beliefs, so accept as truth that we would rather cede a battle than risk offending Rshtra Who Came Back by killing things favoured by her."

Okay, no wonder we couldn't work out why they ran from CRITTURS. Not even the wild guesses had been close.

"Why did you attack humanity?"

"You had the potential to be a worthy opponent. So we goaded you until you challenged us and managed to slay a Mistress. With that, you rose to be a foe we could war against."

"You make war because…?"

"We expand to find consorts and allies. As yet, we have found no allies and few consorts. Human warriors make good consorts, but we must continue. When Galad returns, we must be ready and we cannot stand alone."

"Galad?"

"The progenitors of our race. Rshtra rescued us, and they brood in the outer darks, waiting for a time when the stars align to lead them back to us. But our ancestors were cunning. They turned our world into a vessel and we foray on that, forever a moving target. It buys us time to find allies."

I was now so far out of my depth that my mind was whirling. The Borsen started wars to meet the vague, apocalyptic end-of-times survival dictates of a race-wide religion, derived from their origin mythology? Jackson Spence needed this information, because I had no idea what to do with it.

Thank you, Wakan Tanka. I grinned. The irony was not lost on me in that moment.

"Fshnepri, would you accompany us until we part ways? I shall point you towards your, and our, opponents."

"I have become acclimatised to these great Joyous Ghosts. I would ask to be escorted by them."

"Let's go."

"Scouts, four-step and find our regiment. Then get a direction on Leng."

"Air smells funny, Wolfman."

That was all I needed: "'Ware gas. Move out!"

We sprinted as best we could. In the end, Tundra-Ghost picked up Fshnepri in his massive jaws. I watched terror turn her rigid. It was something I will never forget. A Borsen, the bane of humanity, paralysed by religious fear. Fox-By-Night lowered her off-hand so I could step up into a piggyback. My Dog-Ts were faster than humans by design. With all the slow people mounted, the triple pack really started to move.

At a dimly lit T-junction, Serves-No-Meat pointed to the left.

"Bad guys about a kilometre that way, Wolfman."

I gestured for Tundra-Ghost to place Fshnepri on the floor. She shook like a leaf in a breeze for a whole minute, then stretched. The pops were cartilaginous, not bone sharp. Interesting.

"Fshnepri, your death in combat lies thataway. Kill at will and take many with you."

She grinned fiercely, eyes wide and more than a little maniacal: "They are only humans. To fight again will give joy to my dying."

So the Borsen suffer from stir-crazy as well? I watched her run stiffly into the darkness, her gait smoothing as she warmed up. Mad as it was, I wished her luck. I also hoped she chopped Leng's people to dogmeat and made it back to her Knights. But that was a thought that would never pass my lips aloud.

"Time to go, puppies. At the triple!" I was going to be sore from hanging on to Fox-By-Night when she was in four-step. Then a huge jaw just picked me from her back, and threw me onto another of the Tosak.

"We can carry you with ease and without compromising combat capabilities."

I sucked in air to get round my winding, and just waved agreement to Tundra-Ghost, as Apple-Tea set off, her gait fast and smooth. Far behind us, I heard a firefight start. It continued until we passed Dog-T hearing range. Even wasted after two decades of captivity, it seemed that Fshnepri was very dangerous. Which made me smile - whilst worrying about that sort of resilience.

We pounded down tunnels after the regiment, following scent markers. The splitting of the group meant that there could be no traps left, but I figured that Fshnepri was compensating for that with a will.

A single tail-wagger met us an hour later. He reported facing me, but his eyes were stuck to the Tosaks.

"We're above ground, Wolfman. Chase-The-Stone has got the perimeter up."

Hallelujah for that.

"I see you spotted our new assault pack, Runs-Over-Water. Please let the sentries know that the big CRITTURS with us are Tosak friendlies."

"Yessir!"

A half-hour later I was sitting comfortably in a dugout, ration pack in hand, the sounds of my pack filling the night about me. The Tosaks were wandering about, being marvelled at, and getting to know their new packmates. There were a couple of rank challenges, but, really, they were more for entertainment than anything else: the newcomers being able to ignore everything the Dog-Ts threw at them, and stomp any attacker flat in a single move. One warrior even got a new name: Screams-When-Thrown will never forget the night that the Tosak arrived.

Spark-Ear tapped my shoulder: "Permission to give Apple-Tea full access, sir."

"Do it."

The Tosak settled down in a sphinx-like pose and her compound eyes lit up in rainbow colours. A few minutes later, she turned to look at me, eyes returned to their midnight blue.

"Alpha Commander Wolf-Man-Wendigo, I have oversight."

"Oversight? Explain."

"Chalfont theatre is under my watch. All communications and data structures are compliant."

Not much I could say to that except: "Give me a channel to Thofin two-oh-six-four, and introduce yourself to Wanders-By-Night."

"Done and done."

Wanders-By-Night sounded suitably bemused: "What have you done this time, Wolfman?"

"Found some Tosak, found out why the Borsen are scared of CRITTURS, found out why the Borsen Incursion happened; you know, just a typical Saturday night."

"You're not joking, are you?"

"No. I have priority data for Knife-in-the-Night. It is absolutely critical that he hears what I have got."

"Routing requests now. Who's your new lady friend?"

"A prototype 'full-spectrum warfare server' in a Tosak."

"I have routed that data as well. I suspect our reinforcement window is about to get a lot closer."

That would be good. Gadison Leng was not going to be a happy maniac.

"Wolfman. I have a closed-channel hail on non-standard frequencies. Tightbeam."

"Secure it and make sure we're not traceable. Give Wanders-By-Night listener access. Let's see who wants to chat."

"Done, done and done."

"Is this the leader of Ghost Command forces on the planet you call Chalfont?" A woman's voice, eerily wavering over the tightbeam.

"It is."

"Then I extend my thanks for letting my sister Fshnepri fall in battle. It was a gracious thing to do."

"Execution would have sat badly with me."

"As it would have with us. In acknowledgement, we withdraw. Chalfont is yours."

The channel went dead.

"Wakan Tanka! You're going to be famous, boss." Fox-By-Night was grinning fit to bust.

"Wanders-By-Night, did you get that?"

"I did. I'm not sure where that is on the list of unlikely events for this universe, but I think it's near the top."

I grinned: "Okay, gratuitous surprise and the rest will have to wait. There are still people down here who want to kill us. Apple-Tea, does your oversight include Earth Command channels?"

"It would not be oversight if I only had one side."

Oops. Hit a professional pride nerve: "Apologies. Does your oversight extend to intelligence-data collation and similar functions?"

"Limited, but adequate for gauging what our opponents have left, sir."

"Then do it. Find the tricky buggers as well, if you can."

"Permission to drop their drones, sir."

I just stared at her. What in the name of Turing had the Project Pavlov teams on Chalfont been trying to achieve?

"Hell, yes and not yet, Apple-Tea. Can you feed them data?"

"I will need an upgrade for that, sir. My systems were considered five years beyond bleeding-edge, but that was twenty-two years ago."

Her apologetic tone cracked me up. I couldn't help it: "Then take them down. Take out the ten percent furthest from us first, then drop all remaining ones simultaneously a minute later."

Chase-The-Stone smiled: "You think Leng will fall for that misdirection?"

I shrugged: "We're the thing he hates most, and the thing he fears most too. Ascribing us almost-mystical powers would not be outside the psych profile for his type of madness. If he's coming for us, I'd like him more angry than tactical. That tank trick he pulled was too clever. We're going to have to goad him properly. I also want him verging on superstitious dread, if we can manage it. He likes to think that he's the

nightmare that CRITTURS have. I want us to be his waking
nightmare."

"Suggestions?"

"The silly stuff. Let the pups out. Long range and fast. I want any
leftovers from his Battle Group to disappear, and that includes bodies. I
want Borsen gear retrieved and set in covered dugouts beyond our
combat perimeter, to look like poorly concealed ambush points. Feel
free to rig up any other wrecked gear in suitably convincing ambush
positions. Then put all Safari remains in a long trench beyond the fake
Borsen. Make it three metres wide, three metres deep, and as long as
we have time and wreckage to carpet it with. Oh, and fill the dugouts
and the trench with anti-personnel ordnance of the nastiest kind. I want
bleeding, screaming and paranoia. Stressed troops are crap troops. We
need every edge."

"I'll make it happen."

With that, Chase-The-Stone disappeared. I wandered outside to see
Tundra-Ghost lying on his back, belly armour peeled back, access
panels open and the lower half of my tech sergeant, Spanners-Before-
Guns, protruding from the hole. I strolled up to them.

"If you've broken him, you're going to be digging latrines for a year."

Spanners-Before-Guns twitched in surprise, and a solid thud came
from within Tundra-Ghost. Score one for the boss.

"Not likely, sir. I've never seen this level of reinforcing or
redundancy. Looks like the Beta series were intended to have Ceres-
class gravitic cores, but the budget wouldn't permit. They jury-rigged
body-motion-rechargeable cells, but they're well past it."

"So, if I conjured you up a trio of C-class gravitic cores, are you
saying that the Betas would be more effective?"

"Don't know about more effective, but they'd certainly no longer be in danger of keeling over without warning the next time they come under load."

That's handy to discover before the battle starts. I ran back to my dugout.

"Apple-Tea, get me Wanders-By-Night."

"Done."

"Hello Wolfman. Make it quick; things are a little hectic up here."

"I need three Ceres-class gravitic cores. Now."

"Soon as I can. Get Apple-Tea to send me a bullseye, I don't have time to be subtle."

"Done. Wolfman out."

I pointed out to Apple-Tea where the freightspear could impact. It was the quickest way to get supplies down, without diverting resources. Then I set Fox-By-Night to ensure that no pups wandered into the area.

With that, I realised that I was knackered. I passed command to Chase-The-Stone and hit the sack.

A two-hundred-decibel howl brought me awake, and had me reaching for my guns before consciousness caught up. I looked outside. There was a lot of running, but it was purposeful, not panicked. I had time to dress.

As I finished kitting up, Kitty-In-Disguise jogged over.

"Morning sir. Hostiles are five kilometres out and closing fast. They should hit the first line of diversions in under fifteen minutes. Apple-Tea is waiting over at command."

"Good enough, warrior. Go join your pack."

She saluted and sprinted away. I loped over to command.

"Morning, dogs. Apple-Tea, what are we facing?"

"Eleven hundred effectives coming in three blocks from east, northeast and southeast. The command block is the northeast one. Gadison Leng has been wounded in an encounter with our 'Borsen allies' as he termed it. Seems that Fshnepri was very stubborn about dying. They lost forty-two effectives to her."

Impressive for a one-tentacled woman. Glad we weren't on the receiving end of her dying wish.

"So, our estimates were correct. We've taken eight hundred of them down."

"Close. They've got a hundred effectives guarding their base."

"Which unit took the worst beating?"

"Unit Three. They're down to fifty-eight dogs."

"Send them with a pair of Delta Tosak for heavy support. They go round the forces and take out Leng's base. And I do mean take out. Raze it. After that, they can either loop back or hit Safari in the arse at their discretion."

"Done."

"Where's his armour?"

"Southeast block. Three battle tanks and a crawler."

Damn. Crawlers were impossibly tough.

"Tactical option request."

"Go ahead."

"I noted that Wanders-By-Night is very accurate with freightspears. The last one landed within a metre of the co-ordinates I supplied. If that is her standard deviance, why not spear the armour while it's rolling slow and easy? Just override the braking rockets and parachutes."

I liked it. Unorthodox and, possibly, devastating.

"Do it. Liaise with Wanders-By-Night directly. You have target authorisation. Free fire."

"On it."

Apple-Tea's eyes went colourful again. Just how much kinetic energy could an unbraked freightspear deliver at point of impact? This could be a new tactic.

We waited. A couple of minutes later, we saw flaming streaks in the sky to the southeast. A minute after that, we heard them. The scream was hackle-raising, and the impact blasts threw smoke and debris high into the sky. I wouldn't like to have been under them.

"How did we do?"

"Ascertaining, Wolfman. Please wait."

I waited, starting to hear sporadic fire in the distance, interspersed with the explosions of our surprise packages.

"They are down to one tank and have lost eighty effectives to blast and shrapnel."

"Damn. That tank could ruin our defence."

"Incorrect, Wolfman. Tundra-Ghost and Fury-Bushido have had their gravitic cores fitted. I deferred, as the available time necessitated a bias toward first-line combatants."

I could have kissed her: "So the two Betas can handle the tank?"

"I think they will handle substantially more than the tank."

"Then let them and the Deltas loose on the southeast block as soon as it enters the zone between the fake Borsen dugouts and our combat perimeter."

"Actioned."

I had a good feeling about the coming battle. It persisted as Leng's Battle Group made heavy work of our three diversionary lines. They were particularly incensed by the quarter-kilometre trench carpeted with their fallen, tossed in with the rubbish and wreckage. They spent a lot of their venom on the fake Borsen dugouts and then came at our rocky refuge full-tilt. Well, I had my wish: they were raging.

"Leng is encouraging suicide runs and no quarter. He sounds quite upset."

"All units, this is Wolfman. Free fire. Kill at will. No quarter. We either win or die, and dying would ruin my plans for this evening."

Yips of approval followed that, and there was nothing more to say. We waited.

First blood had been ours, thanks to the traps. Second blood to us as well, with the freightspear trick. Third blood, and coup, arrived as Leng's southeast block became the field-test for the first Tosak pack. I watched it all happen and still do not believe the utter mayhem that heavy assault class CRITTURS walkers can cause. The two Betas went through the block as though the firepower being turned on them was only a rain shower. Their interlaced armour sparkled as it defeated all comers. Then Tundra-Ghost actually bit the tank's main gun barrel in half, before he and Fury-Bushido demonstrated that the turret flange was not immune to the law of levers. Apple-Tea has the recordings of Leng's command channels when that happened. The fear and disbelief is palpable. Meanwhile, the Delta Tosaks were roaming through the south-eastern block almost at will, soaking up incredible amounts of damage and killing with a chillingly cheerful ease.

"Heads up, puppies. Incoming."

The northeast and eastern blocks ignored their fellows to the south and came at us with no consideration of tactics or self-protection. They charged, screaming insults and war cries. Thankfully, their hatred was only toxic for them. Over the command channel, Leng was exhorting his men and women to greater efforts, laying down a rant about their cause making them stronger than the weak-minded fools and their abominations.

For all my levity, it was a vicious battle, and Leng's Battle Group showed that it deserved its fearsome reputation. They may have been fanatics, but they could fight. Unfortunately, when it comes down to it, a soldier in the latest war gear still has skin and bone under his uniform, which only has laminate armour plates to protect the vulnerable bits and armoured mesh reinforcing the joints, all covered in reflective coatings. A Dog-T is a two-metre tall cerasteel knight-in-armour that is lethal and bulletproof even when naked. Geared up, they are fearsome: far more than a half a dozen men can deal with – unless said men have anti-tank weaponry. Leng's troops also had a fatal case of being absolutely sure that they were better than us. They may have been in many other ways, but, in the end, we had their measure this time. They were dogmeat.

Gadison Leng never knew what hit him. Stalks-The-Fences did not even know whose head he tore off: he was coming back with his unit and the Tosaks from levelling Leng's base. Racing in to assist us at a four-step from the northeast, Gadison's command post was the first thing that got in the way. So they hit it hard and then rolled on to join the main battle, leaving Leng and his command team in pieces.

An hour to break them, an hour mopping up. Despite my qualms over execution, there was no way that anything of Project Safari and Battle Group Five could be allowed to survive. We had to send a message and write it in their blood.

The trench was handy: we could just chuck in the remains and backfill. The finishing touch was the Betas dragging the tank turret over and embedding it, by the stub of the barrel, in the middle of the mass grave. I etched the memorial myself:

HERE LIES GADISON LENG,
HIS BATTLE GROUP,
AND
PROJECT SAFARI.

GENOCIDE NEVER WINS.

After that, we just gathered ourselves and waited for upship. The orbital paths and near-space were cluttered with the remains of Project Safari's ships. All except his flagship, which had been making for somewhere else at flank speed. The Dreadnought Crashes-Through-Suns caught it with its proverbial pants down and didn't give it a chance to get them back up. The remains of Leng's flagship are spread across, and embedded in, the outermost planet of the Chalfont system.

Chalfont was 'ours', but it was too far from Ghost Command territory to be defensible. We would just take our victories, and the information that could prove to be even more valuable, plus our new pack, and go home.

I needed to sleep for a week, and my Dog-Ts probably needed a couple of days refitting. Then we could have the coup ceremony, followed by the Mad Dogs and Englishmen gig. After that, I could get down to rebuilding my regiment.

Plus, investigating exactly what Tosaks were capable of. And arguing with research over duplicating Tosak armour, because they'd made tentative queries about taking a Tosak apart and I wasn't having that. At least I had a bargaining chip: Apple-Tea had a copy of the Project Pavlov Tosak research data, right up to the order to destroy the facility and the subjects before some do-gooder Alpha Commander named Jackson Spence discovered them. She was the one who had warned Tundra-Ghost when that order came in.

'Genocide never wins'. Seems to me that the Seventh has discovered a motto to go with the world on our newly feathered banner.

Haunted
(Y581 PA)

The laboratory was too quiet: the sort of silence that indicated a
serious problem and those seeking to avoid blame. The vast expanses of
equipment were idle, as the staff stood observing the huge tank of
faintly luminous green gel half-sunk into the floor. Within the tank,
cables hung unattached, still swaying in the aftermath of the tumultuous
splash when the occupant of the tank had disappeared. In the control
room above, a uniformed officer glared at a bespectacled young man
who stood with his arms spread in the classic pose for protestation of
innocence.

"Where did it go?"

"I have no idea. It should be back in an hour or so."

"Back! You mean it's done this before, and no-one told me?"

The anger escalated to fury and Doctor Padironas wilted in the face of
it.

"This is the tenth time. We wanted to gather more data before
reporting."

Captain Anderson looked at the ceiling as he took a deep breath to
calm himself. Losing his temper with the techs just would not help.
They were so deep in this incredible field of biotechnical science that
they just could not see the realities about them. Jackson Spence had

specifically said that they were to be left in the slightly disconnected intellectual wonderland that allowed them to create. That was why every cadre had a veteran CRITTURS-'feathered' warrior in control. He took a second deep breath and remembered the words of Idiot-Breaker: "The cadre techs have too much scientist in their heads to have belief in their hearts."

He looked down at Padironas.

"I will remain until –" he consulted his pad "- Subject Ee-Dee-oh-oh-four returns. Have someone bring me a coffee and a sandwich."

The Doctor exited the room at speed, calling for an orderly to run the meal errand. Anderson looked into the tank. This was the only octopus CRITTURS cadre working from the biggest of the octopus species; attempting to generate a starship-capable sentient of an alternate line to whale-based splices. His thought train was derailed by a stunningly beautiful woman in a lab coat, who entered the room with a mug of coffee and a triple-stack sandwich on a platter.

"Beef 'n' salad with English mustard, Captain. Black double-strength coffee."

She smiled as Anderson's heels thudded onto the floor.

He knew that he was one of the founding cadre and, thus, quite well-known, but the exactitude of this was unusual: "That's spot on. Thank you. And you are?"

"Doctor Crying-Blade, sir."

Anderson smiled. Most people on Project Spirit had two names, one from their parents and one given by CRITTURS. 'Feathered' humans always used their given names when meeting other feathered in public. Professor Padironas was the first case he knew of where the

CRITTURS had admitted to giving him a name, but had not told him, or any human, what it was.

He bowed his head: "A pleasure. I am Walks-in-Honour."

She smiled at his reply: "I know. Idiot-Breaker speaks highly of you and Death-From-The-Shadows sends her regards. Captain Thunder-Down-the-Walls merely wondered if you have learned how to open doors yet?"

She cocked an eyebrow in query as she finished. Anderson shook his head. That exploit on their first day as corporals was always Theakston's favourite dig at him.

"We were at a site rescuing a CRITTURS. I had to crash a controlled door."

She nodded and turned her gaze to the tank below.

"I'm Stephanie, and we are waiting for Swims-The-Singing-Dream to return."

Anderson sat bolt upright.

"Singing dream? Where he goes is a place where he feels there is music?"

"Yes. He cannot define it, but says that it is a place like deep space or the deep sea, but without stars or prey. He can only visit it because there is somewhere that he can be safely."

Anderson shook his head and hit the prime call on his comm. This was too incredible a coincidence to take chances with. The voice that answered caused Stephanie's eyes to widen in shock.

"Knife-in-the-Night."

"Walks-in-Honour, sir. Need you at Cadre Blue Ten now, and we need Kilo support. I'd like to abuse our friendship and ask for one of Thunder-Star's brethren as well; no questions until we are face to face."

There was a momentary pause.

"Kilos are all deployed, but Blood-Moon will be honoured to make your acquaintance in about ten hours. He's one of Thunder-Star's big brothers, and politely suggests that while Kilos would be good, his squadrons of Hanfins will be better."

Anderson punched the air. He hadn't dared to ask for one of the Generation Four CRITTURS warships, but as usual Alpha Commander Spence had read through his words to his need.

Eleven hours later, Shine II became the primary planet of Ghost Command as Alpha Commander Knife-in-the-Night landed on the surface, while a formidable array of dreadnoughts circled in watchful orbits around it. In a shielded conference room, he regarded Anderson, and all the doctors of the cadre, with raised eyebrows.

"So you have an AWOL octopus CRITTURS that seems to have the ability to visit warp space without assistance. In that place, which until now has been the exclusive domain of the Borsen, he has found somewhere he can dwell safely. I am fascinated, Doctor Padironas. Why exactly did this shattering revelation not warrant notifying me, or Captain Anderson at the very least?"

Padironas' day had gone from bad to unbelievable. He knew the Alpha Commander's reputation for working with the CRITTURS, something he appreciated on an intellectual level but just could not grasp.

"I deemed the CRITTURS observations to be unsubstantiated and did not wish to waste your valuable time. We have a lot of expectations to meet, and it just was not scientifically valid to take the word of a test subject without verification."

Anderson winced when he saw Spence's eyes narrow as he regarded the datapad before him.

"Doctor, I see nine of these excursions reported. All have only been recorded in your private notes. I see cadre-wide orders, issued on your authority, that these 'incidents' are counter-productive and efforts should be made to find ways to prevent them occurring. You have reprimanded five of your staff over their recommendations that Swims-The-Singing-Dream be interviewed at length by psych-techs, to help his understanding of his experiences, and to give him information that would allow him to expand upon his observations and thus report more accurately."

Jackson Spence placed the datapad upon the table carefully, the deliberation of the move betraying intense anger reined in by will alone.

He looked up at Padironas: "Captain Anderson speaks highly of your ability, yet has reservations over your empathy. I can only agree. However, I see that Swims-The-Singing-Dream has a variant genetic imprint credited to you. I believe that you did something unusual to him, outside the scope of your remit. I also believe that you are terrified because you cannot explain what has occurred as a result of your modification."

Doctor Padironas turned an ashen face to Stephanie.

"I used your qualification treatise. The jellyfish nerve-net intrigued me, and seemed to fit in some way, so I spliced it into one test subject to see if it produced anything useful."

Stephanie stood up, anger writ clear on her face: "So that's why you refused my request to do that! You had already done it – and I guess that was why my qualifying treatise was 'lost' in a system crash."

Spence slapped the table hard.

"Enough! Padironas, your decision to splice on a hunch tells me you are wasted in cadre. I need you on Shine One with core research and development. Doctor Crying-Blade, Cadre Blue Ten is yours. Senior Researcher Padironas, you will ship in two hours and your effects will follow. Corporals Danshin and Hadden: accompany him to Shine One and remain until relieved. He is to have no access to systems until I say so. You three are dismissed."

The corporals left with Padironas and Jackson sat down with a sigh. He looked at Doctors Crying-Blade, Never-Gives-Up and Eyes-of-Ice.

"Right. As of now, all cadres are to be headed by feathered Doctors, reporting to a feathered commander. I'll formalise it when I return to Shine One and assess just how much whining is going to occur. Now, we wait for our new star performer to return."

He took a deep breath before pointing at Anderson, his face mock-severe: "Captain, you mentioned that Doctor Crying-Blade has access to English mustard? I do hope you weren't trying to influence my impartial assessment of this situation."

He raised an eyebrow, while sliding a sideways glance toward Stephanie, as muted laughter drained the tension from the room.

Two hours later Jackson walked into the laboratory, behind Stephanie and Anderson. In the tank, a livid red octopus, nearly eight metres long, turned a single eye to regard them.

"Hello, Doctor Crying-Blade and Captain Walks-in-Honour. Greetings, guest. I am Swims-The-Singing-Dream."

"Greetings, warrior. I am Knife-in-the-Night."

The gel in the tank splashed, as the CRITTURS spasmed in surprise.

"I am honoured, my chief."

Jackson walked right up to the tank and leaned on the reinforced crystal pane.

"It is I who am honoured. Smokewalker extends his greeting to one who has found new hunting grounds. Tell me of the singing dream."

"It is a place of grey, like space is black and seas are blue. It sings a forever song and hosts things that may be far-distant kin to me. But in that vastness I dreamed of a place of ours that waited for me. So I went there."

Alpha Commander Jackson Spence had one of those moments of uncanny insight which had guided him so well over the decades since the founding of Ghost Command. He excused himself from the conversation while he had a chat with Blood-Moon, high above. Cadre Blue Ten had just become the most important facility in Ghost Command space. In fact, in the whole of mankind's space, much as Earth Command's deluded military would attack it just as the Borsen would. He left Blood-Moon to liaise with Thunder-Star and start the process of upgrading the defences on Shine II to Category One. Then he returned to Swims-The-Singing-Dream.

"This place that waited for you. Could you bring it, or lead it, back to us?"

Swims-The-Singing-Dream went through a dozen colours while he contemplated. Then he surprised everyone present by disappearing again without warning.

Five minutes later he was back: "I can, but the mind of that place is injured. I will need tutoring in the arts of repairing a Duodene Biomatrix that has had its organic component slain. It says that the singing dream will only permit a synthetic analogue, and suggests that a hyperconductive silica gel will allow it to make ad-hoc connections sufficient to return with me."

Jackson smiled. He knew of only one vessel that had warranted a Biomatrix, but that had been before he left Earth Command. In the intervening time they could have made more. But, if he was right, he was about to be present at the making of history, again. He left the laboratory to arrange for a team of his finest biocomputer techs to rendezvous with his best psych-techs, and for both to get their entire operations here sooner than quickly.

During the following five weeks, Swims-The-Singing-Dream made twice-weekly journeys into what was suspected to be warp space. He was given access to all the information that Ghost Command had on warp space, and agreed that it was likely to be the place he visited. After the specialist teams arrived, he progressed rapidly, to a state where the probable limits of his technical ability were defined. Three months after his tenth journey attracted so much attention, he went into warp space with a canister of specially formulated gel and a toolkit adapted for his tentacles. He was gone for four days. As night fell across Shine II on the fifth day, warp intrusion alarms blared, and the planet readied itself for action.

Suddenly, a huge starship appeared in high orbit. Its hull was pockmarked and torn. The centre section was oddly distorted, as if giant hands had grasped the ends of the ship and twisted it through a quarter-turn or so.

As the warp-flare around the ship faded, Swims-The-Singing-Dream reappeared in his tank. The specialists debriefed him while his vital signs were checked. High above, on the bridge of the Thunder-Star,

Alpha Commander Spence regarded the arrival. It was bigger than Blood-Moon. Blazoned on the twisted flank was the sigil of Earth Command, above the ship's designation:

ECWD/A

EXCALIBUR

Jackson Spence smiled. He had an octopus that could enter warp space, and he had found something thought to be lost. He looked at the Excalibur, gone for nigh-on four decades, and felt that haunted touch he had last felt just before he vowed to liberate the CRITTURS from Project Pavlov's ignorance.

Initial reconnaissance showed signs of scavenging and evacuation throughout the interior. Its memory lattices were corrupted and the inorganic component of its biomatrix barely cognizant, let alone capable of remembering. There had been eleven hundred people on the ship when it left Earth orbit. As he surveyed the empty escape vessel bays, he knew that he had to try to find out what had happened to them.

Reunion
(Y583 PA)

Tara slapped at his arms as Jack lifted her down from the transport. Behind her, Luke and Eva stared out at the distant mountains in awe. Cherry trees lined the edge of the landing-field, and the city beyond looked clean and low-rise. No skyscrapers or girder-framed warrens marred the view.

"You're back?" Her words were more question than exclamation.

Jack grinned. This woman had put up with twenty years of him being a complete and unknowing idiot, as his mind resynchronised after the loss of the regen ship.

"I'm back. A few grey areas, but I have most of it now. He's my dad, she's my mum and you're my granny." He pointed to Luke, Eva and then Tara.

Tara punched him in his rock-hard abs before bursting into floods of tears and collapsing against him.

"Jack, I see you've managed to reduce the poor woman to tears within a minute of her arrival."

Tara released Jack to see an Alpha Commander in field casuals strolling over, humour crinkling the skin around his eyes, for all that his mouth was stern. Jack pivoted to face the new arrival and saluted with vigour, but without precision.

"Sorry, sir. Old habits, sir."

Alpha Commander Leon Stubbs slapped Jack hard in the chest: "Oh, get a grip, Shiro. If she hadn't been in tears I'd be more worried." He turned to Tara with a warm smile: "Lady Shiro, may I welcome you, and your family, to the planet Okuninushi, your new home."

Tara felt the blush rise to the roots of her hair: "Please, call me Tara. That's my son Luke."

Luke glared at her.

"Sorry; Sergeant Luke Shiro of the Twenty-Seventh. The elegant lady at his side is my daughter, Leftenant Eva Shiro, member of the command crew on the Dreadnought Armentieres."

Leon stood to regard the two youngsters, who came to rigid attention and snapped off salutes that their father could learn from. He caught them all out by bursting out laughing.

"I am delighted to meet Commander Shiro's angel from the heavens and his two Borsen-eating progeny at last. Maybe I can get some of his attention now that the moping will hopefully cease."

Tara raised a hand for silence, then pointed at Jack: "Commander?"

Leon stage-whispered: "Busted."

It was Jack's turn to colour up: "Well, you said I should go for something better than piloting, having died eight times and used up my spare lives. So when this lunatic turned up at rehab and asked me to help him build a planetary society from the ground up – because he wanted someone who could read, speak, write, swear and give orders in Japanese – I said yes."

Leon raised both hands: "Before I cause a divorce on the landing pad, I asked Jack because his service record indicated a dedication to a cause and family like I had never seen. I knew he could help shape

Okuninushi into a fitting member of Heaven. He has. We have. Welcome home."

He turned his gaze to Luke and Eva: "You two. Look over the rosters and pick your new postings. I've had your ratings pushed under my nose enough times to know that you're both capable of reaching the upper echelons. But for now, why don't you two and I head for the officer's mess, where you can instantly obtain reputations you don't deserve yet, while your folks rediscover each other?"

Luke and Eva looked at their parents, who seemed to be having some sort of staring match over their intertwined hands.

Luke snapped a quick salute "Yessir. Good idea, sir."

Eva grinned: "Thank you, sir. Classy save from us having an afternoon of pretending not to hear and see things." She looked over at her parents: "We'll make a lot of noise before we come in."

Leon smiled: "That won't be necessary. Families here have houses, not double-accommodation apartments."

Jack and Tara waved distracted acknowledgements, and were distantly aware of the three of them leaving. After a while, they wandered off hand in hand.

"Was I really as much of a pain as I dimly remember being?"

"Yes. But I'll give you the next thirty years to apologise."

"Only thirty years?"

"Then you can start on the backlog from that thirty years."

"Cunning. I always loved that about you."

"You said it was my –"

"That too, but I need to check. Ow. Stop hitting me."

The laughing couple disappeared beyond the cherry trees.

Zen and Ink
(Y584 PA)

Byron was yet another spectacular disaster, and only the fact that it was an uninhabited planet kept the Borsen from warpkill, which meant the grunts on the ground got to experience what a massacre caused by outdated strategies felt like.

Why did Earth Command keep contesting every planet? It wasn't like Byron had anything on it except for our military presence. Then again, as a decorated veteran and one of the very few to survive more than ten battles against the Borsen, perhaps I have more reason than most to ask such questions.

I swing down a drop-cable and hop off at sublevel eighteen; what used to be street level. The sheer mass of humanity concentrated on the six Earth Command base planets used to make me nervous. Now I know they're never in danger from the Borsen.

"Evening, Colonel. Noodles or fakesteak?"

"Chop the pseudomeat into the noodles and add some of your devil sauce, Honchi."

The old boy does as asked and I hold out my hotbox for the steaming, stir-fried mass. Foil bags and even plastics are scarce now. To be able to carry hot food any distance, you have to be an Earth Command officer who can bend the rules a little.

"Enjoy!"

"I will." Of that there is no doubt. I took eight hundred men down onto Byron. I managed to bring back forty-six vacant-eyed veterans, only half of them from the unit I landed with. I was the only senior officer to return, something that I am getting used to. What is the use of getting to be a leader, through all the blood and mayhem, if you promptly sacrifice yourself with your command? How does that help us? The regen ships are long gone. Dead is dead.

I stride over to the next drop and swing on down to sublevel twenty. I guess you'd call it 'colourful'. Previously, it would have been called 'somewhere to avoid after dark'. At this time of day, it's short on residents and long on echoes. But down at the end of the fourteenth on the left – after the local refuge office – I see a light burning. There are people outside the place and I hear laughter, music, and the click of dice tumbling. The air temperature rises, as if life itself can warm the parts that the weather towers can't.

"Colonel Miller! You're back!"

And, just like that, it's like I've never been away. Old Gan waves at me from the far side of a backgammon table, where he's gently thrashing some youngster who I suddenly realise is Ruben. The boy must have had a growth spurt since my last visit. Phil is playing three-string and Hella is pouring beer into his mouth, on demand, so he doesn't have to stop playing. I make my way through the group, waving the hotbox as my reason for not stopping. I push through the door, and the warmth increases. As the door closes, I hear a muted conversation out back, one side of it in heated tones. Amanda is behind the counter, and smiles in relief as I enter. She mouths the word "Help" and points toward the studio. I put the hotbox on the counter, gesture for three portions, and head on out to see who's bothering my only real friends on this planet.

The studio hasn't changed. I pause and smile at the yellowed picture of a twentieth-century racing car, then listen to the conversation taking place just out of sight.

"You want how much for this? I can get it done on the base for a couple of credits."

"Then why did you come here?"

"Because my sergeant said that you tattooed some hardass vets, and thought it would do me good to 'feel the needle', whatever that means."

"So, do you want to get it done? The price is the price."

"I could get you into a lot of trouble for doing this down here, you know."

I do believe that's my cue. I step into the studio and address numbnuts' back while winking at Carl: "The hell you will, son. Because I will, personally, shove any report and the datapack it arrives on so far up your arse that you will have difficulty swallowing for a month."

The soldier on the stool rises and spins round, to freeze under my very best 'merciless' stare. He flicks his eyes to the identity flashes down the sleeves of my dress blacks. His eyes widen. Yup, that's seventeen markers. Sixteen campaigns, and the one at the top that reads 'C5'. I'm a Colonel and you're in the shit, kid.

I have to say that I'm impressed with the speed that he comes to parade attention.

"Sir, sorry, sir!"

"You just missed your chance. Tell your sergeant that Lazarus Miller will be in touch. Get out."

He goes. He and his C1 are tomorrow's entertainment. I'll be in a better mood by then.

"Laz. You look like you always do, mate."

Carl grins and holds his hand out. I shake it as I reach into my pocket and pull out the campaign insignia that the robotatt unit at the base burnt onto a piece of cloth for me.

"Got the patch for your dress blacks?"

I pass him that. He looks at the two.

"I can freehand the colours, and the stencil will take a few minutes. More importantly, do I smell some of Honchi's cookin'?"

"Of course. Would I dare come here without hot food?"

Carl laughs and gestures me to go out ahead of him.

"Confucius always said that chow time comes before ink time."

I grin and follow him out. Amanda has the food in bowls, and the table up. We sit down, crack open three bottles of local brew, and get down to eating.

Carl waves a fork at me: "I hear that things are changing. Hear that the Borsen may be coming too."

I shake my head: "Changing, yes. Borsen, no."

Amanda jumps on that: "Why no Borsen?"

I flip a coin in my head. It comes up heads: tell the truth.

"Because they don't want to conquer. I've seen them fight. In every battle, they have the edge. Sometimes in numbers, but these days it's usually in quality. Earth Command is just throwing forces into each engagement, hoping to find the magic combination that gives them the win."

Carl shakes his head: "Wars at this level are won by smart commanders using the best strategies. Sun Tzu still has the right of it. You taught me that."

"Precisely. The last really smart Alpha Commander we had was called Spence, and you know how that ended."

Amanda grins: "Wishing you had joined the-"

"Don't say it! It's one of the few words that will attract monitor drones, even down here."

Amanda looks scared, and rightly so. Monitors bring Department of Civil Defence militia. Nothing good ever comes from those sorts of visitors.

Carl coughs: "Damn Honchi, that's fierce! What does he make his sauces out of?"

"Best not to ask. Just be grateful he makes them. The food has been rough for a while now, and non-combatants get the poor stuff."

Amanda persists with a smile: "Why no Borsen?"

"Like I said, I've seen them fight. They're not trying. It's like they expect something from us, like they're waiting for something to happen. Until then, they just follow some unknown rules that occasionally let us win, but I'm sure it's only to stop us from giving up completely."

"What is it, do you think?"

"I have a couple of less than popular ideas. On Romala, the rumour is that we took out a Mistress. The same rumour says that incident is what prompted them to switch from raiding to open warfare. If that's true, then possibly they are waiting for us to rise to that level again. To become an opponent that the Mistresses can respect, I guess."

Carl nods: "They want to see signs of strategic intelligence to back the many instances of individual valour, maybe?"

"That works for me. Every battle that I have been in, they could have taken us apart. One hundred percent losses every time. But they didn't. I've seen Mistresses in their hellish power armour just watching battles where their intervention could have saved them countless warriors."

Carl taps the table with his fork: "You have a theory. I can see it in the crease of your brow. You're thinking too hard, on top of the memory of what you've survived."

I sigh. Perceptive as usual: "It's not a theory about the Borsen. It's about Earth Command."

They both look at me.

"I think they have a long-term plan. I've been on classified missions to retrieve downed scoutships that have no reason to be where they are. I see everyone going without, while Earth Command increases its core troop numbers with penal battalions and regiments of people who couldn't even qualify for regular service before the Incursion. It's like a chunk of our best are nowhere near the war and need a lot of the basics. Spence's command did that early on, but cut back their raiding when they got established wherever they are now. This is something different and run from inside our side."

Carl looks thoughtful: "I presume that you're just making an observation, rather than intending to do something heroic and bad for your health?"

I smile at the two of them: "Of course."

With that, the conversation lapses to mundane matters while the food is finished and the beer is drunk. Carl pats me on the shoulder and returns to the studio.

Amanda watches him leave before looking intently at me: "He's not seen them, but the DCD have been lurking."

That, I can do something about. I reach into a back pocket and pull out a diplomatic datapack: "You and Carl need to retina-print this. If any goons turn up, show it to them."

Amanda takes it and raises her eyebrows in query.

"It makes this place, and the both of you, a registered supplier to Earth Command. Commander Braun and I have notarised it. These registrations never require any details of what you supply, because it could be classified materiel. It just states that you are not to be interfered with, because you provide something essential. That statement will be backed by lethal force if necessary."

Carl speaks quietly from the doorway where he'd been leaning unnoticed: "Does this put you in trouble?"

"Hell no. You provide me and Dave Braun with something that is impossible to find elsewhere. Speaking of which, shall we?"

Carl nods and steps out of my way. I hear the datapack beep, verifying two retina prints, before Carl re-enters the studio.

With a smile, I strip off my uniform top and relax into the recliner.

"You've got more scars."

"And a new arm."

"They did a good job. Which one?"

"Right. Borsen Knight's energy blade. If it hadn't already gone through a trooper named Higgins, I'd be an entry on the Byron roll of honour."

"I'm saying nothing. Where's this one going?"

"Left of my navel? Think there's just enough room."

"Your eye is good, as usual. Lean back. You know how this goes."

I do. Commander Braun introduced me to Carl and his ancient art back when he was only a Major, and I was still a grunt. He brought every new soldier down to Carl's place. He and I are now the only survivors of the few who took to this old way of healing mental wounds.

Surviving a campaign against the Borsen leaves you in shock. Earth Command calls it 'carnage-concussion' and they have some awesome drugs that make you forget it, and a lot of other things. The old words are Post-Traumatic Stress Disorder. It can turn heroes into cowards and sane men into lunatics. You have to face what happened, but, more importantly, you have to accept it and live with yourself. My comrades drink, fuck, watch films, party, work out, race every conceivable device that can endanger their lives and similar. Dave and I come down to sublevel twenty and let the needle take the pain away.

Traditional tattooing was nearly wiped out by the arrival of the robotatt unit. You feed it the design you want, and it will render it perfectly – on any part of your anatomy that is approved by the Department of Welfare. But the robots are perfect. Too perfect: it's like photocopying onto your skin. From decision to delivery is a matter of minutes. You just pick a robotatt unit rated for the colour-palette and size. The anaesthetic spray lands, the air-injectors hiss, the gel-gauze covers and that's it: you're inked. Please rinse the cover with antibiotic gel once a day for a week, then peel it off. Do come back soon.

Dave's family has been visiting Carl's ancestors to be tattooed for four generations. Carl's family tattoo business has run from various premises since before the Apocalypse. Every son and daughter has been a master tattooist, learning the craft from childhood like a martial-arts master learns his craft from infancy.

The textures, the colours, the right needle for the skin type and position. How to give a two-dimensional image depth, and even the semblance of a reflection. How to imbue every line with spirit, by understanding why the tattoo is being done. It is a unique art and it should never be lost.

But more importantly for someone like me, it's the pain. There is nothing like the pain delivered by the steel needles of the traditional tattooing gun. I have experienced the usual pains from a rough upbringing and military training. In addition, I've been shot, burned, bludgeoned, impaled, stabbed, and half-decompressed. I've had limbs sliced off, burned off, and blown off. I even had my legs reduced to something that resembled chicken noodle soup by a hand-held warp weapon that they still say cannot possibly exist. As I arrived back on the ship without the puddle of my legs to prove it, I couldn't contest the fact. It's why all serving troops have their identities and service records tattooed on their torsos. Limb loss is fixable. Damage severe enough to get to your torso, through your powered armour, is usually fatal.

The gun hums and the needle tracks across my stomach. I quell the need to flinch that tells me I need to relax more. With that done, my breathing deepens, and I am just not entirely here anymore. The smooth strokes and the steady pain ease me. I cannot describe it adequately, but it sends me into a state where everything is the needle, and the needle is everything. In that pain I can leave behind the anguish of what I have done and seen, the grief of losing comrades and strangers, the anger of knowing that we're being sent in to a slaughterhouse to provide fodder and propaganda, not victors. It all goes down into the mark that is being etched on my skin. All the accumulated distress, that could destroy me, is bound to the pattern being added to me. For me, each tattoo is literally an emblem of survival.

A while later the cool impact of the healing gel, that Carl deliberately keeps in the chiller, brings all of me back to here and now. Amanda has a coffee ready. I put my uniform over the strip of gel-gauze the robotatt unit extruded, along with the etched piece of cloth, earlier. It's the ink that's important, and the gel-gauze is designed to withstand the rigours of military life. I still need to be able to ruck and roll at an hour's notice, fresh ink or not.

"Should we do anything?" Carl seems inattentive, but he rarely misses much.

"Keep yourself in non-black-market supplies. The monthly retainer that comes with your registration should help with that. Make sure you can fortify this place, and possibly the area around it, so your extended family can reside here as well, when things get worse - and have no doubt that things will get worse. Make sure that everyone who comes here, from now on, is someone you trust, otherwise, meet them elsewhere."

Carl nods, and Amanda puts an arm around him, as I head for the door. No time for backgammon and music this trip: I have a regiment to rebuild. Again. I pause in the doorway and look back at the two of them: "I'll be back."

Carl smiles: "Hopefully only for decorative ink. I have a lovely parrot on a bed of flowers that would suit you, Laz."

Amanda cracks up, while I give Carl one of the oldest 'informal' salutes and stroll off into the shadows, laughing.

Look upon My Works
(Y586 PA)

The corridor is long, and broad enough for a trio of Ferines to drive down. Its smooth walls are broken, at intervals, by no less than four sets of blast doors. A casual observer would be unaware, but the trained eye would be caught by the double-layer installation at each point. A pause to examine them would reveal that they are double-layered because they are designed to rise and present impenetrable barriers in both directions. What could necessitate such extreme precautions? Captain Targiven knew, because he had ordered their installation. He smiled as he walked, remembering the shouts of outrage from the engineering teams when he insisted on them being placed exactly as he specified.

He reached the end of the corridor after twenty minutes. He liked his morning walk, eschewing transport to allow him to organise his thoughts and prepare himself for the onslaught that would come as soon as he entered. Hybrid Division deserved its reputation for craziness and terrifying results.

The access portal lifted, and a haze of blue smoke wafted out. While he mentally noted the need for a slight pressure differential with the corridor, to prevent any such emission occurring again, he was more concerned that smoke was coming from the control section of Hybrid

Division. Drawing his pistol, he entered swiftly and flattened himself against the bulkhead to the right of the door.

"Greetings, Captain Smiles-Like-Death. The situation is under control, but I regret that I have had to break one of my siblings."

Targiven regarded the Gora called No-Bananas-Today and braced himself for the worst. Anything that could do that much damage to its yellow painted armour, without heavy weapons, was unknown in his experience. Just what had Professors Padironas and Button come up with, this time, to ensure that he regretted taking some leave?

He holstered his sidearm and looked about the war zone that had been the command section. Walls demolished, conduits spilling torn and sparking cables, desks smashed, and racking reduced to twisted art. All emerging from a floor-concealing haze of blue smoke.

"Padironas! Button! This had better be good!"

He let his anger show in his voice. This sort of mayhem was several steps too far. A white-gloved hand emerged from under a pile of chairs, clutching a piece of paper. It was followed by Professor Anduman Button, teenage prodigy turned twenty-one year old maniac.

"Hello Captain. Professor P was just proving to me that his new mentation, in an enhanced subterranean-insertion Panthac chassis, was stable."

Anduman looked about: "I would have to say that his definition of 'stable' fell somewhat short of accepted usage."

Targiven shook his head. He must not smile: "What was the blend?"

"Leopard base. Badger, mole, bat, wolverine and mink splice."

"Exactly what was that unholy combination for?"

Anduman shrugged: "We'll never know. It splattered the Prof all over procedure rooms two and three."

Targiven leant against the wall. Padironas dead? Alpha Commander Spence had been right. Why kill the man for his stupidity when he would eventually harbon in style. They had gained a couple of years of Padironas' strange insight: for all that he regarded CRITTURS as little more than poorly trained dogs, occasionally he would just add a splice to a blend that produced the most incredible results. He wiped his face, stood up, and strode over to where Anduman now leaned on a desk, smoking a slim panatela, while using his neural interface to gather data from No-Bananas-Today. He paused, realising that trying to get the professor's attention would be useless. As he did so, he caught a movement in his peripheral vision. Turning to get a better look, he saw a long, thin manipulator tentacle teasing a priceless hardback copy of The Art of War from a fallen bookcase. He moved stealthily, following the tentacle and purloined book down two corridors, before arriving at an open atrium. Squatting across it, with landing spikes carefully placed to cause minimal damage, was the strangest CRITTURS spacecraft he had ever seen. He saw it register his presence and the front end canted toward him.

"Greetings, Captain Smiles-Like-Death. I am Creeps-Them-Out."

Targiven nodded.

"A fitting name. What is your designation?"

"I am a fourth-prototype mantis base with black scorpion, mantis shrimp and a hybrid octopus/jellyfish neural net. My drones are spliced from *bathynomus* and *armadillium*."

"So you have warp capability?"

"Not quite. This is why I am not considered production-ready: they do not know where I nearly go."

Targiven nodded. They kept on encountering this in Hybrid Division. You combined some desirable traits with some you felt would be useful, and what happened was that your new blend highlighted a need to revisit some laws of physics previously considered to be concrete. His quantitative-applications team would have been Nobel Laureates several times over for the advances that they had made, if recognition on Earth had been an option.

"Demonstrate."

Creeps-Them-Out did not move, but his entire body suddenly became indistinct, shifting in opacity from misty to completely transparent. It was a disturbing spectacle to observe. Targiven felt parts of his mind recoil in abject, indefinable rejection of what his eyes beheld. He was just contemplating the possible causes of this discomfort when a sleek, half-metre, cerasteel-plated CRITTURS that resembled a streamlined woodlouse scuttled up onto the doorframe by his head. It buzzed happily at him, while waving its quadruple antennae in intricate patterns. He could not help but smile. Some of the smaller CRITTURS had character; no matter that it was frequently incomprehensible to humans without the assistance of a larger CRITTURS.

He pulled his sidearm and rattled off three rapid shots through the not-entirely present Creeps-Them-Out. All three shots 'spanged' harmlessly off the panelling on the far side of the atrium. Well, that was interesting.

"Can you converse in that state?"

The woodlouse analogue by him buzzed briefly, and Creeps-Them-Out returned to the accepted version of reality.

"I cannot, but my drones can reach me. I can also move through manufactured materials in that state, although I am not sure as to the usability of that, as I cannot grasp anything for purchase, and thus would have to be under power. In effect, I would need to fly through the object."

Targiven chuckled: "Or maybe the idea was for things, potentially destructive things, to be able to pass through you?"

"I had not considered that, it was not within my brief. Thank you. May I ask your advice on another topic, Captain?"

"Of course."

"I am lost as to what to call my drones. Woodlouse, louse or roach seems inappropriate and they do not like it. What would you suggest?"

Targiven was immediately presented with a memory of his grandfather showing a very young Targiven the wonders of *Ligia Oceanica* scavenging on the shore near their summer home.

"Call them Slaters. Reference creature with colloquial name 'Sea Slaters' from archives. You have my permission to access, should it be required."

"Thank you. I see the comparisons and the positive associations with human curiosity, and affectionate derivatives of fascinated revulsion."

The slater by Targiven buzzed loudly and rotated clockwise once.

"They like it too. We shall consider that a designation and propagate it to the colonies."

"Colonies?"

"My slaters are merely the latest version of scouting and nuisance raiding drones that are deployed with most CRITTURS units which have reconnaissance, or behind-the-lines insertion, roles."

"So what were you designed for?"

"A question that the late Padironas refused to answer, Captain. Professor Mad-as-a-Hatter is quite baffled as well, but does enjoy playing games of dara with me."

Targiven laughed. The astronomical cost of these new CRITTURS types would make that something not to include in the usage notes. Then a thought occurred.

"You mentioned that you are the fourth prototype? What happened to the previous three?"

"Another good question, Captain. I do know that they were tasked by Padironas as a part of their proving trials. I also know that they have not returned."

Targiven felt that peculiar brand of unease start up in his mind: something unauthorised and substantial had occurred. He disliked the idea of three units as potentially capable as Creeps-Them-Out being AWOL.

"Creeps-Them-Out, what are your data interrogation capabilities?"

"In keeping with my presumed role for espionage-aspected reconnaissance, they are Category Two. It should be noted that I am only an amateur practioner due to lack of experience."

"Acceptable. Please prepare for command interface via my access to Professor Padironas' dataspace. I am guessing that he kept notes about you and yours somewhere out of sight of the normal scrutiny."

"Very well, Captain. Shall I relocate to one of the bays?"

"Good idea. You do obstruct the view a bit up here. Let me know which bay you're in."

Returning to the control section, Targiven was greeted by the sight of a dozen human technicians, Professor Button and both of the Gora; No-Bananas-Today having called in his partner, Gone-Fishing. He made his way under and around the small hives of activity, repeatedly interrupting them, until he was satisfied that all would be restored before the following day. Professor Button was even less enthused with the knowledge that he was going to spend the following day having an in-depth chat with Targiven, covering all extant projects. Anduman's expression clearly conveyed his feelings, but he only had himself to blame for letting his partner-in-crime commit involuntary suicide by enthusiasm.

Several hours later he arrived at bay twenty to find Creeps-Them-Out settled and fully deployed, with twenty slaters scattered around, their manipulator arms deployed to assist with reconnections or fine tuning. Targiven sat at the workbench and cued up Padironas' dataspace, applied his access rights and granted them to Creeps-Them-Out. He spun to face the exotic CRITTURS.

"Let's see how your Category Two finesse is, Creeps-Them-Out. I want a full, granular inventory of all of the late Professor's activity. Take your time but get it all."

"Acknowledged, Captain. I would suggest that you action a core backup of this sector before I attempt access, then I would also recommend that you spend a while making Professor Mad-as-a-Hatter's life interesting. I will contact you when I am done."

Targiven waved as he exited. Giving the Professor a hard time and finding breakfast were two priority subjects. He decided that his need for a late breakfast would sharpen his rematch with the Professor, so headed for the control room first.

It was early evening before Targiven received Creeps-Them-Out's call. He made his way swiftly down to the bay, pausing only to grab Anduman and his long suffering assistant, Sally Hedger. Bay twenty was lit only by the underside lumens of the slaters, something that gave the place an unearthly feel. Targiven paused to query as to why the slaters had underside lighting. He was informed that the facility allowed them to double as rescue, utility or marker units, as well as adding another aspect of possible communication.

"Okay, now I know why your brood glows, let's get down to business. I presume you know Eyes-Like-Midnight?"

"I do. Hello, Sally."

"Hello Seetoh."

"What?"

"Sorry Captain. I found Creeps-Them-Out to be an irritating name to pronounce, so I created an acronym from it. As I was using an informal mode of address, he decided that using my human name was a suitable equivalent."

"This is proving to be an educational day. So, what have you found?"

Creeps-Them-Out projected multiple views, using over a dozen screens and multiple holograms. Using his longest manipulator arm with its tip illuminated, he started to work through his discoveries. It was a laborious process, as Targiven had to assess the relevance of each topic before dismissing it from further consideration. Finally, only a single hologram remained. It showed a young woman, possibly around Sally's age.

"What do we know of this person, Creeps-Them-Out?"

"As far as I can deduce from the reams of personal notes and diary entries that I have not bothered you with, this is Helen Turay. She is a Captain with the Ninety-Eighth, which we know to have taken heavy casualties in the recent defence of Callustrey. She is twenty-seven years old and Professor Padironas' daughter from his first marriage. Her mother was killed on Kursale ten years ago. Communications indicate that she was not enamoured of her father, but had a curiosity as to why he joined Ghost Command that Professor Padironas was desperate to answer."

"How does that bear on where your siblings have – oh hell. Tell me he didn't instigate an entire branch of CRITTURS research to find a way to get a message to his daughter?"

"I would be incorrect if I said that. It would appear that I am the product of one man's fixation with giving his daughter something she may or may not have needed, but which he saw as an apology for being a poor father. In addition, I am not the only line of research he instigated without formal request."

Targiven hung his head. Even in death, Padironas was a pain in the butt.

"Creeps-Them-Out, is it your assessment that your three siblings are currently involved in an attempt to deliver a message to Helen Turay, who was a ranked officer in Earth Command. Furthermore, if she is alive, she is currently on board an Earth Command warship that is quite likely on full battle alert after being involved in combating a major Borsen offensive?"

"Yes."

Targiven looked at the ceiling and swore in a vehement monotone for about a minute. Then he looked at Anduman Button.

"Professor, you are now dedicated, along with Sally, to cataloguing every piece of Padironas' work. You will not deviate from this task until it is completed. Creeps-Them-Out will remain interfaced in this bay and will provide full data query and manipulative support."

Two solemn nods were all the reply he received. He turned his attention back to the shadowed CRITTURS.

"Creeps-Them-Out, we had better hope that your siblings are as exceptional as you in their abilities. Otherwise I fear we may not be seeing them again. Did they have the usual anti-capture protocols embedded?"

"They did, Captain. I can also assure you that in the event of their loss, I would know. So far, they are still extant."

Targiven shook his head. Padironas. What a sad genius that man had proven to be.

Late Delivery
(Y588 PA)

They told me to watch her closely. Even though she plainly detested her father, she had made the mistake of mentioning her idle curiosity as to why he'd joined Ghost Command. Apart from that, she was the captain you wanted. Tougher than troopers three times her weight, never put a man on report for trivial stuff, always handled the serious stuff by investigating thoroughly before she tore someone a new one.

Yeah, she was my captain – and I had to watch her like she was going to turn on the lot of us at the slightest hint of being able to switch sides. It stank to high hell, but the Colonel was giving me points and formal credit, so I stuck it out.

A week ago, we hauled into orbit over the fabled Twin Cities of Conestoga. The Borsen were already down and we had to chuck them back off the planet.

We did it. Or they let us. Doesn't matter in the end. Being involved in any sort of victory is good for everyone in the command line, from Alpha Commander Braen Stuenish all the way down to me, lowly Sergeant Lily Hubert.

The win cost us sixty percent of our forces, a twenty percent drop against the usual casualty figures. Everybody on the troop carrier *ECTV John Rico* was happy about that. The party lasted for a day, before

Captain Turay politely asked us if we'd like to actually soldier. That did it. My squad were down in hangar bay twenty-eight, doing a freefall assault course that she had set up, within two hours. We had full kit on as well. She'd checked our performance stats and seen that my squad had been a little sluggish in action on the moon. So we were going to go back and forth on the course – with her sniping at us, using twenty percent loads – until we improved our stats. After that, we could strip and service our armour. Then we could sleep.

We were just on the way back for the eighth time, when the Borsen delivered their reward for our victory to the fleet orbiting Conestoga: a warpcore attack on the troop carriers.

The Borsen can use warp like we use artillery. Problem is our artillery loads only go bang in various ways, or burn things. The NewsNets mention the use of warpcores, but are careful to avoid details. Civilians I've spoken to seem to think that they are some kind of fancy rocket. The only thing the two have in common is that they travel in a straight line.

My dad was a machinist. If I hadn't seen him at work, I wouldn't have the vaguest idea of how to describe what a warpcore does. So, mount a white-hot food whisk in a lathe. Spin it up to the highest speed. Then crank a big block of chilled cheddar onto it, slow and steady, until the whisk has gone all the way through. Some bits fly off, other bits burn and melt, some do all three.

The cheddar block is the starship, because everything is that soft to a warpcore. The impact end is a direct contact surface between the real world and warp space. Things break down. Things change states. I got to see the insides of several of my mates, through their armour and skin, briefly. The way things get blended is horrible. The noise is awful. But the silence after it passes is worse.

The John Rico took a pair of fifty-metre warpcores: one to the bridge, one amidships, their angles of impact taking them down through the guts of the ship and the troop quarters. Finally, both exited through hangar bay twenty-eight. I was running point, and was trying to keep the Captain's head down, while my squad came up to join me. The rearmost core came down and removed the back half of the bay, along with my squad. The foremost core took out all of the bay entry points, and tore the bay doors off.

The flying mess of twisted and flayed troop carrier went everywhere. Something took my right leg off at mid-thigh, and Captain Turay stopped a piece of H-beam with her stomach. Our armoured suits did what they could. In my case, I would probably survive.

We lay there: her on the upper walkway, where the beam that impaled her pinned them both to a ragged fragment of the port bulkhead; me down on the floor under half of a lift sled.

As the silence deepened, my comm crackled and a weak voice came out.

"Bravo squad. Status."

"Just me, Captain. Lost a leg, but all green otherwise."

"Lily, call me Helen. Ranks seem a little silly right now."

"Affirmative to that. What's your status?"

"I have an H-beam where my guts used to be. The hole is so big that my suit is asking me why I'm still alive, and I have no idea. I never knew the medipacks on these suits could make you feel so damn good while you die."

"It's berserker mode, Helen. If you'd been in battle, the drugs would have sent you at the Borsen, singing battle hymns."

"Silly me. For a moment there I thought it was meant to make things easier."

I had to laugh at that. Helen's sarcasm was something we had all taken a while to get used to. I was going to miss it.

"You're the one that the Colonel got to keep an eye on me, aren't you?"

She knew. I should have guessed: "Yes. Sorry about that."

"No problem. You'll get status from it."

"Can I ask you something?"

"Go ahead."

"Your dad. What's the story? I got the official side and it was smelly and full of more holes than, well, the John Rico has at the moment."

She laughed, which ended in a racking cough. She cursed and I heard only wheezy breathing for a moment.

"Dad was a boffin. A brilliant man. But as a husband and father, he was a non-entity. Didn't have the remotest clue how to interact with people. Mum fell for his genius, had me, and then took us away when she finally realised that he was never going to change. She once said to me that the night they conceived me was the closest he ever came to being human, and he left before she finished because he had a brainwave over some project or other."

"So, no love there?"

"Oh, I loved the idea of a genius dad. But the reality was that he drove me to tears. In the end, I told him exactly what his shortcomings were."

"Like you did with Labbitt on Teysa Four?"

"Worse."

That would certainly ruin a father-daughter relationship.

"What happened after that?"

"A few years of silence. Then the Exodus, and I got USE security and Earth Command police crawling over and through my life for a month."

"Only a month?"

"I told the senior officer what I thought of him and his investigation. In front of his team. They went away the next day."

"Since then?"

"Nothing. Except you, of course."

I had been watching this woman for three years because of that? Seems that the top brass were still hypersensitive about Ghost Command. Helen coughed and it ended in a gurgle.

"Helen?"

"Checkout time, Lily. Hope you get rescued in time. Going to go quiet now, you don't need to hear the end."

With that, she shut off her comm. The silence quickly went from creepy to hideous. Eventually, I had to shut down the non-essential systems in my suit; so, time passed, and I had no idea how long I'd been waiting when I saw a light.

Then I saw several lights. At first I thought they were the spotlights of a rescue team, until I realised that they were too low to the surfaces they moved on, and that was also a problem, because they were on every surface and heading my way.

There were two options. Power up and go down fighting, or power down to minimal life-support only, amp up the external pickups, and hope. I chose hope.

The lights turned out to be the underside armour of half-metre-long CRITTURS that looked like flattened woodlice. They milled about, waving twin sets of antennae, and touching everything. The Captain's body was nearer to them than me, and that let me escape. Because when they encountered her body, they all stopped and then rotated anticlockwise while emitting a buzzing noise.

With a grinding of metal, three medium sized CRITTURS spaceships-with-legs heaved themselves into hangar bay eighteen, through the rents where the doors had been, and made their way over to her body. I watched the little CRITTURS climb back into their hosts through slots on the undersides.

The reedy voices surprised me.

"Helen Turay?"

"Identity positive."

"She has gone to Wakan Tanka?"

"Confirmed."

"We were too late."

"Padironas will be displeased."

"Confirmed."

"Mission complete?"

"Copy onboard logs."

A thin tentacle emerged from the nearest ship, connected briefly to Helen's dataport, then retracted.

"Confirmed."

"Mission complete?"

"No instructions regarding rites."

"Mission parameters override them: no interference."

"Mission complete?"

"Confirmed."

"We depart?"

"Query other life sign?"

I held my breath.

"No interference. Proximity of active vessels dictates immediate withdrawal."

"Confirmed."

"Confirmed."

They turned, with surprising dexterity, and left without further utterance. At the opening, they queued while each pushed off vigorously, flickering into near-invisibility as soon as they did so.

The ruined hangar was quiet again. For my future health and prospects, I think that my post-incident report will skip their visit entirely. I guess that Helen's dad had something important to say to his estranged daughter, because he sent a squad of CRITTURS to find her. Hope it included an apology. She deserved that much, at least.

State of Play
(Y590 PA)

The following is a verbatim reprint, including hand-written annotations, from the original proof. It was considered lost, but had actually been deposited with a distant relative of the author. Unfortunately, the appendices mentioned have not been recovered.

Originally published in the (swiftly withdrawn) first edition of the Calicon University 'CU590' Yearbook, it was excised from all later editions under the provisions of the Y565 Sensitive Information and Public Order Act.

Observations on the Borsen Incursion
After Fifty Years of War.

By Morgan Neath -
Professor Emeritus of Modern History at Calicon University.

It is fifty years since the Borsen declared war upon humanity, and somewhere between eighty years and a century since they started their incursion.

I have decided to simply record what I know or can reasonably extrapolate and let people draw their own conclusions.

The Borsen Incursion commenced with raids upon our outermost settlements. These persisted for some while before the USE let the public know. The exact period of time involved is only known to those with the highest-level access to Earth Command data, but I believe us to be in the eighty-fifth year of the Borsen Incursion.

When it started, mistakes were made. An early offensive was wiped out in circumstances that still produce the most evasive denials when any query or investigation is attempted. We all know of the first 'harbon', the event that created a new low in the annals of strategic incompetence. My research indicates that the fall of Romala may well be a rival in all but the numbers of fatalities.

This highlights my problem. Free media dissemination ended with the Apocalypse, and Earth Command have been burying the truth and the bigger picture ever since.

I am a historian. It is my duty to discover, unearth or piece together truths, then record what actually happened. This document, barely more than an article, is the best that I can do.

It saddens me that possibly the most important work I have ever written could be dismissed as nothing but the ravings of a delusional conspiracy theorist.

Romala marked a shift in operations for both sides. The Borsen started to actively encroach upon USE territory and Earth Command moved to a war footing, radiating confidence in their ability to win back the few worlds taken.

The warp dreadnought Excalibur vanished into that non-space with a muted fanfare and high expectations. That the war did not cease by the end of 543 indicates to me that they failed.

In 551, the War Resources Act changed the face of society on every USE world, forever. Things we took for granted – like cheap technology, plentiful food, and community support – virtually disappeared. Our penal system was turned into something that still funnels people into Earth Command for purposes supposedly benign. Our care and health systems have similar provisions for those without recourse to family assistance.

In 559 the highly publicised rescue of the Twenty-Fifth battalion, from a siege that should have become their mass grave, introduced most of us to the astonishing machine-creatures called CRITTURS. For a bright moment, it seemed that humanity had merged technology and nature to emerge victorious once more. Earth Command started to actually predict victories. Then the silences crept back. The wondrous creations that caught people's minds and hearts ceased to be mentioned. The heroic efforts of human forces were emphasised instead.

In 565, the USE reeled under the revelation of the defection of Alpha Commander Spence, all the forces under his command and every CRITTURS. We were horrified and outraged, not only at the betrayal, but at the scale of it. How did he manage to get away with deceiving so many for so long? Earth Command promised us answers. They have never arrived.

For nearly ten years after that, Ghost Command raided Earth Command worlds for supplies. Occasionally, rogue broadcasts would flash across our screens, purportedly from Ghost Command, claiming that marginalisation and incompetence by Earth Command forced them to leave, or face false accusations of high treason. Earth Command responded vigorously with views of planets like Staten, destroyed when another regiment turned traitor and joined Ghost Command.

The most telling thing is the fact that the use of the term 'Ghost Command' is banned throughout Earth Command. That is not a mandate made by people with nothing to hide or to fear.

Some people wondered if we were being told the whole truth. An underground data-exchange network developed, purveying news and views that swiftly became significantly at odds with what we were being told by the USE and Earth Command.

After the disastrous loss of the Tenth Battle Group in 575, we were given the heroes and heroines of the Fifth Battle Group, under Alpha Commander Leng, to admire, as he led his people forth to combat any threat to the worlds of the USE: be they Borsen, Ghost Command, or merely opportunist brigands. They lasted five years before being wiped out, or 'despicably ambushed and slaughtered by a combined force of Borsen and Ghost Command elites' as the media told us. The underground network whispered of mass murder, but of whom, and upon whose behalf, never became clear.

This brings me to the most recent decade. The war grinds on, and seems to suck more and more from the remaining worlds of the USE. The Borsen are, without doubt, an implacable enemy, but the sheer scale of the losses I am hearing about beggar belief. I have seen reports that present eighty percent fatalities as being acceptable losses! If these reports are correct, then our 'massive ready deployments' and 'reserve bases', on worlds nearer the front lines, are nothing but fiction for public appeasement.

This is my reason for writing this article, regardless of the lack of 'hard' facts available and the possible repercussions for creating it. If all the troops sent out to fight are already dead, then where are all the resources being bled from every world of the USE going?

Of course, once you start asking questions at this level, the next level is stupefying: how many worlds have we actually lost? Is it only forty since Romala? Or are the rumours of over five hundred nearer to the truth?

I can present very little of this as verified fact. I should qualify it with a comment to the effect that it is merely instigation for people to start enquiring as to the real state of this war that is changing mankind.

The appendices will contain easy-to-read statistical charts, demonstrating that what is being sent is way beyond what would be considered excessive, even for a war of this scale.

In Y591, Professor Neath was about to publish an addendum that corrected his misapprehensions, after working with Earth Command sources for the six months following the original article's withdrawal. A short while before the release of the new document, the planet Calicon was targeted by the Borsen. Calicon University, along with Cordreya, the capital city, was annihilated. There were no survivors.

Taken
(Y594 PA)

She had one tentacle around my neck, which could kill me. But, typically, my mind was more concerned about what the other tentacle was wrapped around. Her ruby lips parted, and her bifurcate tongue flicked. Images entirely unrelated to the severity of my situation came to mind.

"Your choice, warrior?"

Her choke-hold loosened so I could speak. I took my mind off my privates, and grated out the only proper reply: "You better kill me, bitch. Because I can still fight without my balls."

She smiled, squeezed me hard at both ends, then released me – applying brutal twists – and exited the featureless room. The door just appeared as she approached what seemed to be a wall.

I blinked my eyes to clear the tears, and waited for the throbbing pains to ease, before examining my situation again. I hung by straps around my elbows, my forearms and hands hanging down, devoid of sensation. The pain in my shoulders was a constant I could live with, now the swinging induced by her last session had stilled. My feet were just clear of the floor, even if I stretched.

How did I get here? I had been on guard duty. Where? The Earth Command fortress on Sardusier! That was it! I had been on the graveyard watch that ended at dawn. What happened? There had been a disturbance... What kind? An attack. Not quite: a portal in the air. It had appeared in the atrium, over the water feature. I had called for backup, and was keeping back the few curious folk around at that time, when the tentacles had lashed out. Yes! They had grabbed a late-shift tech, and I opened fire. The tentacles dropped him, and I moved to stand over him, on the grass verge by the edge of the pool. I remember. His feet, with only one shoe on, were in the water. That's when the tentacles got me, when I was distracted for a moment by the reflection of the portal in the water.

The door opened. A different Borsen Mistress entered. This one was smaller than my previous tormentor. She came over to me and placed the tip of her tentacle on my stomach.

"Who are Ghost Command?"

That question surprised me. They were the Borsen's allies, after all. Easy answer, then: "They're traitors to humanity."

"Why?"

"Because they supported you, while pretending to fight for us."

"You are told that this Ghost Command are not your allies?"

Where was this leading? "Yes."

"What of their strange mechanical warriors?"

"They're called CRITTURS. They are cyborgs, combining instinctive animal traits with technological combat systems. Ghost Command insists that they are sentient, but it's a lie."

She nodded her head and stepped back, looking me over: "You are strong. It is a shame you are reserved."

"What for?"

"My sister wants to breed from you."

Hang on. Breed? I turned the bitch down just now.

The door opens, and the other bitch is back: "Sister. What do you here?"

"I needed to ask this one about Ghost Command. It is as we feared: they are independent of this Earth Command. There is a feud-state between them, driven by Earth Command's fear. It seems that they, too, find the Joyous Ghosts to be an abomination."

"The WarMistress will not welcome that news. It took a long time for her to approve the warp raids, and this one wounded the catcher."

"She has already issued an edict against further warp raiding."

She turned to stare at me again: "Will there be anything left of this one? I find him acceptable."

"I shall endeavour not to let him expire before you rejoin us. These warriors are quite capable, when hydrated adequately."

"Then water him, sister, and soon. May I bring my brood sisters? They have not seen a breeding from this stock."

"I will hydrate him and await your return. The lessoning for them is more important than my desire to spawn."

"Then we shall have a tutoring and breeding session, if that is acceptable. With you being first, of course. Then you can guide the rest of us. How long before he expires under load?"

"Some have lasted two sessions, but this one is not combat-ready despite being fit. I expect him to fail sometime during our session."

"Good enough."

The smaller Mistress exited the room, and the tall one turned to me.

"You will be given water and stimulants. As you are defiant, you will remain restrained. You really should have taken my first offer."

Bitch.

Sister Strange
(Y602 PA)

The man is in uniform and he's trying really hard to be nice, but I don't like him. I don't like this place, because it makes mum and dad look scared. I don't like the men with the big guns, because they're digging up our pond and the wood around it.

"You're not in trouble, Samantha. Just tell us what happened, like you told your parents when you got home."

"Will you put our pond back if I do?"

He looks at me funny, then the woman standing behind him leans forward and points to something on his datapad. He reads it, looks up and smiles at me.

"I'll see what I can do. But it does depend on what you tell us."

I sit up straight like Miss Jammor tells me I should, so I can speak clearly and with 'proper diction': "I was out of bounds. Dad told me not to go beyond our fields, but I wanted to go to the pond in the woods that we go to when we have picnics. So, after I did my housework, I told mum I was going to climb the tree at the back of the cornfield."

He nods: "And then you went straight to the wood? You didn't go anywhere else?"

"That's right. I skipped most of the way because it was a lovely day. Granny says you should skip on sunny days."

"Did you see anything unusual?"

"I'm sorry, I don't understand that word."

"Unusual. It means anything odd, or anything you don't normally see?"

"I saw a big blue eagle over the south pasture. We don't get many of them round here."

"Okay. So you got to the wood."

"Yes. It was nice and cool and the squirretts were singing, and I just followed the path. Dad says that snapping orchids grab kids who leave the path."

"Your dad sounds like a very wise man. So when you got to the pond, what did you see?"

"Water."

He sighs a big sigh and his breath smells of coffee.

"What else did you see?"

"Rocks and grass, and the willows that came all the way from Earth, and the sun pansies were really pretty."

"Nothing else?"

"No."

"So what did you do?"

"I took my smock off and went for a swim. After that, I laid down on the big rock to let the sun dry me. It was nice."

"So she wasn't there?"

"Not then. Later."

"Later? What did you do until later?"

"I went to sleep. It was warm and smelled good and the squirretts were far away, so they weren't loud."

"So you were sleeping and she woke you?"

"Yes."

"How did she do that?"

"By splashing in the pond."

"She splashed you?"

"No. She was just splashing and giggling."

"Giggling?"

"Yes. Like when you have fun."

I see the woman behind him smile.

"So she was splashing and giggling and you ran away?"

"No. I asked if I could splash too."

"I see. What did she say?"

"She said of course I could."

"What happened next?"

"I splashed with her, then we splashed each other. It was fun. We giggled a lot."

"I see. Then what?"

"After a while, she said her arms were tired. I saw that her arms were funny and she said that she had been spawned like it. I guessed that being spawned is the same as being born."

He smiled: "What did you do next?"

"I said that the big rock was a nice place to sit and dry in the sun. I asked her where her clothes were so she could bring them over."

"And she said?"

"She said that she didn't have any because she didn't need them when she was out war-ping."

"Warping?"

"That's what she said. I asked her what that meant and she said that it meant that she was being a bad mistress, and her mother would be very angry, but not for long. I said that was just like my mum."

"Then she told you her name?"

"No. I told her mine, because Granny says that is what polite people do." I looked at him hard. I saw the woman behind him smile again.

"So you told her your name without being asked?"

"Yes."

"Then she told you her name. What was it again?"

"Terr-buth-ah."

"That's a funny name."

"That's what I said. She said my name was the funny one. She tried lots of times to say my name, but it always sounded like Sum-nuth-ah."

"So, after introducing yourselves, what happened?"

"We sat on the big rock and talked about school. She doesn't like it at all. Says there are more fun things to do. I said yes. Then I asked her if she was truanting. I had to explain what that was."

"Did she agree with you after you explained?"

"Yes. She said that she was truanting a long way from home, and no-one could get her until she went back."

"I see. Did you ask why they couldn't get her?"

"Yes! It would be good to be able to do that."

"Why?"

"So I can do what I want, and only get told off when I get home. It's no fun when mum or dad, or both, come and get me before I want to come home."

"So what did she say?"

"She said that she had an ass-pecked that lets her do war-ping. No one else has it yet."

"Yet?"

"She said that she would have to spawn a lot when she grew up. So there would be lots like her."

He frowns and makes note on his datapad. He looks up again without a smile.

"What did you do next?"

"I taught her to play Frisbee."

"She didn't know how?"

"She said that her home was a big four-tress, and throwing games were only for grown-up mistresses."

"Why was that?"

"When I asked, she said that her people's throwing things are only for hitting bad people."

"What then?"

"We played Frisbee and she was really good. We were laughing and throwing the Frisbee up and down the pond, splashing a lot too."

"After that?"

"She stopped. She said a man was coming and whispering my name. She said that he sounded angry."

"That was your father?"

"Yes. He came into the clearing, saw Terr-buth-ah, screamed like mum does when she sees a rubyrat, and then he fell down."

Everyone smiled when I said that.

"What did she do?"

"She went to my dad and touched his neck, because I asked if she had killed him. She said she wouldn't do that to a non-com-bat-ant, and that my dad had only fainted and would wake up soon."

"Then what?"

"She said that she should go, and that I should stay with my dad until he woke up."

"Then she disappeared, like you told your parents?"

"Yes. She just was not there anymore, and the water splashed like it was filling a hole."

"So you waited for your dad to wake up. Then you went home and told your parents what had happened, and they called us."

"No."

"No? What do you mean?"

"You're nearly right, but only after she came back."

He sits up very straight: "What for?"

"She came back, gave me my Frisbee, and said I would have a lot of people pretending to be nice while they asked me questions. She said that I should tell you something."

His head creases like dad's does before he shouts at me.

"What did she tell you to say to me?"

"She said that I am a sweet little mistress, and she can be anywhere she wants, and you can't stop her because if her mother can't, you have no chance at all. She said that you should only question me and my dad."

"Why?"

"She said that she will be very unhappy with you if you do anything nasty. She even made me say the last bit back to her so I would get it right."

"The bit you just said?"

"No."

"Then say it."

"'If you harm my little sister I will bring ray-peen to you and yours'."

He sits there and his face turns a funny colour. He leans back and whispers to the woman who frowns and then nods. He looks back at me.

"Thank you, Samantha. If your sister comes back, I'd like to speak to her."

I smile. Terr-buth-ah said he'd ask something like that: "She said that I would not see her again for a very long time, because of people like you."

His face goes all red.

"Did she say anything else?"

"Yes. She said that she would check on me every now and then. Just to make sure that you behave yourself."

Aces Deep
(Y611 PA)

I flick wing-over-wing and dive, engines howling, as some bright blue nastiness passes through where I was. Half-committed in the dive, I pull the nose up and jink sideways, broadside to the angle of travel. The parachute effect yaws me, and I float for a moment as the world goes slow. Echo One seems to drift across my nose, and I squeeze the teat that causes my railgun to punch a chunk of ferrocored titanium through his centre section. His drive objects to my percussive realignment, and my screens have to flash-compensate as he leaves this life at Mach 9, in pieces. Wanagi Wichothi is not for enemies of the *oyáte*, so I hope his afterlife has a place of honour for warriors.

Even as his pyre dissipates, I bring the hammer down and perfectly bullseye the corona of his demise. Wish I could see that in long shot: a ring of energy, a ring of smoke, a ring of fire and pieces, and my exhaust like a shaft through the middle, with me as the arrowhead.

My proximity-detector flashes amber, and I corkscrew into an inverse slingshot before even looking. Echo Two coming for the title, out of the sun. In this day and age? I continue the dive until he's happy, then shut the back door and open the flue. Still hurtling surfaceward at Mach 8, I flip apex-over-base, so the sharp end is pointing the right way. Echo Two discovers this as he flies head on into a few kilos of iron and titanium doing Mach 20. Ouch. This allows me to close the flue, reopen the back door, and hurtle through his expanding debris-cloud without a scratch.

This is frustrating for Echo Three, as he was expecting me to still be heading down, due to the impossible g-forces involved in attempting sudden manoeuvres at these speeds. Of course, any airbreather would be jelly by now. Forty gees will do that, unless you're some sort of mutant cartilaginous cyber-spawn of a predator from the benthic depths of the Pacific, suspended in a hyperconductive saline gel. Handily enough, that's exactly what I am. I'm callsign Kilo-Ten-Ten. A revered ancestor was callsign Kraken. Got a proud family history of killing things to live up to.

Echo Three pulls a half-loop with a roll out of his attack and ends up screaming down at me, flat out and very angry. Opens fire, way out of range. He could have been dangerous if he'd kept his cool. As it is, I release a nanotube-braced monofilament net, stand myself on my tail and punch it. Echo Three is about to become a cloud of hundred-mil chunks that will be a bigger threat than he ever was.

The skies clear as I ascend, and I click my beak as the blue fades to black and the stars come out. There's always something magical about that transition.

Seven hours to base. One hour for debrief, while the gel is cycled, then I get to go hunting again. The depths of any ocean are nothing to the vasty deeps of space, and I like to think we've made the transition well. Sleepless predators we've always been, but Ghost Command gave me the stars, the enhanced smarts to love them, and the means to defend them.

I pass the moons before engaging Hirsch, then flutter my tentacles to work out the kinks, while my arms cue up some cetacean jazz and sketch three more kill-kanji, for the hull, on my datapad. They need to be ready for the techs to etch on my hull while I'm being debriefed.

Three more down, with hundreds to go. This ocean of stars is rich with wonders - and prey. My siblings and I will continue hunting until the Borsen, and Earth Command, understand that the stars are not theirs for the taking.

Dead Letters
(Yᒪ13 PA)

I take the tear-stained letter from my daughter-in-law and place it in the stasis frame below my son's picture, then I step back, and we look at the four of them, side by side.

Grandpa Levi went to war, and left Marcus to father the man I loved, before he followed his father's path. By the time I married Erde, his father and grandfather were dead: just letters on the wall naming them heroes who gave their lives for mankind.

Erde didn't want to go, but all good men went to fight the implacable foe, so he left me pregnant with Louis and entered service. His letter said he made Captain before they took him.

Yesterday, Natasha received the dread letter. She kept it overnight, then came round in floods of tears, distraught and apologetic that she wasn't pregnant.

I take her by the shoulders: "The fact you didn't conceive is nothing to be ashamed of."

She stares at me disbelievingly, her voice hiccupping: "I let you down. Four generations of service and no-one to carry on."

I kiss her forehead tenderly and smile into the eyes drowning in tears: "You haven't let me down. You've made me happy."

She frowns and more tears flood down her cheeks: "How can you be happy with me? Louis wasn't."

"Louis was my darling boy, but he believed in Earth Command. I stopped doing that when his father died. We don't give birth to soldiers, Natasha. We give birth to babies. Earth Command makes them soldiers, takes them away, and gives nothing back but a piece of paper."

Her tears stop as her eyes widen.

I smile: "We didn't get a say in their plans. From now on, they get no say in ours."

Last Men Standing
(Y621 PA)

Jackson Spence could not get used to being everywhere at once. He had agreed to being transposed into a variant of the CRITTURS intelligence container as his body started to fail with extreme age, but he'd be damned if he could cope with having his awareness spread over more than two rooms simultaneously. It was something that his staff quietly adjusted to, and that his daughter Katie – now Alpha Commander Kathleen Spence – was quite happy to make fun of him over.

But today was a day when his consciousness absolutely needed to be in one place: the bridge of the recently upgraded Thunder-Star. Now wearing the body of a Generation Four Dreadnought, the improvement had been instigated because of Jackson's newly acquired inability to evacuate any vessel he resided upon. Due to him being reliant on external power for anything except very short periods of time, his vessel and home needed to something able to take a lot of damage, deal out more and still be able to exit any such encounter with grace, and power, to spare.

Katie looked up at his camera: "It's confirmed, dad. Earth Command has slowly been contracting its operational spread. They've done it very quietly, but worlds lost to the Borsen are increasing, yet are never truly strategic."

Colonel Mandelsson cut in: "The cynical amongst us are already seeing a pattern of sacrifice. The Borsen meet increased resistance in certain areas, and are gently directed toward planets that they can subject to rapine. Earth Command uses the respite the Borsen always grant after that to consolidate."

So it had happened. Earth Command had finally admitted that it could not defeat the Borsen. The best they could do was maintain a costly, temporary stalemate. The trend for bigger Borsen ships and even more bizarre warp-based technology to arrive every decade or so was almost guaranteed to result in the Borsen gaining an even-more insuperable upper hand within twenty years of any stagnation in hostilities.

"Packet for Alpha Commander Spence!" The courier arrived on the bridge at full pelt.

Katie turned with a beaming smile: "Which one?"

The courier looked panicked for a moment, then saluted with aplomb toward Jackson's camera, before bowing as he handed the packet to Katie.

"I think it was intended for your father, ma'am. But I guess that the sender is unaware of recent developments."

Jackson liked his diplomacy: "That settles it. With immediate effect, there is only one Alpha Commander Spence: my daughter, Kathleen."

Colonel Ching-ko stepped directly in front of Jackson's camera: "You must have a title, Jackson Spence. You cannot be Revered, because you are extant and thus not an ancestor. I suggest Governor. First Governor of Ghost Command. So that those who decide to take the same route as you may become Governors, as it seems likely that static placements for future transferees would make sense."

Jackson felt himself smile, which was strange as he had no face. But advice from one who numbered Emperors of a country that had weathered three millennia in his ancestry was not to be dismissed.

"I agree, Colonel. Alpha Commander, Colonels, may I re-introduce myself: First Governor of Ghost Command, Jackson Spence."

Katie laughed: "You sound comfortable with it already. But it will certainly clear up the confusion and rumours."

"Agreed. Now, let us defer discussion of Earth Command's quiet retreat until we have heard whatever is on that datapack."

Katie loaded the datapack, verified its seals, then turned to Jackson's camera: "Who's 'Mockingbird'?"

"That would be Randolf Tsander, son of former councilman Admiral Tsander and recently promoted to Admiral himself."

Katie rubbed her nose: "That's quick."

Mandelsson shook his head: "They're short of competent commanders. Progression is rapid when any lack of ability is 'highlighted', usually fatally, by the Borsen. In addition, no line officers are allowed to remain if they are found to be responsible for a defeat."

Ching-ko straightened: "Or if they are assigned responsibility for a defeat. As happened to me."

Jackson laughed: "Indeed. It is sadly fortunate that one of our main recruitment avenues for command positions remains those hung out to dry by Earth Command."

Katie loaded the datapack, and all turned to face the screen. It showed a very tired-looking man, sitting on a simple wooden stool in what looked like a ruined restaurant; the icons along the lower edge indicating significant protection about the recording venue, and of the recording itself. He was dressed in worn casual wear and had battered hiking boots on. Running his hand through his regulation crew-cut, he took a deep breath before looking directly at the screen.

"Alpha Commander Spence. My late father's compliments, and apologies. He was unable to halt Servan's rise. He also says that you should not mourn him: he is glad to be out of somewhere he referred to as 'the snake pit' for the last eight months of his life. And, as you may guess, this message is not for the frivolous purposes of getting dad's last words to you.

Dad said that you and he had discussed the stranger projects that Earth Command has been engaged in. The supplements to this pack contain the entire project closedown records of, and addenda to, Project Wells. He said that you really needed to read the addenda headed 'Interviews with Returnee 'Axel One''.

I have continued my father's work, but Servan is becoming increasingly fanatical as he ages. He is scared of dying with no-one he considers 'worthy' to succeed him, yet continues to distrust almost everyone. The result is that his *de facto* Secret Police are everywhere. I believe that dad and yourself discussed the various aspects of The Ragnarok Proposals? I presume so, because his last information for you is only a sentence: 'Project Noah started last year.' – I have no knowledge of Ragnarok or Noah, as the clearance for them, and all similar, has recently been restricted to Servan and his faithful alone."

Randolf paused for a long pull on a water bottle, then he swilled his mouth out and spat. He grinned at the recorder: "I feel that I should mention that the big woodlice with glowing bellies are now the stuff of urban legend on pretty well every planet. Servan is beside himself because everyone except he and his faithful regard them as good things to encounter, and people refuse to report sightings. Whoever decided to insert them on most Earth Command planets, after having them programmed to help out civilians and assist in locating people buried by accident, disaster or battle, is a genius. It is a piece of counter-propaganda that works by deed alone. Superb."

Jackson chuckled. Seetoh and Sally would like that. He paused, mentally slapped himself and routed a message with the details to Hans Targiven's team with only a thought. This new state of being would be handy if he ever got the hang of it.

On the screen, Randolf leaned closer: "Earth Command has started withdrawing. Nothing public, nothing on political channels, but it is happening. Systems thought to be sympathetic to Ghost Command or disenchanted with USE, Earth Command, or the war are the first to be abandoned. Do what you can, because whatever is happening is beyond sane intervention now. Servan has won."

Damn the man, Jackson raged. Although he had been the catalyst for Jackson's decision to cede from Earth Command, Jackson had hoped that Servan's incompetence and increasingly fanatical outlook would have brought about his demise. Instead, the man had risen to the heights of power in the USE, extending Earth Command's influence to the point that the hierarchy of the Unified States of Earth had to be considered as Earth Command's public relations group, rather than as an interplanetary governing body.

Randolf leaned back, looking down to the left of the recorder: "Oh, hello. You'd be the courier, then?"

A cheerful buzzing from off-screen indicated that a Slater CRITTURS had arrived to collect the datapack.

Randolf laughed and pointed toward the CRITTURS whilst looking at the camera: "I've never met one of these before, and I have to say for all the many legs and big insect thing, they just seem, well, friendly. Fun, even." He gathered himself: "Sorry. This is going to be my last message. The scrutiny we're all coming under is too much to risk, but I will continue to do what I can. I strongly recommend seeing what happened to the planets that the Borsen did not warpkill, and there are a lot more of them than the public think." He grinned again: "And for everyone's sake, keep on picking up people who come your way. I know that your vetting is one hundred percent by the hissing and spitting that Servan's spymasters send your collective way in every report they file. The fact that you are proving not to be the monsters portrayed by Earth Command, but another human force fighting the Borsen, is the only good thing for many people, especially Earth Command regulars. Keep on doing what you do."

His smile was completely relaxed. Then he turned away quickly: "I hear vehicles. Time to go. I never met you but wish I had, Mister Spence. I would also have liked to meet a Panthac in person, if only briefly."

With that, he reached toward the recorder and then stopped, his face twisting into a grimace: "I nearly forgot. You may have noted my use of the word 'faithful' in relation to those who align with Servan. It's not an idle naming. The man has a dangerous charisma, and those who follow him show all the markers for a fanaticism verging on religious awe. Be careful."

With that, Randolf closed down the recording, and presumably made his escape. Jackson watched the command staff on the bridge exchanging glances of varying import or confusion.

"I do like the fact that I can see all your expressions. That would have been so handy in the past."

His voice made everyone jump and elicited some embarrassed laughter.

"Now to business, people. Randolf is right, we need to get sight of several occupied planets and we need it to happen yesterday. Katie, talk to Hans Targiven. He mentioned in his last report that he had achieved some spectacular results by hybridising from the splices that gave us Swims-The-Singing-Dream and Creeps-Them-Out. Whatever it is, if it can do what Hans was hinting at, I want it. Also, if we can arrange it, I do think that we should grant Tsander junior's request."

Colonel Ching-ko was smiling so widely that it endangered the top of his head: "You wish to kidnap an Earth Command Admiral?"

"Seems like a good idea. I like to remind Servan we're still here, by doing something close to his comfort zones, every now and then."

After a few minutes' laughter, and discussion of ways to action his outrageous idea, Jackson cut through the humour his previous comment had started.

"Project Noah is the plan for Earth Command to abandon USE space and all non-combatants to the Borsen, then retire far away to regroup for five generations or so before coming back as a warrior caste to save the peasants from the evil tentacled invaders and their collaborators."

Katie said what everyone else felt: "That's insane!"

"I suspect that Earth Command know what happens to the captured planets. They are retreating to preserve their control, at the expense of what they consider to be the expendable members of humanity."

Colonel Mandelsson came to attention: "What are your orders, First Governor, Alpha Commander?"

Katie gestured for her dad to speak. She needed some time to consider the strategic aspects, had teams who could handle the tactical aspects, but her father was the one who had the ability to intuitively extrapolate from information. Various CRITTURS elders said that he received visions from the echo of Inyan in the Thunder, the gift of the farseeing of the Wakinyan. Origin and method arguments aside, Ghost Command was a proof of the power of whatever strange insight that Jackson occasionally brought to bear.

Jackson gathered his thoughts, then, finding nothing perceptive to add as yet, he let his feelings choose his words: "Earth Command are abandoning their duty. Ghost Command could therefore be regarded as only the first rodents to abandon the ship." He paused a moment to let that sink in.

"Humanity is open to rapine, yet Earth Command is leaving. That alone testifies to the majority support of their troops. Which would not be forthcoming unless there was some solid proof that the Borsen will not wage war on non-militarised habitats. If that is true, it is another advantage. Advantages are what we need, because we have to find new ways to fight this war on our own. For everyone we have lost, and everything we have worked for, there can be only one outcome: we must triumph. Until then, we will spear our tether to the ground between the Borsen and humanity. We shall fight and *we* will be the last *oyáte* standing."

As those present cheered and applauded, Katie smiled. Sometimes dad gave them prescient insights. At other times, he produced oratory that inspired everyone and made his chroniclers happy. Today was definitely one of the latter cases.

Now You See Me
(Y622 PA)

"What is that?"

Professor Carmichaels smiled proudly: "It's a specialised field generator that creates a subcategory of the chrono-rephasic effect discovered by Project Wells."

Jackson Spence chuckled: "Okay, I asked for that. What does it do?"

Captain Ruby Daniels, known to CRITTURS and subordinates alike as 'Eyes-of-Lightning', stepped in to save Jackson from potentially lethal exposure to long words.

"It's easier if we show you, sir. Please see if you can detect anything around the two o'clock position between us and the first moon."

Jackson interfaced with the sensor suite. He knew his way round it thanks to regular practice, but he was all too aware that he did not have the instincts of a sensor arrays officer. After a couple of minutes' checking, he decided to cheat. He routed a query to Thunder-Star, the vessel he was still getting used to residing in.

"Thunder-Star, priority query: between Cadre Blue Fourteen and Erebus, please tell me that you have a cloaked object trying to avoid attention."

"Negative, Knife-in-the-Night. Space is clear, as far as my sensors reach, in all directions."

"Thunder-Star, stealth-scan that area. No prior ready state required."

"Ah, we are playing hide and seek with one of Professor Faraway-Eyes' subjects?"

"Correct. Find it for me, old friend."

"I have it. There is a small presence, using unidentified stealth measures, at the midpoint between you and the moon."

Jackson double-checked the sensors, then switched over to the various external view feeds. Any vessel in that position should be silhouetted against the moon. There was nothing, not even a distortion effect.

He addressed the two people in the ship far below Thunder-Star: "I am now impressed. See if you can add happy to that."

Ruby grinned and activated her headware: "Deathdealer, care to rejoin us?"

Suddenly, there was a single Hanfin hanging in space, exactly where nothing had been a few moments before. The sensor suite confirmed that it was really there, had definitely not been there, and that there were no residual effects or data to explain the anomaly.

Jackson laughed: "Now that is impressive. No light show, no weird output, just back again. What's the activation like?"

Ruby grinned even wider: "Deathdealer, please return to CDR and perform a clockwise pass around Thunder-Star, before returning to current position and rejoining us."

Jackson thought he was prepared, but the Hanfin vanished without warning or trace, just like a disappearing-act performed by a conjurer at a children's party.

"Knife-in-the-Night, I have a detectable emission trail commencing six point oh-eight metres behind Deathdealer. I am only able to be that precise because I have Hanfin signature data available."

"Thank you, Thunder-Star."

Jackson regarded the pair of grinning people in front of his lens: "How the hell did you come up with this? Give me the short version for non-scientific people, please."

Professor Carmichaels pondered for a moment: "We have a lot of Earth Command data on Borsen warp technology, despite having no access to the actual relics. On reading the Project Wells data, something in it reminded me of some notes made during the early Project Wallaby trials. Then I added some of Swims-The-Singing-Dream's expedition data. After that, it seemed sensible to factor in the Padironas Corona effect as manifested in Creeps-Them-Out and his brethren. From there, I cannot give you a simple explanation."

Jackson laughed again: "Brilliant! So, how do we deploy this?"

Ruby gestured toward Deathdealer: "We chose the Hanfin because of its power-to-weight ratio. A Kilo cannot run one of these generators. We'll have to run peak-load specifications on the whole fleet to see which vessels can handle it. We are sure that Generation Four dreadnoughts like Thunder-Star can be Starclad."

"For some reason, this effect seems familiar. Why is that?"

"Earth Command equipped one or two of their observation ships with a variant of this. It used brute power to induce the effect, which impacted the firing- and manoeuvring-capability of ships equipped with it. The project was abandoned and the equipped vessels will only retain it until it fails. The surveillance dreadnought Thunderchild definitely has it. We're also sure about the problems because we equipped our dreadnought Storm-Surfer with an equivalent unit a while ago."

"That would explain a few things. So, what are the limitations of the field?"

"As Thunder-Star showed, the Starclad vessel has to be completely passive. No emissions at all, if it wants to be undetectable. However, we are very sure that engaging in combat while Starclad will give opposing targeting systems seizures, until someone works out the predictive aspects necessary to work round the advantage granted. If stealth-scan technology becomes standard kit, the advantage disappears. Unless Professor Faraway-Eyes, and his team, have created the next generation of CDR by then. Plus, the vessel can still be collided with. Chrono-Detectile Rephasing does not remove the physical object from real space."

"Acceptable. This is something that will allow me to act on some old information. Colonel Blades-of-Life from the Takuman Provisioning Cadre will be in touch very soon. Thank you."

Jackson felt a grin spread across his non-existent features. This was a decisive edge. It was up to him to work out how best to use it to cut away his opponent's advantages.

Seeds
(Y623 PA)

The planet hung in space, the blue of the narrow oceans separated by the many shades of the great landmasses. The top and tail showed the white and grey of small polar regions.

Mist-In-The-Sun surveyed the whole spectrum available to him. Telluride had been ceded to the Borsen in Y615. There had been a brief skirmish with the Borsen prior to that, then the resident Commander evacuated his regiment, as he had no chance of winning any bigger conflict. The colonists had been abandoned, as the Commander had no spare capacity on his ship.

There were no detectable threats. The planet was habitable and qualified as 'highly desirable for colonisation'. The moon hosted nothing but the remains of the Earth Command base. The system showed not the slightest trace of a Borsen presence.

Mist-In-The-Sun weighed the risks, and emerged fully from his cloaking fields, shutting them down to avoid any chance of interference with his scans.

Still nothing.

He orbited closer, continuing to scan for anything he had a chance of detecting. Then, resuming his cloaking, he descended into atmosphere over the southern pole.

After the bright path of his entry dissipated, he orbited the planet for two days, scanning and accumulating data. The results did not match Earth Command's official description of a Borsen-captured, non-warpkilled, world. It was meant to be a ravaged wasteland. This was a prosperous agricultural colony, with bountiful crops approaching harvest. The people lived in small communities, and the only unusual things were the lack of advanced technologies and complex weapons. Ox-drawn ploughs and steam threshing machines were the norm, and range weapons were bow and arrow at best.

Telluride was the last of five worlds that he had surveyed. Apart from the fact that the planets lay light-years behind what was considered to be the front line of the Borsen advance, any of them could be one of the fabled Lost Colonies, a settlement that had survived from the time of the first subluminal colony ships, launched in the late twenty-first century.

They also shared a complete absence of Borsen. Not even a picket ship or monitoring installation.

Mist-In-The-Sun exited the atmosphere over the north pole and, as soon as he had completed another system scan, which acquired no new data, he dove into warp and headed for home.

Jackson was worrying about Ghost Command's future. After sixty years of nomadic existence, with makeshift outposts hidden in out-of-the-way places, the numbers were becoming insurmountable: the task of stealthily supplying the two million people spread across the fringes of Earth Command and Borsen space was approaching impossible. In truth, the operation had only lasted this long due to the reduction in population suffered by Ghost Command over the last decade. Earth

Command seemed intent on having the last punch before they quit, and had become quite merciless when a Ghost Command outpost, planetary or otherwise, was found.

If he didn't come up with a solution soon, things were going to become grim for the people who had placed their trust in him.

"First Governor Knife-in-the-Night."

Jackson activated his main viewer to see Kyle Maclachlan, an officer in the overworked logistics division, standing at ease in the audience room.

"Major Parts-the-Deer. What's gone wrong this time?"

Kyle grinned: "Nothing new has broken. But I do come with an idea that seems sufficiently crazed to be worth sharing."

"I'm intrigued. Seeing that it's early in the morning for you, let's hear it."

"Mist-In-The-Sun's discoveries had been nagging at me. Not in a threatening way, but in that annoying 'missing the obvious' way. Early yesterday I saw a report from Blood-Moon, about a Borsen raiding fleet warping out of a system as soon as they detected an entirely CRITTURS force arrayed against them. That gave me an idea."

Jackson thought it over: "Still not seeing it. But that's your point, I think."

Kyle nodded: "We should adopt, and adapt, the key strategy from Earth Command's desertion. Plant colonies behind Borsen lines. Just set up on the opposite side of the world from the USE colony, complying with the technological limitations we've seen. Work with the locals if possible, scavenge any Earth Command or Borsen leftovers if we can. Thus settling our non-combatants somewhere that the remaining Earth Command cannot reach. In emergency, I'm sure that a picket using a pair of Apafin would keep any Borsen at bay. Plus, we can get some detailed information about how the Borsen manage 'their' colonies."

"Major Maclachlan, you're insane. But inspired. Work up the details, task Mist-In-The-Sun and several of his siblings to reconnoitre as many worlds as possible. Define half a dozen clusters with wide separation. One world in each cluster is to have a colony for three months. If that works, we distribute to each cluster, one planet at a time, until all of our non-combatant elements are safely groundside." Jackson paused, "Kyle, you may just have saved Ghost Command. It's a thankless reward, but you're promoted to Colonel and dedicated to what we'll call 'camping expeditions' until they settle, or we have to abandon the concept."

Kyle laughed and executed a florid bow: "My pleasure." He straightened up, spun on his heel and walked out, shaking his head after he turned the corner: "Camping? Good grief."

Jackson chuckled from the speaker closest to Kyle: "I can still hear you. Now go and organise some campers."

Slash and Grab
(Y625 PA)

Randolf Tsander sat in the padded back of the 'relocation van' and
wondered what he had done wrong. He knew they hadn't discovered
his involvement in smuggling information to Ghost Command because
he had only been detained, instead of being executed on the spot.
Muted conversation between his escorts had hinted at further
questioning regarding his father's *ex-officio* work, in conjunction with
his own recent activities. That could be awkward. Revealing that his
father had been trying to limit Servan's influence upon, and damage to,
Earth Command strategies was not something his interrogators would
want to hear. The fact that he had continued his father's work as best he
could would also be unwelcome. Except for the names of his
correspondents, of course.

Could he kill himself? He regarded the snapstraps about his wrists and
ankles. The restraints attached to the snapstraps precluded any
movement violent enough to break his neck. So, the only choice was to
withhold information for as long as possible, trying to bait them into
using harsher techniques that would lead to his death. If that failed, he
had to hold out until they broke him or he died. Every minute bought
was another for friends and sympathisers to get away. They would all
realise the threat that his detention posed.

He heard the loud 'beep' of an incoming warning for the officers up front. The muffled conversation had overtones of disbelief that swiftly turned to panic. Shouting ensued, and the truck swerved off the road, bumping down an embankment, before turning back the way it had come. Running for cover, possibly?

A rumbling blast shook the truck, and the shouting increased in volume. The next blast lifted the truck into the air. Randolf joined in the shouting, then braced himself as best he could and waited for the end.

He came round being dragged by the snapstraps around his wrists. Looking back, he saw the truck in its roof. Smoke rose from several craters on either side of the highway. In the distance, raid sirens wailed. But this was Earth Command Base Five, one of the six most fortified and heavily defended planets in the whole of the USE!

More worryingly, his escorts were showing all the signs of men trapped in hostile territory.

"Lemil, anything?"

"Nothing, Serge. It's like whatever hit the truck just disappeared."

"Damn warpers!"

"Aye. Get under the bridge, lads. Whatever's doing the shooting won't be interested in us. After they finish their raid, we can call for transport."

"That will be unnecessary." The voice was low, feminine and rumbling.

Randolf twisted his head, but whatever spoke was ahead of the group, out of his sight.

"*Madre de dios!*" The whispered imprecation came from the escort dragging Randolf.

"Shut it, Marco. It's a CRITTURS. We make enough noise and it'll move on for an easier target."

"You are our target." Another rumbling voice, this time from the top of the embankment to Randolf's left.

Randolf whipped his head round. Atop the embankment, neatly spotlighted by a highway luminance, was a man-high feline composed of grey-blue armour. Ruby-red sensor eyes glowed, and the twin pulse-cannon deployed from its shoulder bays tracked wherever the CRITTURS looked. Randolf stared. Panthacs! On ECB5! Servan would be apoplectic.

"Back-to-back. Put the prisoner in the middle!"

The four escorts arranged themselves quickly. Randolf found his vision obscured by armoured boots and trouser legs.

"Lemil, Marco, take the one under the bridge. Victor and I will do the one on the highway."

"What about me?" A third rumbling voice, feminine and above.

"There's another one! On the bridge!"

"Steady, lads. Reinforcements will be rolling."

"Until they reach the section of road we demolished." The fourth voice was male and came from the direction of the truck, rumbling with suppressed humour.

"Serge, can we take four of them?"

"You know the answer to that. But if they're after us, these robocats want our prisoner. So we have a bargaining chip."

"Listen up, fuckers! You take one step closer and we'll kill him."

There was a deafening yowl of feral joy. Something hit the escort from the side, and Randolf suddenly had an unobstructed view of the sky. To his left, screams clawed at the night as the sounds of gruesome death increased. He was just wiggling about to sit up when a massive metallic paw descended on his chest, pressing him down gently but with unarguable strength.

"You do not want to witness that."

Randolf looked up into a pair of ruby-red eyes: "Okay."

The Panthac looked to one side, and Randolf twisted his neck to see. A cheerful buzzing preceded half a dozen Slaters scuttling into view as the water of the canal churned, heaved and splashed. Something long, large and invisible heaved itself out of the water, and, guessing from the ground-shaking concussions that accompanied the move, stepped up onto the bank using piledrivers as feet. After that, there was silence, except for distant sirens and the sound of water running from the unseen something that Randolf presumed was a CRITTURS.

"Randolf Tsander."

The purring masculine voice came from the Panthac that approached from where the sounds of carnage had now ceased. Its grey-blue armour was spattered with blood.

"First Governor Spence would like to invite you on an extended visit to Ghost Command. Duration being as long as you want."

Randolf found he was shaking with relief: "I'd be delighted. Good thing you were passing."

He watched in awe as the Panthac on the bridge leapt down to join them with pure feline grace - and a tank-like 'thud' upon landing. She turned and moved to regard Randolf.

"We came for you. Knife-in-the-Night said you had expressed an affinity for Panthacs, so we volunteered. You also said nice things about his Slaters, so No-See-Eye wished to behold you."

With an electrical crackle, the hiss of water turning to steam, and a sudden waft of ozone, a fifty-metre CRITTURS that looked like nothing less than a cross between a Praying Mantis and a high-manoeuvrability stealth-raider appeared. Standing on four segmented legs, each of its raised forelegs ended in weapons of a type Randolf had never seen.

"It is a pleasure to meet an animal-lover in this compassionless desert." The voice was scratchy, like some recordings of very old music that Randolf had heard.

"Slice-And-Dice, we must be gone. There are a lot of unhappy Earth Command forces coming with alacrity. Knife-in-the-Night will be disappointed if we have to break any of them."

"Very well. Hidden-In-Dream, Death-With-Grace: throw the remains into the truck, front and rear. No-See-Eye: we need the slaughter area scorched and the truck blasted. Randolf, may we have your clothes? All the more proof that you have died."

"You could, but – hey!"

With much vari-pitched happy buzzing, the Slaters extruded little blades from their foremost four legs, and neatly extricated Randolf from his bonds and clothing. As he stood, shivering in the night, one of the Panthacs scooped up his shredded garments in its mouth and made for the truck.

"There is an overall on board. Please hurry to the forward hatch. The Panthacs use the loading doors. Three minute warning!"

Within three minutes, all four Panthacs, the half-dozen Slaters, and Randolf were on board No-See-Eye. There were a series of deep thrumming sounds as it blasted the area to remove as much trace of the real event as possible.

"Admiral Tsander, please lie down and relax. Transit to near-phase state can be disorienting for humans."

Randolf lay down with a smile. His vision blurred, a migraine flashed through his head like lightning, and his gut squirmed.

"Transited. Three, two, one. Upship!"

No-See-Eye climbed vertically, exited into free space, and carried on in a straight line, interrupted only by an impact that shook the CRITTURS.

"No cause for alarm. It is a very large and very 'loud' explosive device packed with all sorts of nuisances for those about. When it goes off, we will depart."

Randolf lay where the G-forces of the ascent had pressed him. His body was disinclined to move for a while, having been thoroughly tenderised.

"Dive dive dive!"

Randolf heard the singing void. His eyes must have betrayed his fear of the unknown changing to profound awe, as he heard words amidst the harmonic chaos.

"You have been warp-touched, Admiral Randolf Tsander. You are changed by this. How and why may become clear one day. Until then, welcome to Ghost Command."

Diversion
(Y631 PA)

"Dive dive dive!"

"Six more Hirsch rainbows, Captain!"

That meant we had a full Pursuit Group after us. Standing orders are 'no engagement'. Earth Command may be led by bastards, but the rank and file used to be our shipmates.

"Grey-Weaver, how long can we stay under?"

"Ten minutes, Rides-the-Nightmare. No more."

I watch as our viewscreens go black, then grey. In the back of my mind, and at the base of the place where my hearing registers, the song of warp space resumes. The CRITTURS call this subspace the 'Singing Void' and only those who have experienced it can fully understand why.

"Leftenant. Let's use the recharge time to make sure the weapons and shields are up to capacity. We're going to have a fight on our hands when we come up."

"What about standing orders, sir?"

"Defence is permitted, and I have no illusions about why that Pursuit Group has been lurking about our patrol area for the last month. They've been using warp intrusion detectors to map our breaching. Wherever we go, they'll be minutes behind. Did you see the Hirsch ratings on those ships? Every one is running double-drive so they can jump with one while the other recharges. They must have worked out that Grey-Weaver and his siblings can only follow routes determined before we set out on patrol. Hell, they don't even have to shoot us. All they have to do is force us to dive wild, to avoid certain doom, and warp space will do their job for them."

"Grim truth. I know some of those ships."

"Me too. But it won't change a thing."

A hideous thought matures from my understanding of how the Pursuit Group have trapped us.

"Grey-Weaver, what's our maximum drift when coming up?"

"Ten kilometres or less."

I reach for the comm: "Leftenant Makinoh. What's the blast radius of a counter-intrusion mine?"

"Used to be that the type dictated that, sir. Type one was a two kilometre blast, type two was four kilometres, and so on."

"Sergeant Futhard, what was the standard deployment load for Pursuit Cruisers of the class we are trying to evade?"

"Types three through eight, sir. Quads of the lower three, pairs of the upper. I would hazard a guess that fitting double-drive would reduce that. Depends if their tacticians thought it through, and ignored the strategists."

"Open forum. If you knew about our breaching points, had no way to pursue us into warp, and knew you had to get us when we emerged, before we could move off and Starclad, would you think of using a combination of battle groups big enough to take us and counter-intrusion mines for the breach points you didn't have the battle groups to cover?"

The majority say yes. I agree, and we have a big problem. Facing ships would actually be better.

"Okay, still to open forum. Do we breach and take what comes, or do we ride the void and breach wild?"

"Can we dive wild if we breach and the Earth Command forces have too much grief for us to handle?" A good question from an unidentified ensign.

Grey-Weaver replies: "We will have to remain up for five minutes."

Which would be equivalent to committing suicide.

"Call it, people. Grey-Weaver, you get a vote as well."

"I say we ride and breach wild, Major. The void is a home to us, it will not let us down."

One by one, everyone agrees that taking a chance is preferable to certain death, because if they don't get us the first time, they will eventually.

"Grey-Weaver, please use what residual charge we have remaining to transit and breach."

Breaching at our assigned co-ordinates is simple because they are 'fixed' by quantum determination – as they are calculated in real space, it means they will apply; or something like that. I paid attention to all the lectures and the workshops and still emerged baffled. It's a damnable black art, navigating warp. We lost several early vessels without trace, and still do, occasionally. The danger is messing with the calculations while you're in warp, or entering warp without determining where you will breach. So what I just asked Grey-Weaver to do will probably place us outside the reach of the Pursuit Group. Whether it places us beyond the reach of reality, as we know it, is a moot point.

"Breach in three, two, one."

The grey spins into black and real space surrounds us. Cheers of relief turn to confusion.

"Where are we?"

"Canopus Spur."

"What? That's light-years from where we were!"

"The void does not obey our reality, Rides-the-Nightmare. The fact it let us out is a blessing."

All of the Warptopii do this, whether they have taken a full CRITTURS transformation like Grey-Weaver or remained in their hybrid, mainly organic, form like Swims-The-Singing-Dream. They talk about warp space as if it is an entity as well as a place. We just add their every utterance on this to the Warptopii databanks under the heading 'Mystical Aspects'.

"Contact!"

That's all we need.

"What in the name of all the gods is that?"

I turn to look at the viewscreens, and sit down hard as my legs give out.

It's a spacecraft, but nothing Ghost Command, Earth Command or - hopefully - the Borsen ever produced. It looks like a spiralling spray of oil, over five kilometres long, frozen as it gushes from a valve. 'Black quicksilver in stasis' is the description that comes to my mind. You can see through it in places, between the arches and thickenings.

"We have a tightbeam hail."

I look at the Captain. He shrugs. I get a partial grip: "Record everything, full spectrum. Open channel."

"This is Major Helmut Delaney of Ghost Command Privateer Grey-Weaver."

"We know." The voice is clear and genderless.

What the hell? I look at the Captain and he rolls his hands in a 'keep going' gesture.

"Say again?"

"This is Confederacy Strike Vessel Stormbringer. The dive and breach co-ordinates you require follow. Please recharge and dive as soon as possible. We will remain."

"Grey-Weaver, how long?"

"One hour preferably, but I have reservations that I cannot define."

From the looks on the faces around the bridge, he's not the only one.

"They say dive and breach, so charge for single transit and let's get hell-and-gone from Rossiter's Locker."

The retrieval of the inexplicably abandoned Excalibur from warp space had triggered the naming of all sorts of warp phenomena and improbable destinations from Earth's old sea tales. It seems that sailors are always superstitious, regardless of the seas they ply or the technology they use to do so.

"Twelve minutes."

"Stormbringer, we will need twelve minutes."

"Well done, Major. Any other answer would have been fatal."

I keep it together by act of will alone: "Good to know, Stormbringer. Any other tips for us?"

"Hard-a-port when you breach, Grey-Weaver. Stormbringer out."

I can hear the underlying laughter. I repeat: What the hell?

We record everything we can, which isn't much. The Stormbringer seems to have the big brother of our CDR technology built-in and always on. Apart from that, space around here is empty. Or, as I start to suspect, it could be hidden from us by the increasingly disturbing vessel off our bow.

Twelve minutes later we're ready.

"Major, by your command?"

"Grey-Weaver: dive dive dive."

And we're gone into the realm of the wordless chorus once more. Five minutes later, Grey-Weaver issues the breach warning.

"Hard left on exit, Grey-Weaver."

"Seriously, Rides-the-Nightmare?"

"Let's savour the lingering flavour of this weird excursion, shall we?"

"Very well."

The void spins into black and we breach, Grey-Weaver's manoeuvring drives already humming. With a howl, the drives peak and the wall of armoured hull-plating rushing at us slides to the right. For a moment, I can clearly see our shadow on that hull, as we are silhouetted by our fading warp-flare. A minute later, we're hanging in space above a planet, as a lot of ships hurtle towards us, and our comms board lights up.

"Rides-the-Nightmare, I suspect that someone was making a point."

"Do tell."

"The manoeuvre we were warned to perform, and I had prepared for at your instruction, was the only viable course to avoid our destruction in collision with the flank armour of the Excalibur. We are in orbit over Shine Two."

I sit down hard again. Something momentous just happened. Wish I knew what it was. But as we've arrived here, I know damn well who I'm meant to tell: "Get me First Governor Spence."

Plus Ça Change
(Y636 PA)

They said it was for the best. All the soldiers went away, leaving our planet without defences. All the weapons were removed. Nothing that could even remotely be considered as military equipment was left. We cried and protested, but Earth Command was adamant.

The whole planet came to a standstill on the day they left. We all gathered in parks and open spaces to watch contrails in the daylight, or the rainbow coronas of Hirsch transit stain the night. There were fewer of both than we expected.

Life settled over the next few months. Some harsh revisions to civil law enforcement had been suggested, and they worked. No one wanted to risk death or maiming, even if the possible rewards were lucrative.

Eight months after the last Earth Command ship left, we awoke one morning to find strange vessels blocking the overways. Troops in battle armour, that seemed to come in every colour of the rainbow, patrolled the streets. We huddled indoors for a day or so, but when atrocities did not occur, the need for survival and routine drove us to continue. The strangely disproportionate armoured forms were courteous, stepping out of our way, and even stooping to help in those little situations that inevitably interrupt the day.

A week after that, it was announced that we were now a Borsen colony. We could export to them, or to a small selection of our neighbours. If the results of a year of that arrangement were without incident, we would be allowed to trade intergalactically with other 'bonded' planets as well.

Eventually people would be permitted to volunteer for service with The Borsen, but that would not be for at least a decade.

With that, they left, after commending our recently enforced harsher civil penalties for lawlessness. They also repealed some statutes regarding censorship, drugs, prostitution, and freedom of worship, while adding some death penalties for profiteering and racketeering.

Life goes on. It really is like we were never at war. We visit the graves of those we lost, but the resistance and defiance Earth Command told us to foster is just not forthcoming, because we are actually living in a better, more peaceful, and less restricted society.

It has been remarked upon that Earth Command's final announcement, regarding the fact that their retreat would be all the better for us, is the first time they had ever been truthful with us.

No God but Me
(Y640 PA)

"You're looking well, Servan."

"The new longevity treatments are working well, thank you, Admiral Purbetch."

"They seem to be of variable effect. Mine, not so good."

"A shame. But progress is being made every day, there may yet be a compound that works better for you."

"Let's hope so. Now, I know you're busy, but I needed to discuss Project Saviour ahead of this afternoon's meeting."

"Very well. What is your query?"

"How on Earth do we do this, Servan?"

"We use eugenics and every other form of population control that we need. A completely orchestrated society with one focus. The return to, and liberation of, United States of Earth territories from Borsen control."

"That's inhuman."

"It may seem like that to people who grew up with the freedoms that the next generations out here will never know, but it is the only way. My teams have been running projections and there is no alternative."

"Why not start over? We did it after the Apocalypse: we can do it again, and avoid the mistakes, the flaws that brought us down."

"The only flaws were traitors and weaklings in our own ranks! Spence and his cohorts cost us the Earth!"

"I don't think that is strictly true, Servan. Analysis of our strategies has highlighted some embarrassing flaws."

"Analysis? Who authorised that?"

"I did."

"Good god, Purbetch! We don't have time for navel-gazing and maudlin reflection!"

"It's not wasted. The lessons from our failings will ensure that they never happen again."

"Leftenant Cade."

"Yes, Lord Servan."

"Lord? What happened to Commodore?"

"It was not fitting for the architect of a new stage of mankind's evolution."

"Good god, man. You're deranged."

"Leftenant Cade. The Admiral is revealed as an undesirable."

With a single movement, the armoured officer levelled his compressor-pulse shotgun at Admiral Purbetch and shot him point-blank.

"He is purged, Lord Servan."

"Thank you, Leftenant. Please call the cleaning staff and let's get back to my suite. How have the other negotiations progressed?"

"Fifty-three purgings. Nine carried out by desirables upon their senior."

"Excellent. Ratify the nine promotions, and gather all executive officers in the meeting hall after lunch. We shall discuss the new order and how it is to be implemented. The groundwork is done, now I must ensure that true humanity survives, purged of weakness and doubt."

"You will, sir. You've brought us this far."

"Thank you, Leftenant. While I'm resting before lunch, please have Purbetch's possessions reassigned as you see fit."

"And his family?"

"Like I said, his possessions are to be reassigned as you see fit."

"Thank you, sir."

Epitaph
(Y651 PA)

Spence reviewed the message from the datapack once more. It made
for sad reading: this log of a nine-month maiden voyage that ended
with a discovery so devastating the volunteer crew realised that their
entire mission had been futile.

He wished that Excalibur's databanks had been uncorrupted, so people
could have been spared the agonising wait for news of their loved ones.
At least some answers had finally arrived.

Adding the information to that from the few handwritten scraps found
aboard the Excalibur, and the actual state of planets 'captured' by the
Borsen, he called up the grainy pictures of the mysterious
Stormbringer. Then he reread the final interviews with Axel One.

He felt that lightening of thought which presaged a moment of clarity.
Then it came, and he knew that if he'd still had a body, he'd have
collapsed.

"First Governor! Are you well?"

"I'm fine, Doctor. Just had another one of those intuitive leaps. I
presume your distress means you got readings?"

"We did, sir. I'm relieved. Your transition to containment was the
first, and largely experimental. I cannot help but be nervous."

"Never as nervous as I am, Doctor. Go and relax, or oversee your analysis team. I need to take the helm of Ghost Command for a while."

He contacted his daughter: "Katie, drop everything. I finally got it."

Her voice hitched, then her words gushed: "You did? We have the win?"

"No, daughter mine. But with some effort, I think we can change the game forever."

"I'll be there in four hours. Who shall I bring?"

"Let's start with the Admirals."

He paused. Even in this machine state, he needed to prepare himself for some things. Finally, he opened a line down on to Shine II. In his mind's eye, he could see the little farmstead where the comm lit up. While waiting for an answer, he routed a priority call to the nearest emergency medical station down there.

A rugged man in a worn check shirt stared at the screen: "First Governor. This is a pleasant surprise. Can I scan you a drink?"

Jackson laughed. The man had no respect at all, which was probably why they got on so well.

"Kind offer, but I'll pass. Sit down, John."

"I'll stand."

"I cannot tell you the details, but I am now sure that Janet is dead. I also know she died saving her people from something utterly terrifying, and it didn't faze her one bit. She also left information that may lead to the end of this war."

John Rossiter slumped down into the chair by the comm, face turning ashen grey.

"Oh, my girl. Captain Mum to the end."

He raised eyes filled with tears to the screen: "Thank you, Jackson. Millie will be glad to know, at last."

Jackson Spence wished he could cry as well. Millicent Rossiter had been fatally wounded off Busarius by Earth Command ships from her mother's former battle group. John's trip to tell her would be a sorrowful walk to the grave in the shade of the apple tree in his garden.

"At least I can stop the longevity treatments now. They really hurt the last half-dozen times."

Jackson saw the splash of strobing light on the wall behind John as the emergency team arrived. He pushed bare-bones details to their preparedness datapads, then cut the transmission. There really was nothing to say. Some personal tragedies are so monstrous that silence is the only fitting acknowledgement.

The End of Ways
(Y652 PA)

Alpha Commander Alison Cruetes looked out at the second impossible thing she'd seen this week. If one of her subordinates had told her last week that a spaceship bigger than Jupiter would be parked one-quarter of a solar orbit from half of Ghost Command's forces that currently existed 'next Friday', she would have sent that subordinate for psych evaluation.

"Eyes-Never-Changing, you're going pale again."

She blinked. The damn thing was hypnotic in its size and reflectiveness: "Thanks, Race-The-Starlight. It nearly sucked me in again."

"It is a force majeure, Alpha Commander. If you think it is fascinating here, you should hear the void around it. It is so dangerous that Swims-The-Singing-Dream has banned all warp work until it departs."

"Tell me again how this happened. I lost the plot around the point that WarpMistress unpronounceable-name with the huge breasts and hissing hair came aboard to play dara with Swims-The-Singing-Dream."

"They played dara for a day and discussed many things. Four times they went into warp space and returned. Then she took eight ceremonial dara sets and returned to the Avallea."

"The significance of dara sets being?"

"I have no idea. Why not ask?"

"No thanks. Is that little Mistress still in his tank?"

"She is. Comes up for air about once every five and a half hours. She is teaching him something about warp manipulation."

"As if he needs more ways to make our scientists gibber."

"Knife-in-the-Night insists that Swims-The-Singing-Dream is essential to our diplomacy."

"Diplomacy? What are we diploming, exactly?" Her voice dropped to a whisper as her eyes returned to the monstrous vessel.

"We are at the fulcrum of history. Sometime in the next few hours, either there will be a new alliance formed, or the Borsen will annihilate us."

Alison sat up like she'd been shocked: "What!"

There was a chuckle: "Apologies. You looked like you were drifting again."

She shook her head and swung the seat to face away from the view: "Now tell me the truth."

"Swims-The-Singing-Dream brokered a cessation of hostilities, as you know. Now he and Knife-in-the-Night, along with all of our Admirals, several Commodores and two Governors, are hammering out the terms of an alliance."

"How did he broker the ceasefire? Reports are vague."

"We have been giving the Borsen a hard time of late. Every time they breach to attack, they find themselves faced by CRITTURS warships. So they retreat. The last time, they found only a farming world devoid of military presence. Then Swims-The-Singing-Dream breached on their bridge. He actually used the line 'Take me to your leader'. Much to everyone's surprise, they did."

"Ah yes, their mysterious leader. Can you tell me about her?"

"The Matriarch is apparently a WarpMistress who has mastered many of their facets of warp manipulation, before being chosen from several contenders by the current Matriarch. She is trained to become the heart of the Borsen: the living core of Avallea, their world-turned-spaceship. There she remains, until she tires of the role and hands over to her chosen successor. There are contenders in training all the time, because, many generations ago, the Matriarch keeled over without warning. She muttered a few dire sentences regarding this Galad thing, and then died. They were in chaos for a decade until a new Matriarch could be found. Since then, there are always heiresses to the throne, so to speak."

"Okay. I get that. I know this Galad thing is their end-of-days destroyer death-god. But why did they cave?"

Alison stifled a scream as a large red octopus CRITTURS materialised in the huge bowl-shaped depression in the floor next to her. With only the slightest hesitation, Swims-The-Singing-Dream took up the narration.

"Because they have a morbid religious fear of CRITTURS. Their perceptions go places we don't understand, but, simply put with clumsy words, they see souls and spirits if they exist within physical objects. Or if they happen to be passing by. To them, CRITTURS should be banshees of the dead, not happy citizens of the galaxy. First Governor Knife-in-the-Night is regarded as partially divine."

Race-The-Starlight chuckled: "You're being modest, and I'm not going to let you get away with it. Tell her the other bit."

The octopus flushed yellow in embarrassment: "They think that I am an avatar of the Chosen of Galad, that first race who rebelled against

Galad, by assisting Rshtra to free the Borsen, and were struck down for doing so."

There was an audible 'pop', and a small Mistress with green hair and tea-coloured tentacles appeared above Swims-The-Singing-Dream. With a movement that Alison couldn't follow, he caught her.

"Eyes-Never-Changing and Race-The-Starlight, may I present Trbtha, WarpMistress of the Eleventh, and thus WarpMistress-Elect: a contender for the Matriarchy. She is also the only surviving daughter of the current Matriarch, Shtubreth."

"Oh, gods. Royalty on the bridge," Ensign Karlmat muttered quietly from his post far to the left.

"I am Trbtha, not royalty. Swims-The-Singing-Dream is correct. You are not, warrior."

Alison turned to regard the mortified junior officer: "Still here, Karlmat?"

He saluted, rose, saluted, bowed toward Trbtha, and then double-timed himself off the bridge. Alison laughed.

"He was amusing?" Trbtha sounded uncertain.

"Yes, he was."

"Ah, so, for his antics, you permitted him to live. I understand."

Alison spun about to see Swims-The-Singing-Dream making 'no-no' gestures above and behind Trbtha's head.

She improvised: "I am feeling lenient today. It is an auspicious one, after all."

The tentacle went from 'no-no' to the octopod imitation of a thumbs-up.

Trbtha relaxed and slumped down in the nest of tentacles around her: "You are right. I missed that. Mother always says that I lack imminence perception. I fear that I'll never master it."

Swims-The-Singing-Dream place a tentacle-tip on her shoulder: "Would it not show imminence perception if you were to flip yourself over to the grand hall to witness first-hand the momentous events transpiring there? It is, after all, a moment of worth."

Trbtha beamed up at Swims-The-Singing-Dream: "You would let me go?"

"We have covered your teaching, and I have demonstrated my refinement to your satisfaction. Away with you, contender, you have greater things to prepare for."

With a gleeful laugh and a crackle of green lightning in her hair, Trbtha vanished. Swims-The-Singing-Dream visibly wilted down into his bowl.

"That child is terrifying."

Alison leaned forward, resting her chin on her hands: "Really? I though she was kind of cute for a one and a half metre tall warp-heiress."

"Not funny. She showed me several warp tricks I had never even thought of, and then she interpreted the singing void for me, for a while."

Race-The-Starlight emitted a sound like a startled cat from every speaker on his bridge: "You're joking!"

"I'm not. She understands some of it. Apparently, all Borsen Mistresses do during their growing years. Now, I think I recognise snippets, and it's even less comfortable in warp space than it used to be."

Alison moved from her seat to the edge of the bowl: "So what's it singing about?"

"It's not a song. It's the blended resonance-echo of everything that has ever passed through, or will ever pass through, that piece of warp space."

"Past, present and future?"

"Yes. All interwoven and inseparable, except in the minds of the juvenile females of a race who claim to have been partially conceived by warp space itself. Another fact for the Borsen religion file, I fear. As for me? I'm just glad I came back sane."

A broadcast cut in from the speakers above: "Race-The-Starlight, priority for Eyes-Never-Changing."

Alison stood up: "Go for Eyes-Never-Changing."

Jackson Spence chuckled: "Please thank Swims-The-Singing-Dream for sending Trbtha back: the hyperactive child of the Matriarch is wonderful for driving her mother to distraction. Anyway, we have a ratified treaty."

Everyone on the bridge stopped what they were doing.

He continued: "As of eight minutes ago, Ghost Command and The Borsen have declared Confederacy. This term will be a collective, a definition, and a demarcation of areas of control and influence. The subtleties will keep academics in employment for decades. Either way, the Borsen part of The Borsen Incursion is ended. Now all we have to do is turn this monstrous combined force, the planets captured, those still free, the various disgruntled elements, and eight sentient races beaten into subservience and confined to reservation planets, into a single united community. Because Galad is coming, and before he, she or it gets here, I'm betting that Earth Command's progeny will be back mob-handed to take their grandparent's playground back again."

Alison just stood there. All of a sudden, it was over. She felt changed and terrified. After the ages of struggle and sacrifice, to have it end in a few sentences seemed anti-climatic. But there were interesting times ahead.

"Race-The-Starlight, please relay my words from 'as of eight minutes' to all former Ghost Command units, bases and homeworlds. Add the line: 'But above all, I am proud of every member of Ghost Command, and proud to be a part of this triumphant *oyáte*.' That is all."

Fall from Grace
(Y657 PA)

Servan looked out across the parade ground and smiled. His personal banners fluttered in the warm morning breeze. Arcadia was the world that centred his empire, home to the start of the perfect war machine that he would lead to the pinnacle of human development, and then unleash on Spence's rabble and their tentacled bedmates.

"We are ready, Lord."

He straightened his pristine white uniform and flicked his robe behind him. Taking a deep breath, he strode out onto the podium as the gathered faithful roared in approval.

Gripping the sides of the lectern firmly, and with a stern gaze, captured perfectly by the live feed, he looked out at the core of the new Earth Command. His command. Servan's Legion was the elite, utterly dedicated to his vision of perfection. Not one short person. No cripples, no deviants, no bleeding hearts. Iron-willed warriors with iron discipline.

"My people. Today marks the twentieth anniversary of our arrival in Heaven: the eighteen worlds of the new order. But here on Arcadia, we know the truth. We know what is important. We know that Heaven is just a stepping stone on our journey back to the territory we were forced to leave by the actions of dross with weak moral fibre. We will never be like them. We are the sword that will cut the cancer from humanity. I am proud to be your leader. I am proud to be your inspiration. I am proud that you have placed your faith in my ideals."

The cheering and the beating of armoured fists upon breastplates was heady; he had succeeded. Tomorrow his people would go forth into the eighteen worlds, ready to implement Project Unity: the removal of the weak leaders that had accompanied him to Heaven.

He turned to Alpha Commander Peters: his aide and a warrior of sterling qualities. He had doubted the man's commitment at first, but in the ten years since the death of his wife, he had laboured without faltering toward Servan's vision, leading the Legion with ruthlessness and by example.

"They're fine men and women, Vance. You have done exceptionally well in recruiting all those who sympathised from across Heaven. Tomorrow we will start the rise we all deserve, shaking off the taint of former foolishness."

Vance Peters turned to look down at Lord Elgin Servan, a man who would not meet his own requirements for service in the legion that bore his name.

"It was easy, Lord. I just picked the arrogant, the ignorant, the bigoted, the selfish and the treacherous."

Servan's brow creased: "What did you just say?"

Peters leaned down to stare Servan in the eyes from a few centimetres distance. Servan flinched.

"Heaven does need a new start. Being forced to follow the petty psychoses and vengeful wishes of a failed megalomaniac is not it. Tomorrow will indeed be a new start, but not for you."

Servan mumbled in confusion, so Peters placed an armoured hand on the thin shoulder and shook him to get his attention: "Look up, you horrible little man."

High above, a single contrail arced across the clear blue sky. The distant rumble of powerful engines was just becoming discernible.

"I led the men and women that built the eighteen planets of Heaven from bare rock and grass. I did not dedicate ninety years of my life to let scum like you take a power trip off the back of so much loyalty, suffering and sacrifice. I serve Earth Command. For nine years, I have been the sole agent of Project Lucifer. I volunteered for it. I wanted to see your face as ten kilotons of hellfire purge your dreams and your regime from the annals of history."

Servan whimpered and uttered imprecations. Alpha Commander Vance Peters had held himself back for a long time. As the missile hammered down from the heavens, he leaned down by Servan's ear for a little personal revenge. He whispered to Servan, telling the madman something he was sure would be true, if only his former academy comrade knew what was about to occur.

"Jackson Spence says: 'Burn'."

We Ran
(YᏮᏮᏰ PA)

The white sunlight cut lines through the dust motes hanging in the air of the classroom. She had adjusted the auto screens to not close fully, so the children would adjust to the brightness. Against parental wishes, but adaptation to their new home was essential.

Her class were heads-down to their consoles, finishing the mathematics test. With a rich chime, the assessor locked all the screens as the allocated time expired. Dana carefully rose from her recliner and seated herself on the edge of the tutor's master panel. It was staggering just how tired and weak an extra one-tenth of a gravity could make you feel.

As was her way, while the assessor graded the results, she held an open-forum session for the fifty-eight pupils. Johnny Treaden stood with a smooth ease she envied and awaited her acknowledgment. She nodded to him.

"Fem Dana, why did we run? My father says we should have fought to the bitter end."

Bitter end? That had to be a direct quote. She looked at the poster on the far wall, a misty Scottish loch in the dawn, while gathering her thoughts for a reply. The class all stared at her, their level gazes reminding her of that last meeting. She shook her head to clear the overlaid imagery, and replied,

"It was the bitter end, Johnny. We did not understand what we faced, all the old ways of waging war were useless, but we did not comprehend that until too late. I was there when President Cheung-Hma declared the Mandate of Retreat. She really did cry all the way through reading it."

Johnny looked unconvinced. She smiled and gestured to the consoles. "Look up 'Ant' and scroll to 'supercolonies'."

They did so quickly and then looked up again, waiting for the lesson.

"The ant was an incredibly successful life-form on Earth, able to spread across landmasses in organised arrays, despite many predators and man's repeated control efforts. They did this without thought, just working through difficulties and accepting losses on the way. Man did not realise how far they extended because they were unseen, and rarely came into direct conflict, due to their size."

There were a few glimmers of comprehension. Dana flagged their names in the register.

"Those we left behind are to become human ants, in effect. The Borsen are the new man. We cannot fight the Borsen yet. It may be centuries before we can. But non-combatant humans are ignored by the Borsen, so they can spread quietly, establish colonies, and make alliances with other overtaken races, if they exist. As long as they do not become militarised, they are safe. By the time the warrior caste of man can return to clear the Borsen out, humanity should have recovered and spread, using our adaptive nature to survive and thrive."

Johnny stared at me, no understanding in his gaze. Then he looked down and nodded. I flagged his name for a parental orientation check.

The 'No Retreat' factions were only potentially problematical, and with careful monitoring, would remain that way. Diversity and opposition were essential traits to experience. We were still in the early stages of the Mandate, and the plan predicted two generations before the psychological adaptations became learned behaviour. Two or three generations after that, we should be ready to start.

We ran once. Never again.

Eternal Witness
(Y752 PA)

Jackson Spence was tired. A century had passed since the Borsen had moved from being strange opponents to stranger allies. In that time, the span of the Confederacy had quadrupled, and the long process of bringing the eight races suppressed by Earth Command back to where they had been had started. For all the assistance, it would be centuries before they trusted humanity fully. All that could be done was to let them redevelop at their own pace, and maintain a single embassy on each planet, without any military presence.

As for the thirty-six races encountered by the Borsen on their long journey, he had no idea how to approach them. The total rapine of a civilisation undoubtedly left scars that would influence subsequent redevelopment. Some would certainly have rebuilt as militarised empires. He had decided to defer contact missions until the threat of Earth Command's return had been resolved, one way or another.

His containment was expected to let him live for as long as he wished, because all the medical teams agreed that the ability of the human mind to cope with such longevity was the one unknown factor. He had come to agree with them, and had recently started giving serious consideration to letting them euthanise him. Especially as everything seemed to be going so well. The tedium was becoming insufferable.

The prospect of Earth Command returning from the far strongholds they had withdrawn to had kept everyone on edge for the first forty years, but after that, it seemed like the crazed plan to return after five generations could possibly be a real objective for the departed host. In which case, the Confederacy had nothing to fear for a while. Then again, with forced-growth techniques and cloning, backed by a ruthless dictatorship which Commodore Servan would certainly institute, they could have returned in as little as eighty years. When they didn't, people started to relax, just a little.

When all possible sources of locating Earth Command's haven had been exhausted, he and Shtubreth had laid out the broad actions to be taken, should they return. It was likely they would come with a full invasion, and the last thing either of them wanted was a repeat of the protracted grief that their kin had engaged in. So they laid some plans, making some fairly weighty guesses from both of their understandings of regime-led or indoctrinated societies. Shtubreth was quite open with the fact that her experience was actual, but could be partially inapplicable on a psychological level, given the differences between Borsen and humans.

Integrating the Borsen had been a difficult task. Their Mistresses were used to absolute subservience from males, and the males of their species were brutes of low intelligence and precisely zero imagination. After a couple of failed attempts, it was decided that Borsen males would be restricted to Avallea. The next challenge that Jackson had dreaded was their breeding methods: how to change the centuries-old custom of capturing males of compatible species and mating with them until they died.

Katie made a few suggestions that made Jackson queasy. But she had based her ideas on data from the fall of the Eighty-Second, and observing the reactions of some human males around Mistresses. He gave her leave to trial the concept and, to his surprise, Borsen 'breeding temples' quickly became an established part of many cities. Some human men found Mistresses incredibly attractive. Some human women did too, and the ramifications of that revelation were yet to be fully realised. It seemed that the Borsen had been largely unaware of the full possibilities, and impact, of sex for fun.

Meanwhile, men who visited the Borsen edifices got slightly more pleasure than they could bear, and the Mistresses got what they needed without having to kidnap, murder or inflict rapine upon anyone.

After a couple of years, performance-boosting and recovery venues had opened near every temple, and local business revenues picked up: an unexpected side effect.

Another, and even more unexpected, side-effect had been the number of females born without tentacles. Apparently, it had happened very occasionally in the past, but now it occurred in eight percent of females spawned by Borsen Mistresses, but only Mistresses. Borsen women with 'human' arms produced babies, of both sexes, that were human in appearance, while they retained the mental disparity of 'true' Borsen spawnings. The men were taller than those descended from Mistresses and the women were indistinguishable from human women, apart from a tendency toward lurid hair colours and an affinity for warp. The integration of those women into human society had initially been problematical, but now they were accepted, and even sought-after as partners, in some areas.

The men were also capable of fitting in, something their Mistress-spawned brethren were still unable to do. Investigating the causal psychological aspects of that had created a new discipline almost overnight, and the medical ramifications of the whole thing were still being hotly disputed. The 'common ancestor' theorists frequently clashed with the 'dominant human DNA' theorists on various media and at scientific conventions. Jackson suspected that the controversy would continue, whilst the truth remained a mystery.

Mistresses from pre-Incursion remained aloof from humanity, but all progeny spawned during and since found human worlds to be fascinating. We had so many, and they only had one: a purposeful fortress since time immemorial. Trbtha's progeny added the complication of being able to go where they pleased at will, which resulted in some stern admonitions and edicts by Shtubreth to prevent any more security nightmares, moments of excruciating embarrassment, and incidents of violence through misunderstanding.

But things had settled. For twenty years, the Confederacy had been peaceful.

Jackson had spent a lot of time visiting the CRITTURS planets, all natural wonderlands devoid of all but the slightest traces of civilisation. Thunder-Star would enter orbit and various delegations would eagerly visit Knife-in-the-Night to discuss a range of subjects and to obtain his guidance on others.

Down below, the CRITTURS did whatever deeply spiritual sentient war machines do when peace has arrived. Which in practice meant that, apart from a few vague hints and a lot of rumour, no-one outside the CRITTURS community had the remotest clue what went on.

The CRITTURS were a greater boon than any suspected. In conversations with Shtubreth, he discovered that warp space was inaccessible by purely mechanical means. You could detect it, even open minute portals – if you expended impractical amounts of power. But to actually journey within warp space, you had to have a mind attuned to it. Alternatively, prolonged immersive exposure could attune most minds, even those who would not have developed attunement otherwise. Which explained why the Excalibur had worked in the first place, worked to dodge the Borsen projectile that should have destroyed it, but did not return after that. The damage sustained during that desperate warp transit must have breached the containment of the Duodene Biomatrix's organic component and Captain Rossiter, being unaware of the fact that her entire crew were now capable of enabling Excalibur to breach, had made the logical conclusion that they were marooned in the singing void.

This explained why CRITTURS vessels could traverse warp while Earth Command had signally failed after the Excalibur. They had blamed the failure of Project Lancelot on a flaw in the experimental biomatrix, and resorted to pure hardware. The removal of the organic element also removed any chance of them ever succeeding.

"First Governor."

Jackson brought his attention back to the world beyond his mind and saw that a Borsen Knight had entered his audience room. He did a double-take. Those old body-stealing artificial intelligences never left the Avallea. Their line had ended when consorts ceased to be taken. The figure brought its arm forward to show the Confederacy 'C6' emblem etched on its rerebrace.

Jackson laughed: "Svalten! How many times do I have to tell you to always enter with that emblem showing?"

The armoured figure assumed a cross-legged pose on the floor before replying: "I like to watch your focus rings twitch."

Svalten had come far from the Earth Command battle suit trooper rescued by the surveillance dreadnought Thunderchild. Back then it had been Earth Command rostered but collaborating with Ghost Command as well. He had transferred to her permanent roster, and eventually taken command of the vessel, by which time he had become the first human to voluntarily become a cyborg in a Borsen Knight's armour. His long-time companion, Isla, would no doubt be making Jackson's technical research teams' lives hell while Svalten had a chat up here. Her decision to take transition into a Panthac chassis had caused many raised eyebrows, but Jackson loved and envied the two of them for choosing unique methods of eternal service which allowed them to remain independently mobile, and together.

"Thunderchild is not due for resupply or refit any time soon, so I'm guessing that either you have something for me, or Isla read about some of the new stuff my research teams have come up with."

Svalten canted his head: "Isla wanted them to check over a tremor she's developed, and we needed to see you in private. So if you don't mind, can we just put the Confederacy to rights while we wait?"

Jackson had no objection at all, having not seen either of them in person for over two decades.

About two hours later, Isla prowled in.

"Hello, Uncle Ghost."

"Not you as well."

"Trbtha may be the most dangerous over-sexed brat in all creation, but she has a way with naming things."

"Really? What did she name you two?"

Isla sank into a sphinx position and growled: "Mistress Ghost."

Svalten chuckled: "Brother Ghost."

Jackson laughed: "It seems that human intelligences in machines get to be ghosts. I'm sure there's some deeper meaning. I'll just relay it to the semantics kids and let them play. Now, you two had something to tell me?"

If they'd been human, he'd have joked about pregnancy. For transitioned humans, as with CRITTURS, that was considered to be a nasty quip.

Svalten reached back and drew a datapack from Isla's ventral bay: "Take a look at this on your private net."

Jackson lit the relevant socket on his master board, and Svalten slotted the pack in. The timestamp was barely a month old. The Thunderchild must have blazed a direct route to Shine Two after it had been recorded.

The enhanced-light video showed the twisted skeleton and pitted remnants of a derelict. The light from outside was dim, and the only interior lighting came from Isla's 'third-eye' headlight. The size of the derelict became clear over the next hour, as did its extreme age and the massive damage it had taken. Deep within, Isla entered a room that Svalten would have had difficulty accessing, the entranceway being designed for something barely a metre tall but over two metres in width. Within the room, a single bier of black metal hosted a vast skeleton. As Isla moved about, it became clear that the being had vaguely resembled an octopus in form, except that it had only six tentacles and they each possessed a bone structure similar to that of a snake. The great skull had four eye sockets. Even though long-dead, it gave Jackson a feeling of brooding menace. Finally, Isla shone her light on the back of the bier. Wrought into the metallic material, in a lighter shade of presumably the same stuff, was a single symbol. One that Jackson and a few others knew well. With that, the recording stopped.

"At that point, we realised what we'd found and high-tailed it here. The co-ordinates are included. There is definitely no viable tech left and the hulk shows signs of having been salvaged soon after being destroyed."

"You did the right thing. That symbol must be the original from which the Borsen's Sigil of Galad was derived."

"We thought that. Initial estimates place the hulk at circa eight thousand years old."

"You need to visit the Avallea. Find one of Swims-The-Singing-Dream's clan and get them to find Trbtha for you. She'll inform her mother, the Matriarch. Offer to take a research group back there with you, or to lead one of their ships there. I suspect that Galad may be a dead civilisation by now, but let's not take any chances. This could be a way to break down the Borsen's infernal need to keep moving."

"What if they don't want to come with us?"

"It's a possibility. In that case, pick up scientific and archaeological teams, making sure they include our best xenotechs, and get there fast. At the very least, get full spectrum readings off the hulk. Every piece of information that could allow future detection and identification is crucial."

"We'll report as soon as we're done and drop a datapack regarding how the Borsen are taking it before we depart."

"Good enough. Isla; Svalten mentioned a tremor?"

"One of my biosheaths had deteriorated. Been replaced, along with the affected nerve tissue, and secured away from the edge it had been rubbing against for thirty years."

"Excellent. Can't have one of the Borsen's venerated ghosts breaking down."

Isla chuckled as they both rose smoothly and then departed quickly with their customary near-silent gait, Svalten's hand resting lightly on Isla's flank.

Jackson Spence realised that he too could not 'break down'. Not until he ascertained just how critical his continued existence was to keeping the Borsen in check.

Maybe this discovery would help with their integration. Realising that their ancient nemesis was 'only' a millennia-old race of spacefarers should improve their outlook; after the initial hideous shock, of course.

They would need to reassess every piece of Galad mythology. What if Galad, or whatever they actually called themselves, were still about, somewhere out there in the uncharted reaches? What had happened so long ago, when the Borsen came to be? More importantly, was that unknown event sufficiently monumental for Galad to bear a grudge for this long?

Sympathiser
(Y862 PA)

Marshal Cielan Dhevar looked down from his judgement seat on the group of citizens gathered before him. He knew many of them, had even been in child-bearing partnerships with two. That they would come here was an indicator of something big.

"You wanted to see me?"

Trudi Montosores stepped forward, her smile still engaging: "We want you to petition Concilium Command."

He stood quickly and several below flinched. He gestured to the guards: "Leave the room."

When they had gone, he quickly descended the steps to stand in front of the group.

"That's a dangerous thing to ask, with potentially ruinous results for you and yours. So tell me, informally, what you want."

Trudi's husband Davor stepped up beside her: "Simple enough, Cielan. We think that this 'go back and make war' thing has passed its time."

Cielan sat down on the lowest stair and waved his hands for everyone else present to relax.

"That's a seriously contrary standpoint. You know what some of the other Marshals would do to you for even mentioning it?"

Trudi smiled: "That's why we waited until you were sitting in judgement."

You raise a child with a woman, and she has an advantage for life! Cielan grinned: "Okay, so you picked your soft target with care. What do you expect me to do? I dare not approach Concilium Command with this. They're very nervous about the fact that seventeen of the Eighteen Kings back your stance."

Doctor Sharbills came forward and sat on the step next to Cielan.

"We only used the petition gambit to get you to clear the guards from the room. We don't want you to take one in. What we want you to do is gauge the level of sympathy for our campaign within Concilium forces."

Trudi added: "You command the Tau. Surely the commander of that elite, gifted force can bring some pressure to bear?"

Cielan folded his arms atop his knees and then rested his forehead on his crossed forearms. This moment had to have come now.

He looked up: "We're going back within a decade. The preparations have been going on for a year."

The looks of surprise around him would have been comical, if it were not so sad.

"So it's going to happen?"

He nodded: "Nothing can stop the Crusade from going out."

Trudi caught his careful word choice: "But?"

Cielan looked about at the people around him; people whose opinions he knew were mirrored by over three-quarters of the civilian population of Heaven. This was why Project Crusade had been instigated. It had to go now, before Concilium Command had their mandate revoked.

He smiled: "I already know the level of sympathy amongst the forces. While I cannot do a damned thing about preventing this ancient madness from sending them out, I intend to bring as many back as possible. The rhetoric about 'or die trying' has already been rightly condemned as Servanic."

Davor extended his hand and Cielan took it, letting Davor pull him to his feet with a grunt of effort, because trained soldiers were tailored to be good at what they did. It made them bigger and heavier.

Davor smiled: "So you're with us?"

Cielan raised an open hand and rocked it in a so-so gesture: "I will not compromise my duty to the Concilium. That being said, I will not let people be wasted. I read the treatises on Earth Command. That will never happen again, and I know that some of my fellow Marshals feel the same way."

Trudi nodded: "Better than we hoped for."

Cielan watched them leave. He agreed wholeheartedly with their view, but duty bound him to the other way, for now. He had read the analyses by the Department of Strategic Affairs. They were fine for Concilium forces, but they contained not the slightest hint of what the legendary Borsen and their hated allies Ghost Command could have developed into while the Concilium spent two centuries preparing to invade them.

He had a very bad feeling about this. Despite 'bad feelings' being officially deemed as nonsense, his 'subconscious assessment of potential outcomes' was in complete agreement.

The Tau
(Y871 PA)

They ran like herd beasts, crashing through their own domiciles in a desperate attempt to evade their coming doom.

Newly promoted Praetor Cielan Dhevar looked at a clump of them, gathered about an antique piece of agricultural machinery that flagged as having the potential to be weaponised, then blinked, to pass the target to the nearest interdictors. Infotags showed them to be the Second Squad, Boston Company, under Centurion Idunn. Their tripartite drives left vapour trails rimmed in scads of blue energy as they descended.

Using body-dynamics profiling, they identified the leader of the group, and Soldier Blue used his manda-pulse to turn her into chunks. Several of the group were taken out by the more solid bits of their erstwhile leader and the rest fled, their dynamics showing a return to flock-flight behaviour.

Soldier Red categorised the antique, uploaded data for preservation and then slagged it. Soldier Black ran DNA analysis on the downed targets while 2-Squad mustered on him, a commendable use of spare combat-readiness time to save Concilium analytical squads valuable seconds. Satisfied with Boston Company's efficiency, Dhevar was about to bounce his attention to the cohort taking the second continent when his bloodline flag turned red and flashed rapidly.

He pushed a 'hold' directive to the 2-Squad and pulled the DNA feed, to see the giveaway purple trace on the teenage fem. He dropped to voice-comms as Squads did not have in-head capability.

"Two Squad retrieve fem at nine o' clock to slag. Patch and watch until Tau arrival."

There was exactly forty-three seconds of silence on the comm.

"Two Squad implemented, Praetor. We abide."

Truly exceptional. He decided that 2-Squad, Idunn, Boston Co. were worth watching and deserved recognition. He could have pulled their details with a couple of thoughts, but the morale of the troops was paramount, especially during this first implementation of 'total war'. Cielan had already decided that it was something that no amount of training could prepare anybody for, because it was abhorrent. He did his duty, but he knew that his sleep would be ruined for years to come.

2-Squad were performing the increasingly grim task with expedience. Therefore he should make them feel like they shone brightly.

"Two Squad, immaculate; identify for commend."

There was no hesitation. All three spoke simultaneously.

"Black Harold Bundeberg, Praetor."

"Red Michelle Ganner, Praetor."

"Blue Rufus Smith, Praetor."

He saw their motivation, team and loyalty graphics turn from green to black while their empathic synchronisation hit a remarkable ninety-eight percent.

"Red request observational comment, Praetor."

Cielan raised an eyebrow. It was almost unheard of for a trooper to dare to say a word to a senior exec, let alone request a verbal. He patched in her squadmates before replying.

"Granted."

"Target fem displays no physiology unique to Borsen, appearing to be full homosap. Yet she has warp-attuned hair."

Now that was interesting. The fem was definitely of interest, but the fact that... Michelle... could tell him that, bare-eyed, without the fortune in sensors that Tau Tech Division needed, was frankly astonishing.

"Two Squad, state detection used for analysis."

"Black replies, Praetor. Mich-, Red has always had an eye for Borsen fems, tech- and warp-touched. Blue has sensitivity for warp. In all cases, only functional at Squad cohesion. Been denied status because of it four times now."

Cielan offlined momentarily and swore egregiously. Execs across the command centre become very busy. He picked up again and linked to Boston Company command with a bridge to bring London Cohort command in. All parties chorused.

"Praetor Dhevar?"

"Two Squad, Idunn, Boston Company. Query denial of status for valid Tau talent?"

That straightened them out. Cielan would not have the grunts picking on the specials by the simple expedient of denying them recognition. The Concilium, and Heaven itself, needed Tau-rated people so desperately. He listened to the excuses for twelve seconds, while the monitoring graphics told him the tale of who was guilty and who was surprised. Then Cielan actioned transfer directives to break the chain of anti-Tau command he had found: demoted two, had one shot by his second, then promoted the second. After that, he dropped the command lines and picked up 2-Squad again, with a bridge to the Tau unit en route to them.

"Two Squad, reassign immediate, Tau, transfer immediate, join unit vectoring to you now. New designation: Unit Twenty-Six, Tau."

"Black, Praetor. Query command line."

"Unit Twenty-Six. Your line is now to Tau alone and culminates at me. End."

He muted their line.

"Unit Four, amend pickup, fem target and new Unit Twenty-Six. Transfer back via their former base ship to retrieve personal effects."

"Level of animosity, Praetor?"

That's what he liked about the Tau. They knew his preferences and expectations without a script, and had no trouble discussing things with their commander.

"Whatever is needed, Four, whatever is needed. Unit Twenty-Six has been actively blocked for two years. If their former command plays up, permission to be extremely prejudicial is granted."

Cielan hated the superstitious dogma that had spread through the ranks about Tau ability and privilege. But, as his fellow Marshalls refused to acknowledge it and his Consul seemed to actively encourage that sort of discrimination, he would use it to gather the gifted into his command, where at least he could ensure they worked within a command structure that could utilise and appreciate their talents.

He had wondered, in moments that would have got him executed if his thoughts had been known, if this was how Jackson Spence had felt. From there, his contemplations of why Ghost Command came to be, and the balances of cause and effect, had taken his thinking down some dangerous and revelatory avenues. The implications were devastating, and, given his personal views on the entire invasion, they had been impossible to shake off.

Now the Concilium had returned to the territories forfeited by Earth Command so long before, and what they had found was beyond even the outer limits of the Mandate. While they had been away, the non-combatant humanity left behind had become Borsen indigens.

So, as this devastating opening action continued to find only civilians and local law enforcement officers to wage war upon, the Consul had decided that they were going to liberate them all whether they wanted it or not.

Cielan had sided with the significant opposition to that decision, but had been circumspect about it. Something he had been grateful for, when Consul Varides had the chosen representatives of the 'there is nothing here to liberate' faction executed.

Cielan had been given Praetor status, as the position had suddenly become vacant. From that position, he resolved to limit the Consul's pointless bloodlust.

Tau had found Borsen women without tentacles living with families, and having human husbands, with no apparent stigma attached. They had found Borsen men working as casual labourers. Things had obviously changed drastically, and there needed to be a re-evaluation of the plans made in Heaven, without any consideration or knowledge of the plainly momentous evolution of 'the enemy' in the centuries since Earth Command fled.

He could use that description now. Somewhere in his mind, he realised that some of the 'treasonous' missives stored in the

Concilium's intelligence archives probably held greater truths than the mandated history of the origins of Heaven. Accepting that changed the definition of his legion's 'Tau' talents so completely that he went cold to his core.

Cielan took himself offline while he calmed his breathing and realigned his view of reality.

He had no wish to go down in history as a senior officer in the 'New Borsen', let alone the one who had recognised, and then formed, a legion of warp-attuned soldiers to better track down anyone sensitive to warp effects.

His thoughts took a new turn: the existence of the Tau conveniently placed all of the Concilium's warp-attuned personnel in one place; a useful bonus if a purge were mandated to remove the last taint of warp from humanity. He took a very deep breath and let it out slowly, while a cold certainty settled in his gut.

Would his fellow Marshals understand that this invasion was in very real danger of echoing the actions that had led to the retreat from Earth in the first place, and quite possibly becoming something far worse?

He doubted it. Which meant that he needed to bide his time. The opportunity he required would be a singular thing, to be taken whole, or missed at terrible cost.

Step into My Parlour
(Y871 PA)

They're back. Two hundred and thirty-six years after fleeing to save their privileges, the descendants of power-obsessed greedy incompetents have returned to claim the empire their ancestors abandoned.

I wonder what they have become? Because I certainly don't recognise a lot of the humanity and civilisation I see out there these days, and I pretty well started the damn thing. Thankfully, my descendants act as my interface, and Governors from recent generations can interpret when I get out of my depth.

"Scan-do warp space under quadrant Cherryh-Fifteen."

"Actioning. Resolution three minutes."

"Summon-all C7 and up, include G1."

"Actioning. Resolution two hours."

"Warp space inactive and unbridged."

So they Hirsched their way all the way home? That must have been tedious.

"Req-route Matriarch."

"Actioning. Done."

"You called?"

Her voice is so sultry. Like every wet dream rolled into one nightmare. Even from this far away, she makes my long-lost skin crawl.

"Shtubreth. They have returned."

"I am aware. Sisters lost on Colony Nine-thousand Four. Warp distress noted. Mistresses clamouring for rapine."

"Slowly, Shtubreth. Let this progress as the void decreed. Let my people open the net, before we show them the Confederacy."

"Very well, Uncle Ghost. We will pend."

If I live for another thousand years, I will never get used to them. The recent generations are increasingly personable, but the few surviving Mistresses from pre-Incursion remain far too strange.

A hundred minutes are all that is needed for the rulers of the Confederacy to conference in to me.

"Summon-all resolved, First Governor."

"Ladies, gentlemen and WarpMistresses. At oh-seven fifty-three hours today, Agriworld Lalludorn was attacked and captured by forces from beyond the Confederacy. I have confirmed the initial reports and warp distress. Earth Command have returned. They now call themselves the 'Concilium'."

The hissing and silence indicates the level of disbelieving shock. After this long, even I had considered their return to be an outside possibility.

"What action?" WarpMistress Pnteth is direct as ever.

"We do as we planned, revising for point of encounter and strengths."

"Are you sure, First Governor? Surely we should strike?"

"No, Commodore Pastrin. We should not. The Matriarch and I agreed steps for this occurrence. She would regard it a mortal insult for our joint action to be compromised."

That was unfair, but I will use their persistent fear of Shtubreth to save arguing the toss with people who weren't even conceived when these contingencies were laid out.

"Ladies, gentlemen and WarpMistresses. You know exactly what to do – or, if not, I expect you to within the hour. Consult your action schedules and implement everything, as stated, without delay or discussion. We will have only one chance to prevent a new Incursion. The Confederacy will not weaken its preparations for Galad with lesser threats."

I hear the WarpMistresses hiss happily. I started off using their beliefs as a lever, but after the discoveries of the last hundred and thirty years, I know that the origin of their religious fear was an ancient space-faring race that probably predates humanity. I reluctantly have to admit there is a slim possibility they are still extant. But that is something for another day, long after the Concilium are dealt with.

We could also do with a few dissidents in the coming invasion force. I just hope there are a few men or women with vision left in their command structure.

Sleight of Tentacle
(Y871 PA)

The operations room is quiet. It is what the rank and file call 'the dog watch': these long hours of the morning before the arbitrary dawn on a warship. Our Hirsch drives will be under maintenance for hours yet. The multiple transits required to get here from Heaven have revealed unexpected weaknesses.

"Consul Varides. We have an unscheduled tightbeam transmission with pre-Mandate Earth Command security codes."

I had expected something like this. The pleading always comes first.

"Route it to me. Trace the source."

"Implemented, Consul."

"This is Consul Evan Varides of the Concilium warship Liberator. Who am I speaking to?"

"First Governor Spence of the Confederacy."

"So the traitor founded a ruling line? How quickly he became what he despised."

"Something like that."

"So, are you contacting us to discuss terms?"

"Not in the way that you mean. Over two centuries have passed since your ancestors departed. The Confederacy is now an alliance of ten races. We respectfully offer The Concilium membership, as a fellow star-spanning race."

Unexpected. But the Mandate is clear.

"There will be no alliance. The Concilium will reclaim all Unified States of Earth territories from any who contest our primacy. Those who object will be subject to total war. We are not the technologically inferior remnants your predecessor forced to flee by his betrayal."

"Yet you travelled all the way here using Hirsch jumps."

"Warp space is a chaotic domain that cannot be relied upon. It also has a detrimental effect upon the discipline and sanity of all who attempt to use it."

"In other words, you just can't get to it, and it's driving your research teams crazy."

I feel my jaw clench at his jaunty tone: "We have experienced some difficulties with portal calibration." A reluctant admission, but one that confers no strategic advantage.

"Back to the matter at hand, Consul: how do you want to do this? Shall we wage decades of sporadic and guerrilla warfare across the vast span of what used to be USE space, with the commensurate devastation to civilian populations once again, or shall we decide it all in a pitched battle and subsequent ancillary actions in a deserted system of your choosing?"

Intriguing. I look at the sensor execs with a raised eyebrow. They indicate no fix. Obviously some warp trick. Which a system of my choosing, with suitable preparation, could obviate with ease.

"Much as I am deeply suspicious of your motives, your point regarding civilian populations is germane. How will I re-establish contact with you?"

"Tightbeam toward Earth from your current position. Your communication will be received before scatter renders it unintelligible."

"Very well. Concilium out."

The channel has just gone dead when our primary data system crashes, and a modicum of chaos ensues. After a short while, a Data Executive rushes to my side.

"Consul. Please grant your presence."

"Very well. Lead on."

Down in the shielded depths of the Liberator lie the system vaults where our critical processors reside, safe from all but the total destruction of this vessel. My personal guard part the crowd as they lead me through the multiple sets of blast doors, airlocks and corridors. Finally, I peer into a room labelled 'Primary Data Vault'. There are three dead Blues, all mutilated. The primary data core has already been removed for repair. While I conversed with Spence, his agents breached my ship from warp space to attempt at sabotage! I should have seen it coming!

"How long until the primary data core is repaired?"

"Consul. We have not removed it. It is gone."

"Gone? Define immediate."

"Alarm raised upon weapons discharge in Primary Data Vault. Access procedure requires two minutes eighteen seconds. On arrival, security teams found the scenario as you see now. Note that the presumed-blood near the door is blue-green."

Borsen! Their damnable alliance included the destroyers of humanity!

"Immediate. All ships will run with warp suppression systems active, or within the effective range of warp suppression vessels, at all times."

"Implementing."

"Marshals to gather for war conference on liberated world Lalludorn immediately. Fleet will split between there and here."

"Implementing."

"Prepare transit for me to Lalludorn."

"Cruiser *New Dawn* will be alongside within twenty minutes."

"The fleet is to move to imminent combat status."

"Implementing."

Damn them. They will have their 'pitched battle'. It will be their last.

As No-See-Eye slipped into warp, on the far side of a moon from Liberator and its escorts, Jackson Spence switched views to the loading bay, where three pallid Mistresses were fussing over a fourth, while human medical crews stood around and passed equipment and dressings as demanded.

Ten minutes later, the fourth Mistress was resting comfortably in the tentacles of Voidghost, a distant descendant of Swims-The-Singing-Dream, who had chosen not to transfer to containment nearly two centuries before.

"I trust you will be hale, Pthefra?"

The reclining and heavily bandaged Mistress waved her undamaged tentacle at the lens: "I will. The third guardian was resting on duty and away from his companions. He managed a commendable response before being slaughtered."

The other three Mistresses nodded agreement.

"Did you succeed in destroying their data core?"

"The Matriarch suggested another path, if we could manage the load."

Pthefra pointed to one side, where a large data repository, of foreign design, stood at a slight angle upon the floor.

"She stated that we are to tell you that it is a gift. She knows that your ghostly perceptions can gain far more than any would expect from that device."

"Please extend my thanks to the Matriarch. Also, take my commendation of the four of you for a truly precise application of rapine."

The Mistresses hissed in appreciation and promptly vanished. Voidghost sighed.

"I am not entirely happy with this new generation of natively warp-capable Mistresses. Trbtha is all too fond of breeding."

"Agreed on both points. But this time, they're on our side."

"True. On the topic of sides: if traditional strategies fail, let's hope Shtubreth's precision-harmonic-gate plan works."

"I prefer not to think of the consequences if it doesn't."

"Oh, I don't know. The 'Concilium Incursion' has a nice ring to it."

"I'm going to have you chucked out of an airlock."

"Wouldn't keep me out and you know it. Would you settle for thrashing me at dara, while the techs figure out how to hook that Concilium data store up?"

"Done."

Over the Top
(Y872 PA)

"Opposing forces are deploying, Consul."

"What are we facing?"

"Unit composition is undetermined, but the total is under four thousand."

Consul Varides smiled. They were outnumbered to start with.

"Dreadnoughts?"

"Five hundred and fifteen."

That was inconvenient. He had numerical superiority but they had more capital ships.

"Very well. Set the Tactical Executives on the problem. Flagship?"

"Undetermined."

So they had dispensed with that liability as well? This could prove to be interesting.

"Likelihood of them having broken the encryption on the stolen data store, given the disposition of their forces and warp usage?"

"Low. All capital ships used warp to arrive. Lesser vessels used Hirsch or piggybacked on Hirsch capable vessels."

"Warp intrusions?"

"None. Only the dreadnoughts highlighted in quadrant four have warp activity."

So they were intending tactical usage of warp in some way. Or thought they were going to, anyway.

"All vessels. This battle is the one we have waited two hundred years to win. The Mandate emphasises the dangers of permitting survivors to flee. Therefore, this will be a total war action."

The replies were all approving.

"They are here. We are here. Detonate the moons."

Jackson Spence regarded the incoming data. He expected the Concilium fleet to open with something spectacular and distracting. It was a key facet of their tactical action guidelines.

"All ships, be ready for something big, loud, and dangerous for the unprepared."

He switched channels: "Do we have their warp suppressors identified?"

"Yessir. The cruiser class with the destroyer screens and capital ship shadows are the suppressor ships. However, as they are toward the rear of the deployed forces, the suppression field peters out half way to us."

Static sleeted across the channels as all six moons orbiting the four worlds detonated.

"All ships, beware rocks."

Jackson chuckled. Governor Kathleen Spence had inherited her father's humour.

"Here they come."

"All ships. The Concilium will not be taking prisoners. Be aware that until this dies down, rescue will be unlikely. Fight wisely. Wakan Tanka needs no tails this day."

"Are we taking prisoners?"

"All ships. No action is to be taken against enemy vessels rendered non-combative."

He switched channels: "Take us to war, Katie."

"All ships. The Confederacy will engage. Free fire, kill at will."

The Borsen dreadnought Claflame encountered the problem first. Warp-fields stuttered and then died. The WarpMistress collapsed. WarMistress Nthfra thanked the Matriarch for her foresight in having all Borsen craft retrofitted with Hirsch drives.

"Claflame to Thunder-Star. Nthfra for either Spence."

A feminine voice replied: "Governor Kathleen. What is it, WarMistress?"

"Our warp-fields have been interdicted."

"Noted. Combat in Hirsch, we will be in touch."

WarMistress Nthfra smiled. Pointing in the direction of the Concilium ships, she screamed her battle order: "To the rapine, Mistresses!"

"First Governor, we are getting reports of warp suppression."

"Damn."

Jackson had expected something, but this was annoying. They had swept the environs for picket ships and booster satellites.

"Zero-Master, Knife-in-the-Night; they are suppressing warp on our leading edge and in the Borsen battle groups. We need to find out how and deal with it."

"All monitors, Zero-Master; warp interdictions are in play and they need to stop."

"Knife-in-the-Night, No-See-Eye; I suspect the debris of the moons. The scatter is not as random as it should be."

"All monitors, Zero-Master; check warp suppression origins on moon debris."

"Knife-in-the-Night. Zero-Master; confirm warp suppression using a resonant booster web hosted on the larger moon debris."

"Zero-Master, Knife-in-the-Night; is interdiction possible?"

"Knife-in-the-Night, Zero-Master; negative, over a thousand origin points and still correlating. The only way is to remove the originating warp suppression ships."

Jackson swore to himself. A very effective trick.

"Knife-in-the-Night, all ships; warp suppression cannot be interdicted. Time to apply the lesson the old way."

"Opposing forces are now negative for warp activity, accelerating fast using system drives or real-space Hirsch."

Varides grinned. Ambushing from warp, and dragging ships into warp, was impossible. Now to test their mettle.

"All vessels. Enemy warp capability has been nullified. Go and bring freedom to them!

Five thousand replies of "Implementing!" crackled from the comms. Varides permitted himself a broad smile.

Jackson remembered the days when space dreadnoughts fought like their 'wet' navy counterparts: stately manoeuvring, thundering 'broadsides', tactical considerations, environmental compensation, and simple evasion. He recalled when he saw his first Generation Four Hanfin in action; the enhanced drives made it seem unreachably fast.

Now he watched ships over a kilometre long swinging in a mutated dogfight, as each had weapons able to bear in most directions, unlike fighters. The calculations were performed by incredibly fast computers: where degrees of heading and attack vector factored against the firepower that could be brought to bear from the facing parts of each vessel. From long range, it was a frenetic ballet in three dimensions, punctuated by the occasional ball of energy as a ship exploded, the blue flash of a ship imploding, or a Hirsch rainbow as a ship dropped out of combat.

The speed of the capital ships may have improved, but the fighters were beyond his ability to grasp. Down at the individual combat level, the dogfight had become an art form where pilot ability augmented the computational aspect. The CRITTURS fighters were easy to identify as they pulled turns and other insane manoeuvres involving G-forces that would have killed a human pilot, even with the phenomenal damping systems available. He knew that they still pushed their tolerances to the limit to gain further advantage.

The grace of a Hanfin pack savaging a Concilium fighter squad caught his attention as it whirled into bright light momentarily; the whole melee being stalked by a squadron of Concilium fighters coming to reinforce their beleaguered companions. Then he was lost in awe as one of the few Katafin-class strikeships took out all of the reinforcements, using a brutal combination of ramming to disable and close-range precision shooting.

His distraction ended when the warship Racing-Sunlight disappeared in a blast of debris, swiftly followed by the detonation of its drives. He backtracked the video of the impact and saw the ship fold inwards as if hit by a huge centre punch. Railgun! He pre-empted some long-range viewers and followed the line of impact back. Toward the rear of the Concilium fleet, in amongst the heavily defended warp suppression ships, he saw half a dozen gunships, each looking like cruiser-size vessels built around the breech end of a massive railgun. They were dangerous weapons to fire into a mixed battle, but the phenomenal damage they inflicted could be deemed an acceptable trade-off.

He opened the private line: "Katie, they have half-a-dozen artillery ships in the pack of warp suppressors."

"Not good, dad. We're whittling them down, but those big capital ships on the right flank? They're actually the same inside as the next ones down. The difference in size is purely armour. Nothing has managed to get through to them."

"That's rude."

Another CRITTURS warship fell to a railgun hit that cut it in half. Moments later, a Borsen dreadnought exploded, after seemingly wrapping around itself.

Katie came back on: "We can't spread out yet because, for the next little while, they would have the advantage in mixed skirmishing. But the sphere of engagement means those railguns cannot fail to hit us, and they time their firing to pass between their bigger ships. They seem to have deemed their fighter squadrons to be entirely expendable."

"Knife-in-the-Night, No-See-Eye; confirm they are operating a battle-group of destroyer classes specifically targeting Confederacy vessels rendered non-combative."

Jackson Spence didn't want to play their game. He still believed that the Concilium contained people the Confederacy needed. But it was obvious that this battle was going to result in catastrophic losses of good people, for no good reason, if he persisted.

"Jackson Spence for WarpMistress Trbtha."

"Greetings, Uncle Ghost."

"Please inform your mother that she was right. Zero-Master will provide real-space co-ordinates for her."

Her reply rang with utter conviction: "Of course she was right. They ran. You stayed."

"The railguns are taking toll, Consul."

Varides nodded. It would not be long now. His scavenger group was picking off any enemy that dropped out of combat. Concilium forces were taking quite severe casualties, but continued to perform within acceptable parameters.

"Bring in the remaining ships, deployed above and to the right of our position."

"Implementing."

Praetor Dhevar saw the signal arrive. The entirety of Tau had been consigned to secondary-fleet position, along with the troop carriers, and a screen of warships with a single warp suppression vessel. It rankled, but he could do nothing. The Consul was always right, even when he was a bloodthirsty, arrogant elitist.

"All ships, prepare for Hirsch. Tau and troop carriers will deploy on right flank, Tau as screen. Other vessels to resume their usual fleet-attack positions within stated deployment zones."

There was no reason to deny capable men and women participation because he was having a bad day.

"Implemented."

"I'm showing a seven-hundred-vessel deployment, three hundred on the right flank, and four hundred more, above the command group.

Right flank are troop carriers and mixed in-system and cruiser-class combat vessels, with a capital ship and a dreadnought which are deploying fighters. The other deployments are fleet, including another forty capital ships. Some vessels from the four-hundred unit arrival are moving to take position with what we presume to be their designated battle groups."

Jackson swore with relief. The Concilium were fully committed with not a moment to spare: "All ships, partial disengagement as opportunity presents. Get your tails to our hemisphere of the system, if you can."

"They are manoeuvring, Consul. Tactical Executives expect them to reform with in their system zone."

Varides raised a hand in acknowledgement. His decision was awaited. The obvious one was to pursue, to chase them down one by one. Hardly the actions of an overwhelmingly superior force. Alternatively, he could let them gather themselves, think themselves prepared, and then crush them using the classic Arcadia Academy twin-axis pincer movement. That would be a far more suitable show of superiority.

"All vessels. Permit enemy disengagement and reinforce your formations."

Dhevar beat his fist on his console, as his execs bent to their tasks to avoid attracting his wrath: "No! Pursue! Pursue! Don't let them regroup, they're up to something!"

He had a sudden thought: "Sensor teams. Scan rear and flanking quadrants of main fleet to extent of sensor range."

"Implementing."

He waited. To be useful, whatever it was would need to be close.

"Single nascent warp intrusion emanating from rear quadrant at beyond a hundred thousand kilometres."

Dhevar heaved a sigh of relief – that stopped as his long-ago tutoring in warp detection put that result into perspective.

"Query scope of emergence to detect at that range."

"Somewhere beyond super-massive, Praetor."

"Open secure line to Consul Varides."

"Implemented."

"Dhevar. A little late for observations from the ranks?"

Cielan held his temper. He had worked his way up from trooper. The Consul had arrived via connections, and never missed a chance to emphasise his heritage: "Consul, there is an aberrant warp intrusion radiating from behind us. The projected size could indicate a combat-moon as discussed in the outer-edge strategy briefings."

"Dhevar, Dhevar. The combat-moon concept was discounted because of the sheer time it would take to construct one. And that was as a limited-mobility free-space fortification. A warp-capable one would take centuries."

"Well, would you look at that." Jackson Spence's voice was filled with wonder.

On all Confederacy vessel viewscreens, the entire Concilium fleet was suddenly silhouetted against the glaring blue-white warp-flare of a huge object breaching close behind them.

Consul Varides became aware of consternation amongst his bridge staff, as he closed the line to Dhevar. He felt the ship's station-keeping thrusters fire violently.

"Define immediate."

"All vessels report occlusion of rear sensor fields, visual monitoring is in whiteout, and severe gravitational influences are being felt. We have lost contact with all vessels in the warp suppression and railgun group."

"Dhevar for Varides."

"Maintain comms protocol at all times, Praetor. Now what is it?"

"'It' is behind you."

"Attention all ships of the Concilium. This is Avallea. Stand down, depart or face rapine. The co-ordinates of Heaven are appended, to show that we have the knowledge as well as the means to annihilate your civilisation.

Should your departure be a strategy to regroup, the next attack within Confederacy territories will be responded to by warpkilling one planet of Heaven. Thus, we permit you seventeen warnings before the total rapine of your territory. Which is seventeen more than you gave Lalludorn."

Jackson sighed. At least Shtubreth had kept to the script, except for the final two sentences, which were actually a nice touch.

Garish threats had been the *braggadocio* of pre-battle confrontations and blustering politics before the Borsen arrived. Now he knew, without question, that every Mistress in Confederacy space was praying the Concilium did something stupid, so they could gleefully traverse half a galaxy to commit atrocity.

He would let them. Having watched and witnessed for hundreds of years, he understood that a threat was useless if it was not acted upon when its conditions were met, and it had to be acted upon fully - without diminishment or leniency - at least in the first instance.

Dhevar heard the message and saw the Avallea, as much as he could comprehend. To move this planetary warship via warp was beyond credence. For it to be able to emerge from warp with a precision that placed the leading edge only a thousand kilometres from the rearmost Concilium vessel was terrifying.

"Praetor Dhevar to all Tau vessels and troop carriers. Recall fighters and Hirsch for waypoint twelve, immediate."

"Dhevar! What are you doing?"

"Going home, Consul. This war is over."

"I'll have you executed! The damn thing is too big to manoeuvre! We can outrun it! There will be no surrender!"

"Who said anything about surrender? They have asked us to leave, which is surprisingly decent of them given what we did on Lalludorn. So I'm taking my legion, and the troop carriers, and everyone on them, back to their families. We have Heaven's territory to expand, because we're not going to be conquering anywhere that has warp-capable warships the size of gas giants!"

"It's some kind of bluff, Dhevar. A desperate ploy by those who have recognised us as the superior force."

Dhevar sighed. Had Varides not seen the size of the railguns that snuffed the warp suppressor vessels and gunships like a man would crumple paper?

In a searing coda to that thought, an energy-beam of colossal magnitude annihilated the entire destroyer battle group that had been picking off damaged Confederate vessels.

"Praetor Dhevar to all vessels. Will somebody please execute former Consul Varides before he gets us all killed? Thank you."

There was silence over the command channel for five minutes. Then a woman's nervous voice came on.

"Consul Dhevar?"

"I remain Praetor. Identify immediate."

"Legate Serena Connors, Praetor."

"Legate? Where are your Marshals, Serena?"

"Dead. Borsen appeared on command vessels across the fleet and assassinated all Marshalls, the Consul and any who opposed them. This is why I am surprised at your continuance."

Dhevar heard two of his executives scream behind him. Without turning, he ended the transmission and issued a command to save lives: "Stand down."

"I am WarpMistress Trbtha of the Confederacy. You are Dhevar, are you not?"

The tone was light and the voice lilting. He turned slowly. Standing on the command tier of his bridge, within her striking distance, was a woman with the most attractive face he had ever seen, framed by green hair that moved of its own accord and crackled quietly. Her arms were tentacles and they caressed the edges of his command consoles, while her breasts quivered with what he presumed was repressed laughter.

"I am he."

"First Governor Spence thanks you for your resolute action in standing down. He said to tell you that some of my daughters are rescuing the captives you took. He also thanks you for taking them, instead of obeying your orders. Personally, the other Mistresses and I would relish a chance to bring rapine to your worlds, so do not give us justification."

She pouted prettily: "Couldn't we have just one?"

Alpha Commander Dancing-Blade watched as the Concilium ships dropped into Hirsch, the thousands of rainbows making it look like night-time rain falling on an oil-slicked pond. He turned to the screen.

"First Governor, permission to stand down, and rescue what and who we can."

"Granted, and salvage examples of as much Concilium technology as possible. Everything else goes into the star, to provide a guard of honour for the ships and people that have fallen. They will go to Wakan Tanka with full honours, before we depart."

Even as he mourned the grievous losses, Jackson was routing orders that would place surveillance, using Starclad vessels, upon the system known as Heaven. The first ship of that potentially eternal watch would arrive in time to witness the Concilium fleet returning home.

High Time
(Y874 PA)

Five thousand seven hundred ships went out. Two thousand four hundred and ten returned. Consul Voight read the action reports as Marshal Dhevar made his way to Asgard. He had just finished when Dhevar entered his office unannounced.

"You are forward, Marshal."

"I am tired, Consul. I want to finish here, see to the Tau, and then go home to my family."

Voight steepled his fingers: "It's a good thing that the Borsen killed Varides. If anyone had obeyed your command, they would have been executed alongside you."

"I understand that, sir."

"Good. Now, your return, and the decisions leading to it, have actually received broad approval. I would expect promotion to Consul to be ratified by the Eighteen Kings soon."

"They contacted me on the way down, sir. I am to report to Camelot next week."

"Good, good. While you're there, I would appreciate it if you'd put in a few good words regarding the budget for rebuilding the fleet."

Dhevar's eyebrows rose: "We have sufficient for an excellent standing defence, while maintaining multiple expeditionary forces."

Voight smiled: "Indeed. But what if the Confederacy decides to come after us anyway? We had better be ready. I think a fifty-percent war-footing with a suitably increased budget, would be the best option."

Dhevar smiled: "It would be a boon to the military industries sir, but it would be wasted should the Confederacy come for us. You didn't see the Avallea. If they come, we turn our swords to ploughshares and don't study war no more."

Voight laughed: "Oh, Dhevar. Your soldier's mindset is so simple. The budget increase will let us start a suitable response."

He brought up the artistic impressions of what the whole of the Avallea looked like, and rubbed his hands together, before touching the screens almost reverently. He was oblivious to Dhevar's look of horror.

"We need an Avallea. I *want* one." The Consul's tone was reverent.

Dhevar drew his pistol and shot Voight in the back of the head. Servanic megalomania was now a very rare malady, but remained utterly incurable, even if detected in its early stages.

He looked down at the body: "I may be a simple soldier, but I think that it is high time for Heaven to have a proper civilisation, not just a war machine with civilian ancillaries."

With a smile, Cielan Dhevar holstered his weapon.

With that single unwitnessed sentence, uttered nearly four centuries after Athshper first introduced herself to humanity, hostilities finally ceased.

Prelude

Many centuries before the Apocalypse.
Far beyond the Milky Way.

Against All Odds
(Y4091 BA)

"It has been eight days since Ensign Rammett dropped us into warp without course or hope: a last, desperate gamble against certain death. The warp transit was rough, and we have discovered that warp space is a lot worse when you are becalmed in it.

The Excalibur sustained significant damage on entry, and the biomatrix that underpinned our core systems is dead. Without that, calculation of an egress point that would return us to known space is impossible. The inorganic part of the system has restored itself to limited functionality, but, as the master control computer for an experimental warp dreadnought, it is useless.

Leftenant Slingsby has had an idea. We are retro-fitting all of the escape vessels with crude warp-egress generators cannibalised from whatever is needed. In a short while, I will give the order, and we will all take another gamble with death.

The escape vessels are not designed to handle warp. Everyone will be suited-up and each crew will activate the egress protocols as soon as we have cleared the hull. If we make it anywhere, I will be astonished. But we should have been killed by the Borsen worldship, so any extra time is a bonus won from hostile fates."

Captain Janet Rossiter looked up from her log as she locked it down and cloned it to her personal data system. One copy would remain, the other would go with her. Around the bridge, panels hung loose, and wires trailed in knotted disarray. The damage from entering warp had been exacerbated by the ruthless drive to fit all fifty escape vessels with warp-egress portal-generators. There was still no guarantee that they would work.

She powered up her suit, and left the bridge echoing and filled with almost imperceptible swirls of grey.

They were ready. Command personnel were spread across all the vessels, so no matter what, there would be a command team available.

"Captain Rossiter to all pods. Launch on my mark. Three, two, one: mark!"

Ensign Emelia Rammett counted them away.

"Two clear, six clear, eleven clear, seventeen clear. All clear, Captain."

"Very good, Ensign. Mister Slingsby, at your leisure."

She was compressed lightly as the depleted rail system slid, rather then hurled, them clear of the hull.

"Here goes nothing. Ensign, since you dropped us in, do get us the hell out."

Emelia Rammett coloured slightly and then pulled down the lever attached to the wire-enshrouded mass of the makeshift portal-generator. The wrenching, spinning sensation was impossibly painful, and seemed to last just long enough to think it would never end. Suddenly, the singing stopped, and the 'beep-tak-beep' of normal space navigation became audible.

After the screaming relief faded, she set them to finding out where they were. 'A long way from home' went without saying, but it would be nice to have some bearings.

Navigator Adan Jeffries looked up from the scopes with a look of confusion: "There are no reference points, Captain. Nothing at all. I would surmise that we are beyond the Milky Way, at an acute angle, as that could be what I see at a distance; or we are in another universe. Good news: we have an inhabitable planet nearby. Match to Earth is better than seventy percent, with slightly higher oxygen and less gravity."

That was a welcome surprise.

"Ensign, how many pods in our fleet?"

"All of them, Captain. Nine seem to have sustained similar twisting damage to the ship. Apart from that, everyone seems to be good to go."

"Switch the living from the damaged pods, and balance with non-essentials. Then put the lot of us down on the best-choice landmass as selected by Xeno Officer Khones."

"Sir."

The landing went disgustingly smoothly for the amount of worry beforehand. I emerged from the pod, into what could have been a beautiful late afternoon on the African savannah. Apart from the fact I weighed three-quarters of my usual weight, and felt superb, due to that and the ten percent oxygen increase.

I turned to the crew, who stood about in groups, marvelling at our continued survival: "Heads up! Sundown in three hours. I want to be watching it with a coffee in hand, from the balcony of a fully grounded and deployed Pod One, hereby designated 'Tintagel'. Move!"

They set to and I looked into the distance. Where the hell were we?

Deal With the Devil
(Y4084 BA)

My daughter has tentacles where her arms should be. Just like every other girl born in the two years since we accepted the help of the strange beings that inhabited the Shrine of Galad. I would never have agreed to this, had I known what their help would cost. All the boys are robust and well, although Doctor Femsar has assessed them as being of below-average intellectual capability.

Every day I hold counselling sessions for the mothers of daughters. It is no consolation to know that they are of way-above-average intelligence, health and strength, and are all looking to be at least two metres tall, if our growth metrics are on target. They look like baby Borsen, and that is giving many of us nightmares.

The Bledarne Plague caught us in the fifth year here on Avallea, as we have named our planet. The emergency clone banks had saved us, after we spent a worrying few months trying to get the prototype gestation unit up and running, but it is now churning out fauna and flora with sufficient genetic diversity to establish us. We really thought we had achieved the impossible - then Mary and Stuart Dellene were found dead on their farm, one of the furthest from Tintagel.

The following days were desperate, marked only by acts of courage
and sacrifice. It was Professor Adrianna Bledarne who deliberately
infected herself, and then documented the whole dissolution and
transformation process, all the while dosing herself with damn near our
entire range of pharmaceuticals to test their effects. That is why we
named the plague after her.

Amidst the rising death toll, one of my scout runs returned with
incredible news. A huge citadel, made from a blue, gem-like substance,
stood on an island in the middle of a lake five hundred kilometres west
of us. With nothing that I could do for the sick and dying, I put together
a team and headed out in the only gravsled capable of navigating large
bodies of water. Anything that gave hope, and presented a slim chance,
was worth pursuing.

The place was imposing, and very old. The weathering to the azure
crystal of its construction spoke volumes, when we discovered that our
blades, bludgeons and energy beams could not mark it. The single
entrance faced north and was six metres wide by three metres high.
After discussion, we decided to enter and be damned. It is fair to say
that our survival, against all odds, had given us a certain positive
attitude toward our luck, despite the plague.

The entrance led to a corridor that spiralled down into the bedrock of
the planet; and deeper, until we felt the heat of the magma fires below
warming the environment. It was here that we entered a single
hemispherical hall. The five-hundred-metre diameter floor was covered
in azure slabs, and upon those slabs stood strange metallic blue trestles,
and in those alien chairs were the desiccated bodies of an unknown race
that probably died while we were still killing each other with rocks
back on Earth. We walked past the groups and pairs and rows of these

narrow bodies, their limbs articulated like snakes, and their heads too narrow for the four eye sockets that spanned them. Their mouths were wide, and the teeth were all pointed. Whatever else these beings had been, descendants of predators was definite.

Our long walk paused as we approached an enormous raised dais, upon which lay a ten-metre cadaver very different from those about us. Jonas defined it accurately and humorously as a 'sextopus with a skeleton'. The four eye sockets were huge, and the limbs long, still possessed of a radiant strength, even in death. As we rounded the end of the dais, we were shocked into immobility by the sight of six of the smaller aliens turning toward us on their trestle rests, turning away from what appeared to be lectern-like consoles where pastel lights flashed and moved. The one nearest to us extended an arm, comprising at least six elbows, back to its console, and a voice boomed from below the instrumentation.

"Welcome, inheritors of Galad. We have waited long for your arrival and still feared we would be lost before you came across the waters."

I stepped forward.

"Thank you. I am Captain Janet Rossiter of Earth Command. Who do I have the honour of addressing?"

"I am Talk Maker Blue, the last of my line. We are each the last of our lines and will not see another cycle of seasons. We must go to join Galad and our programme pools."

I bowed a little.

"How is it that you can converse in my language?"

"I am Talk Maker Blue. My programme is language. I have listened to you and divined your syntax, just as my companion Body Maker Red has sampled your leavings and divined your vulnerability to Shlerlm."

"Shlerlm? The disease that we call Bledarne Plague?"

"Yes. Your Body Maker provided us with many reference points we lacked during her final sacrifice."

We exchanged glances. Body Maker equalled Doctor or Professor. Now that could be useful.

"Can you help us defend against Shlerlm?"

"Body Making for you will not be easy. We divine the process to be strenuous for your form. There would be pain. But we expect better than seventy in one hundred and ten to survive."

I paused and looked at my team. So far the plague had been one hundred percent fatal. There were nods and querying looks. I turned back and bowed again.

"We would be honoured to accept your assistance. What can we do in return?"

"When we six pass, we ask that you destroy all cadavers upon the rests in this place, leaving only the body of Galad upon his throne." It gestured toward the enormous cadaver.

"Very well. That is a task we will accomplish. How can the immunity to Shlerlm be given?"

"We will need one of you to step forward so that we may refine the programme. Be warned that it will be a sacrificial act."

Without hesitation, Leftenant Mollen stepped forward. I nodded; she had lost her family to the plague.

"Nobly done. What will ensue will be difficult to endure and unpleasant to observe. We would recommend that you take your distance."

I waved the team away, indicating that I would stay. A Captain's responsibilities are sometimes unpleasant.

Ten hours later, I wished that I'd gone away. In truth, I wished that we'd never found the shrine. What Mollen had gone through to provide the bag of green crystals I clutched in my shaking hand, as I tottered back to the team, would haunt me forever. The fact that two of the six beings had also died was not a relief. I could not even bring Mollen back for burial, because people would see and smell something beyond horror. As I approached the team, I held up the bag. I could see questions on their faces over what I bore, and about the horrific noises they had heard. I quelled them all with a simple statement: "These are Mollen crystals."

We survived the plague, and, six months later, I returned alone to the shrine to find all of the strange beings dead. There was no trace of the strange lectern-consoles to be found. So I set my specially programmed utility-droid to raze every trestle clean of alien corpses while I burned the twisted, attenuated remains of Leftenant Mollen to ashes. After a day, the little droid returned. I erased its memory before loading it onto the gravsled. Whatever these beings had been, and despite their assistance, I could not help but feel that we had been taken advantage of in ways we would eventually regret. It is the only time in my life that I have felt unclean.

Legacy
(Y3088 BA)

Today we laid my mother to rest: the last of the survivors and our
Captain for so long. She had been keen of mind, despite her physical
deterioration, and had been assigning duties and doing all the things she
had taught me so well, right until the evening of her death.

After the funeral, there was another ceremony. This one to mark my
ascension to the Captaincy. It felt wrong to be so overjoyed at
something that my mother had to die for me to receive.

I sit and regard the datapack she left me: the hidden one she had
showed me a decade before, as she gave me a single instruction: "This
is for the Captain on the day that the last survivor is buried. Until then,
it does not exist." With a sigh, I break the seal and, after a momentary
struggle with a closure designed for fingers, action the playback.
Mother's head appears in hologram form. It is obvious that she had
been crying before she started the recording.

"This is Janet Rossiter, First Captain of Avallea. I am recording this at
the start of the twentieth year for the Avallea Colony. I do not expect it
to be watched for some time, so please forgive any anachronistic
references.

Ten years ago, my science officers started to piece together
information about this planet we are on, and our position in the cosmos.

After four years, they moved on to other things, considering the information-gathering as complete as possible. Sergeant Emelia Rammett was the only one to continue until she could extrapolate some remarkable conclusions, that she duly brought to my sole attention. She and I have sat up late many nights over the past few months, and have finally concluded that this datapack is the only record that we will leave. As to why we leave it at all, I hope you will understand that this is something we cannot just conceal, but simultaneously dare not reveal, until all of the original founders of the colony are dead. As to what you do with it, I leave that to your discretion.

When we arrived here, we swiftly determined that we were nowhere within known, proposed or even distantly mapped space. For all intents and purposes, we were cut off from humanity and its desperate struggle against the Borsen. Navigator Jeffries postulated that we were on the far side of the Milky Way and at an acute angle to it. He refined his observations in the years before he died, yet still could not fathom out exactly where we were. It is his observations that gave Sergeant Rammett the hints necessary for her to continue, which led her to an explanation that I believe to be the truth.

My recording of this datapack is also a memorial for Sergeant Emelia Rammett, who, in her actions to save us from the retaliation of the Borsen worldship, and in her inspired understanding of our situation, has been far more pivotal to the fate of the human race than any one person has any right to be. Those are her words, not mine."

Mother dips her head, wipes her eyes, and takes a swig of something, before looking steadily into the recorder again.

"Emelia Rammett has worked out exactly where we are. Avallea is the fourth planet of the Borsen system. More importantly, she worked out

when. As I speak, on Earth it is around two thousand years Before
Common Era in old calendar notation. That is just over four thousand
years Before Apocalypse. Our warp-journeying took us approximately
four and a half astronomical units closer to the sun in this system, and
over four and a half thousand years back in time."

I feel the shock rush through me, my gut cold and my brow hot. I
know what is coming, and I know that I will destroy this datapack
before the night is through. Mother smiles one of her knowing smiles,
pausing deliberately to allow the viewer's shock to pass.

"We set out to survive on Avallea, against all odds. We made a
bargain with strange beings that mutated our children, but we survived.
Those outside this room hope to start a civilisation that will survive to
eventually reunite with humanity."

She looks down at her hands before looking up again, her gaze steely,
the Captain Rossiter that led her crew and this colony to accomplish the
impossible.

"Our distant descendants will be the Borsen. Neither Emelia nor I
know, or can predict, what will cause them to empty this star system to
make the worldship, or what will prompt them to launch all-out war
against the USE. But we are sure that we absolutely cannot attempt to
change events. We shall abide by the history we know, taking comfort
from the knowledge that Avallea Colony will thrive. Earth may actually
be improved by the onset of our descendants, because both Emelia and
I agree that Earth Command, and the Unified States of Earth, is no
longer a beneficial regime. Maybe our legacy is to be the agents of
change for a humanity that is beyond hope of changing itself."

Mother reaches to one side and retrieves her Captain's cap. She sits
up, straightens her jacket, and places it upon her head.

"My daughter back on Earth used to call me Captain Mum. There is something in me that makes me think she would smile at this. I know John would."

She raises her hand in a formal salute.

"This is Alpha Commander Janet Rossiter, formerly Captain of Earth Command Warp Dreadnought Alpha, designated Excalibur. I am First Captain of Avallea Colony One, named Tintagel. I end this memoir with the honesty that is demanded from all officers of my rank."

She smiles.

That is the mother I remember: smiling and resolute. As tears start to run down my cheeks, I swear that I will forever strive to live up to her standards, and will raise my children to respect her legacy.

Her smile vanishes and she lowers her hand.

"I am Janet Louise Rossiter, Mother of the Borsen. May the gods have mercy on us all."

Appendices

Appendix One: Lexicon

NB: Named CRITTURS are listed at the end of Appendix Three

Afya	Type of CRITTURS
	– see Appendix Three for details
Apafin	Type of CRITTURS
	– see Appendix Three for details
Athshper	Borsen WarpMistress
Cegila	Type of CRITTURS
	– see Appendix Three for details
Charon	Earth Command's primary multi-environment interceptor.
Chetan	Type of CRITTURS
	– see Appendix Three for details
Crthani	Borsen WarMistress
	– duelled with Trooper Almiraz
CSV	Confederacy Strike Vessel
Dog-T	Type of CRITTURS
	– see Appendix Three for details
ECB	Earth Command Base
ECD	Earth Command Dreadnought
ECEI	Earth Command Enhanced Interceptor
ECI	Earth Command Interceptor
ECS	Earth Command Ship

ECSV	Earth Command Specialised Vessel
ECOC	Earth Command Operations Control
ECTV	Earth Command Troop Vessel
ECWD	Earth Command Warp Dreadnought
Eshebth	Borsen WarMistress
Ferine	Type of CRITTURS
	– see Appendix Three for details
Fshnepri	Borsen Mistress
Gora	Type of CRITTURS
	– see Appendix Three for details
Graw	Type of CRITTURS
	– see Appendix Three for details
Halhata	Type of CRITTURS
	– see Appendix Three for details
Hanfin	Type of CRITTURS
	– see Appendix Three for details
Hellion	Earth Command's only dedicated free-space fighter.
Hirsch	The faster-than-light drive system designed by Emil Hirsch, based upon research by his wife, Emelia.
Hlfri	Borsen Mistress
	- brood sister of Fshnepri; ceded Chalfont
Hyfin	Type of CRITTURS
	– see Appendix Three for details
Katafin	Type of CRITTURS
	– see Appendix Three for details
Kilo	Type of CRITTURS
	– see Appendix Three for details

Mako	Type of CRITTURS
	– *see Appendix Three for details*
Mateyu	Type of CRITTURS
	– *see Appendix Three for details*
Mayas	Type of CRITTURS
	– *see Appendix Three for details*
Nthfra	Borsen WarMistress
Panthac	Type of CRITTURS
	– *see Appendix Three for details*
Pnteth	Borsen WarpMistress
Pthefra	Borsen WarMistress
Sapafin	Type of CRITTURS
	– *see Appendix Three for details*
Shnthae	Borsen Mistress
	– *killed on Romala by Commodore Baneff*
Shtubreth	Matriarch of the Borsen
Slater	Type of CRITTURS
	– *see Appendix Three for details*
Sthtera	Borsen WarMistress
Taku	Type of CRITTURS
	– *see Appendix Three for details*
Takuman	Type of CRITTURS
	– *see Appendix Three for details*
Thofin	Type of CRITTURS
	– *see Appendix Three for details*
Tosak	Type of CRITTURS
	– *see Appendix Three for details*

Trbtha   Borsen WarpMistress Elect

                    – daughter of Shtubreth

USE   Unified States of Earth

Appendix Two: Timeline

The first year of the Borsen Incursion is USE Calendar Year 501 PA (post apocalypse) or 2623 OC (old calendar); the five hundred and first year after the global apocalypse in 2122.

Dates prior to the apocalypse are referred to as BA, the number of years prior to that event. (Thus 2010 would be Y112 BA.)

In the interests of brevity, only the Earth Command projects that feature within this book have been included.

Year 501	Chant of the Betrayed (*Ethan's remembering*)
Year 502	Terms
Year 508	*Project Noble commences*
Year 512	Chant of the Betrayed
Year 517	*Project Lancelot commences*
Year 519	*Project Samurai commences*
Year 521	The Power That Seeks
Year 525	*Project Wallaby commences*
Year 526	*Project Noble is abandoned*
	Project Pavlov commences
Year 529	Arms Race
	Projects Samurai and Wallaby are abandoned
	Project White Knight commences
Year 535	Police Action

Year 540	Harsh Lessons
	Project Joust commences and is written off
	Project White Knight is written off
Year 542	Dreadnought
Year 547	*Project Lancelot is written off*
Year 549	*Project Wells (the chrono-trooper initiative)* *commences*
Year 551	Sacrifices
Year 555	Ghosts (*Commander Spence discovers* *Smokewalker)*
Year 556	To Kill and Kill Again
Year 557	*Project Pavlov is abandoned*
	Project Spirit commences
Year 559	*The rescue of the Twenty-Fifth*
Year 560	*Project Wells is abandoned*
Year 562	Ghosts (*Commander Spence's journal and decision*)
Year 563	Childcare
Year 564	My Name is Vengeance
	A Farewell to Fools
Year 565	*Jackson Spence is tried and convicted (in absentia)* *of high treason*
Year 566	*Project Thule commences*
Year 567	Privateers
Year 570	Out of Time (*Axel One's reappearance*)
Year 572	Truth in Blood
Year 573	And Far Away
Year 575	Observers
Year 577	Leng's Crusade

Year 651	Epitaph
	Excalibur's last transmission reaches Earth
Year 652	The End of Ways
Year 654	*Project Unity commences*
Year 657	Fall From Grace
	Project Lucifer resolves
	Project Unity ceases to exist
	Project Saviour is written off
Year 668	We Ran
Year 752	Eternal Witness
Year 861	*Project Crusade commences*
Year 862	Sympathiser
Year 871	The Tau
	Step Into My Parlour
	Sleight of Tentacle
Year 872	Over the Top
	Project Crusade is written off
Year 874	High Time

Appendix Three:
CRITTURS

C.R.I.T.T.U.R.S. is a patently forced acronym, officially recorded as meaning 'Combat Relevant Instinct Transferral To Upgrade Robotic Sentience'. It first appeared in the Project Pavlov Master Strategy Document (MSD), tendered in response to Earth Command's request to find a successor to Project Noble.

The primary aim of Project Noble had been to create biologically engineered combatants from Earth's nonhuman predators, citing such things as reproductive rates and lack of moral restraints in its MSD. As it had only achieved marginal successes in fifteen years (from its sponsors point of view) alternatives were sought.

Project Pavlov presented arguments for the use of only the 'useful bits' of Earth fauna in cyborg bodies. Despite the cost effectiveness of the methods and processes clearly being misrepresented, the Project was selected unanimously at the end of the three-year tendering process.

The exact influences applied to achieve the selection are unknown, as are the numbers of creatures vivisected and/or effectively sentenced to agonising deaths to derive the techniques that allowed CRITTURS to be produced in adequate numbers for combat deployment.

It should be noted that the presence of human components in CRITTURS organic makeup means it is almost certain that many humans met similarly gruesome ends. Unfortunately, those responsible were all-too aware of the crimes they were committing, and took highly effective steps to erase themselves and their victims from history.

Project Noble's groundbreaking techniques for drastically increasing fauna intelligence are legendary. Regrettably that is all they are, as all data was lost during a system purge when Project Noble was closed down. Subsequent to that, the relevant information archives that had been transferred to Project Pavlov were found to be irretrievably corrupted.

The KILO series of deep space hunter-killers are the only viable result that survived the demise of Project Noble, although Project Noble's work with various breeds of octopuses would become pivotal to research by Ghost Command that led to the genesis of the Warptopii.

From the outset, CRITTURS form followed two distinct paths: Aniframe and Deviframe. The former were shaped like robotic equivalents or slight variants of their primary source fauna. The latter were shaped as the role they were to fulfil dictated, based on traditional military designs. In both cases, CRITTURS are asexual and gender is purely a facet of each CRITTURS psyche.

Any 'remnants' from Project Noble were designated as the Generation Zero of Project Pavlov. Generations One and Two were created by Project Pavlov teams. Generation Three was created by Project Spirit teams. Generations Four and Five are creations of Ghost Command, while Generation Six are creations of The Confederacy and, in addition, created solely by CRITTURS teams on the CRITTURS homeworlds.

The primary source of each type provides the dominant psyche. However, no CRITTURS are derived from a pure strain. Standard 'packs' of neurological grafts are used to add features that may be lacking in the primary source. Simple examples would be chimpanzee for bipedal movement, leopard or chimpanzee for climbing (dependant on chassis), and so on.

The inclusion of human neurological grafts for data interface and language comprehension is tentatively identified as the origin of the part-organic, part technological sentiences that arose.

While the acronym that gave these entities their name was considered nothing but a facet of a slick presentation, the use of the acronym as a name swiftly overwhelmed any attempt by Earth Command to introduce a 'proper' name. Thus CRITTURS has become the singular and plural form; the only acknowledgement of origin being the capitalisation.

CRITTURS are listed by their generation of first creation. However, a KILO or similar pre-Generation Four design created by Ghost Command would be considered to be a Generation Four CRITTURS due to the improved techniques and technology involved.

CRITTURS named within this book are identified at the end of this appendix.

Generation Zero (Gen-0)

KILO - A long-range, Hirsch-capable hunter-killer and interceptor designed around a bio-engineered giant squid, with its primary modification being a cartilaginous partial skeleton derived from the whale shark.

Generation One (G1)

GRAW - A deviframe free space nuclear missile using the great white's hunting instincts for guidance. After Project Spirit replaced Project Pavlov, production was halted. The few GRAW sentiences that remained sane were given the opportunity to become MAKO (see below).

HANFIN - An aniframe medium range space-escort fighter using the Sand Tiger shark as primary source.

MAKO - A Hanfin chassis with a transferred Graw sentience. Most now lead Hanfin packs attached to Thofin (see under Generation Four, below).

TOSAK - A heavy-weapons aniframe combat platform using a large quadrupedal chassis styled on Tibetan Mastiff. Primary source is Karabas. Beta chassis are 40% large than the production Delta chassis.

Generation Two (G2)

PANTHAC - A multi-role combat aniframe styled on the leopard and using leopard or panther as primary source.

FERINE - A deviframe main battle tank using a four-track, multi-turret configuration. Primary source is polar bear (despite the legends of it being wolverine).

GORA - A heavy-combat aniframe styled on the classic 'silverback' gorilla and using gorilla as primary source.

HYFIN - The first class of CRITTURS warship, a deviframe, Hirsch (and later warp) capable battleship with increased load-carrying capacity. Primary source is sperm whale.

Generation Three (G3)

HALHATA - An aniframe fast scout ship styled on the classic corvid and using magpie as primary source.

AFYA - An aniframe surgeon (or specialist for any technology requiring microprecision) using an eight-limbed chassis. Unique in having no primary source, being a hybrid of various small and medium octopi.

APAFIN - A Hirsch (and later warp) capable deviframe space dreadnought using humpback whale as its primary source.

DOG-T - A multi-role aniframe warrior using bipedal medium or light combat chassis, styled on the classic wolfman. Primary source is Belgian shepherd dog.

Generation Four (G4)

THOFIN - A Hirsch (and later warp) capable aniframe-deviframe hybrid space dreadnought using blue whale as its primary source.

SAPAFIN - A Hirsch (and later warp) capable deviframe space raider using a heavy cruiser template. Primary source is orca.

TAKU - A prototype aniframe scoutship redesigned to take advantage of unusual near-space warp capabilities manifested by its splice. All Taku carry Slater colonies.

SLATER - An aniframe multi-role drone using giant isopod as its primary source.

Generation Five (G5)

TAKUMAN - An evolved version of the Taku with full warp, Hirsch and near-space warp capabilities. A multi-purpose stealth warship with Slater colonies.

CEGILA - The largest deviframe ever built and the first true warp dreadnought, using Giant Pacific Octopus as its primary source.

KATAFIN - A few Mako sentiences expressed an interest in solitary long-range work like the roaming variants of the Kilos. This filled a vacant niche for a strike vessel with the manoeuvrability for atmospheric work combined with the ability to hold it's own against heavier classes of warship for short periods. Using the Sapafin frame as a basis, this vessel eschews all cargo and passenger capability in favour of increased firepower, better shielding and more powerful drives.

Generation Six (G6)

MAYAS - An aniframe multi-role scout, styled on the coyote. Primary source is coyote.

MATEYU - A medium assault aniframe, styled on the hyena. Primary sources are hyena and terrier.

CHETAN - An aniframe, in-atmosphere, multi-role fighter. Primary source is harpy eagle.

Named CRITTURS by Gender, Generation and Type

Able-Doom	F	G3 Gora
Apple-Tea	M	G1 Beta Tosak
Bold-By-Nature	M	G1 Delta Tosak
Bites-Down-Hard	M	G4 Mako
Bleed-No-More	M	G1 Delta Tosak
Blood-Moon	M	G4 Thofin
Chase-The-Stone	M	G2 Dog-T
Crashes-Through-Suns	F	G3 Apafin
Creeps-Them-Out	M	G4 Taku
Death-From-The-Shadows	F	G2 Panthac
Death-With-Grace	F	G3 Panthac
Deathdealer	M	G2 Hanfin
Digs-Like-Mole	M	G1 Delta Tosak
Drinks-No-Water	M	G1 Dog-T
Drummer-Dog	F	G2 Dog-T
Faster-Than-Dawn	M	G1 Delta Tosak
Fox-By-Night	F	G3 Dog-T
Fury-Bushido	M	G1 Beta Tosak
Gone-Fishing	M	G2 Gora
Grey-Weaver	M	G5 Cegila
Hidden-In-Dream	M	G3 Panthac
Idiot-Breaker	F	G2 Gora
Kilo-Ten-Ten (Krakensdötter)	M	G0 Kilo
Kitty-In-Disguise	F	G2 Dog-T
Leap-No-Cliffs	M	G1 Dog-T
Mist-In-The-Sun	F	G4 Takuman
Never-Caught	M	G3 Halhata

No-Bananas-Today	M	G2 Gora
No-See-Eye	M	G4 Takuman
Punch-Drunk	M	G2 Gora
Race-The-Starlight	M	G5 Thofin
Rides-The-Sundown	M	G3 Hyfin
Runs-Over-Water	F	G1 Dog-T
Runs-The-Rivers	M	G1 Dog-T
Scratch-Back	M	G1 Dog-T
Screams-When-Thrown	M	G3 Dog-T
Screaming-Vengeance	F	G2 Panthac
Serves-No-Meat	M	G2 Dog-T
Shame-The-Storm	M	G3 Apafin
Sings-The-Night	M	G3 Hyfin
Skies-Of-Dawn	M	G4 Thofin
Slam-Dunk	F	G3 Gora
Slaughter-Child	M	G3 Panthac
Slice-And-Dice	M	G2 Panthac
Smokewalker	M	G2 Ferine
Spanners-Before-Guns	M	G1 Dog-T
Spark-Dancer	F	G2 Ferine
Spark-Ear	M	G3 Dog-T
Stalks-The-Dark	M	G3 Panthac
Stalks-The-Fences	F	G1 Dog-T
Storm-Surfer	M	G4 Thofin
Racing-Sunlight	M	G3 Hyfin
Thistle-Maw	M	G2 Dog-T
Thunder-Howler	M	G1 Delta Tosak
Thunder-Star (*pre 620 PA*)	M	G2 Hyfin

Thunder-Star (*620 > 753 PA*)	M	G4 Thofin
Thunder-Star (*post 754 PA*)	M	G5 Thofin
Touches-The-Stars	M	G3 Hyfin
Truck-Stopper	M	G1 Delta Tosak
Tundra-Ghost	M	G1 Beta Tosak
Twilight-Killer	M	G1 Delta Tosak
Wanders-By-Night	F	G4 Thofin
Weaving-Hannah	F	G3 Afya
Zero-Master	F	G4 Takuman

Appendix Four: Ranks

The vast disparity of ranks between the survivors of the apocalypse caused considerable confusion. Earth Command standardised all military ranks in Year 011 PA. When Jackson Spence formed Ghost Command, he saw no need to change something that all of his people were used to, except to define when exactly a Commodore outranks an Admiral.

In Year 621 PA he took the title of First Governor, establishing the precedent for senior officers who had transferred from their bodies into artificial containment to become Governors, a rank superior to all military and civilian titles, but under him. In Year 631 he authorised the creation of the Commissioner rank, for civilians of note who chose to take a similar role of perpetual service to Ghost Command.

C1: Sergeant

C2: Leftenant

C3: Captain (*The Captain of a spaceship has authority over all other officers while on his or her ship, even if they are of higher rank. An officer of any rank will be called Captain whilst on board and commanding a spaceship*)

C4: Major

C5: Colonel

C6: Commander

C7: Alpha Commander

C8: Commodore (*outranks an Admiral in civilian matters*)

C9: Admiral (*outranks a Commodore in military matters*)

G1: Commissioner (*ex-civilian, loosely equivalent to C6*)

G2: Governor (*ex-military, loosely equivalent to C8*)

G3: First Governor

Borsen society is dictated by ranks. There are no 'civilians' in the way that humanity understands the term.

Consort	The lowest of the low, destined to be slain during breeding or have their bodies taken over by a Mistress' artificial intelligence.
Warrior	The male of the Borsen species. Brute force incarnate and not much else, apart from a slavish devotion to Borsen females.
Knight	A Borsen Mistress' artificial intelligence in its consort host body. Equivalent of C1.
Mistress	All female Borsen. Within Borsen communities, there are a host of social, political, military and family factors that dictate an individual's standing within this. Equivalent of C3.
WarMistress	A Mistress who excels in strategy and tactics. Equivalent of C7.
WarpMistress	A Mistress who controls at least one of the many aspects of warp-field manipulation. There are hundreds skilled in a single aspect, yet very few achieve mastery of two or more. Equivalent of C9.

Matriarch The current leader of the Borsen. This position
changes tentacles infrequently as the requirements
include mastery of at least eight aspects of warp
field manipulation. Equivalent of G3.

The Concilium officially streamlined their command structure in the transition from their former incarnation as Earth Command.

O1: Soldier Black (*equivalent of C2*)
O2: Centurion (*equivalent of C3*)
O3: Executive (*equivalent of C4*)
O4: Archon (*equivalent of C5*)
O5: Marshal (*equivalent of C7*)
O6: Consul (*equivalent of C9*)

In practice the Consul will appoint a Marshal to be a Praetor (*equivalent of C8*), to act as final authority in operations involving several Marshals. Similarly, Marshals frequently appoint one or two Archons to be Legates (*equivalents of C6*) in war zones that require swift responses without waiting for a Marshal's authorisation.

Soldier Blue and Soldier Red are the standard terms for male and female troopers respectively. A number is suffixed if there are more than one of either in a Soldier Black's group. In addition, any large group will have blue and red officers (*both equivalents of C1*) appointed by the Black. They always have the suffix 'One'.

Appendix Five:
Dara

This two player game comes from Africa and is considered to be early nineteenth century in origin, although it is likely that it had existed in similar form for far longer.

Games last far into the night, traditionally for as long as the moon shines brightly. Good Dara players are highly regarded and champions travel from village to village, challenging the local players. Secrets for playing the game are passed from generation to generation.

Materials.

Two types of counters; twelve of each.

A board consisting of thirty squares, arranged in a grid six squares by five.

Playing the Game.

1. Each player or team takes turns putting a counter on the squares of the board until all 24 counters are on the board.

2. Each player takes a turn moving a counter into an adjacent empty square. Counters may be moved up, down, or sideways, but not diagonally.

3. When a player gets three counters in a row, they get to remove one of their opponent's counters. This is known as 'eating' the enemy.

Special Rules:

1. Players may not have more than three counters in a row at any time.

2. A row made when placing counters on the board in Step one does not count.

3. Only one counter at a time may be removed from the board, even if more than one row is formed by a move.

Winning the Game.

A game is won when your opponent can no longer make a row.

14336754R00189

Printed in Great Britain
by Amazon.co.uk, Ltd.,
Marston Gate.